Scriptures used consist of the following:

King James Version - KJ®

New King James Version ® - NKJ ®

New International Version ® - NIV ®

Copyright © 2009 by Peggy Seay All rights reserved
This book or parts thereof may not be reproduced in any form, stored in a retrieval system, or transmitted in any form by any means – electronic, mechanical, photocopy, recording, or otherwise – without prior written permission of the publisher, except as provided by the United States of America copyright law.

Published by Women Mentoring Women, Fort Worth, Texas
letsdiscuss@sistersletstalk.com

International Standard Book Number: 978-1-59712-306-8

Edited by Sandy Richardson
Printed by Catawba Publishing Company, Charlotte, NC, 28213
info@catawbapublishing.com

ACKNOWLEDGEMENTS

The Trinity: God the Father, God the Son, and The Holy Spirit; for without your presence in our lives and the grace that only you can give, this work would not have made it to fruition. Praise your Holy name, El Shaddai.

Sandy Richardson, Editor – What a blessing to work with Sandy. Her knowledge and expertise helped to make this work become a calm reality. Thank you, Sandy!

DEDICATION

We would like to dedicate this work to each reader. As you pass through your personal 'Seasons of Life' we pray you will reflect on God's Words, using this devotional, *God's Word Day Upon Day*. We pray your relationship with Jesus is enriched by these words and may you enjoy each page with the love and care they are presented.

TABLE OF CONTENTS

PREFACE IX

I. SPRING.. 1
    He Gives Us Hope for Everyday........................... 5
    Lips of Love... 12
    Passion Week... 19
    Who is in Control?.. 26
    For Sale... 33
    Jesus and the Seven RE's of Us........................... 40
    Patience.. 47
    Speech 54
    Our Mansion.. 61
    Wisdom 68
    Righteous!... 75
    May 'Flower'.. 82
    Father's Day 89

II. SUMMER.. 99
    Elohim 103
    His Refreshing Preparations 110
    Songs.. 117
    What Waiting Can Bring................................... 124
    Church of Philadelphia..................................... 131
    "Our Father".. 138
    You Are God's Specialty................................... 145
    Letting Go and Letting God............................... 152
    Faith 159
    Unquenchable Love 166
    Know.. 173
    Sleep 180
    Ultimate Sacrifice... 187

III. AUTUMN.. 197
    Adoration of Our Holy Father............................. 201
    Prosperity 208
    Directions 215
    Words 222
    A Week of Thanksgiving 229
    Hezekiah – Added Days.................................... 236
    A Way of Life... 243
    From The Cross.. 250
    Prayer of Jabez 257
    Designing Us 264
    His Teaching Continues 271
    The Beginning.. 278
    Freedom From the Laws of Sin.......................... 285

IV. WINTER 295

    'IF' 299
    Micah 306
    Senses 313
    Phrases We Often Use... 320
    Is it 'Worth' it? 327
    Defining You 334
    Patience for Coming Events 341
    Flowers in December.. 348
    Love & Hate--War & Peace...................................... 355
    God's Provision in Your Wilderness 362
    Keeping Resolutions 369
    Waiting 376
    Safe In His Arms 383

V. BIBLE BOOK INDEX... 393

VI. TOPIC INDEX... 410

PREFACE

What an adventurous mission this book has been! I say mission because wherever God plants us becomes our mission field. I say adventurous because when we sisters started this project, we had three things: (1) Our trust in God's nudging. (2) A minute experience writing manuals for the different companies for which we worked. (3) Our belief that staying close to Jesus Christ means staying in God's Word daily.

To begin our trek into *God's Word Day Upon Day* wilderness, we started a website: www.sistersletstalk.com. At first we were unsure devotions on the website was God's plan for us. But we soon saw the need as more and more individuals visited the website, even though we didn't have advertising for it in any way. It didn't take long before we felt the Lord nudging us to take one more step on the path of His plan. God urged us to create something all people could use no matter their place or position. We knew that whatever He was leading us to do had to be useful to all, give the opportunity for each person to grow from their own personal experiences, and had to provide directions from God for each daily life it touched. There also had to be an opportunity for personal reflection for what God might be saying.

We believe life is made up of daily situations we do not always feel equipped to handle. Many times these situations come about by our own daily choices and decisions. Some things we experience only once in a lifetime, and some things we struggle with day after day. No matter the situation or trial, God always has a plan for each of us. His plan requires that we turn to Him for every decision we make—no matter if that decision is only for what we are to eat today or a decision that will affect the world—we are to consider His divine ways. There is but one way to draw close enough to Him to hear His pleas for our lives, and that is to know Him. Since we cannot look Him in the face to have a conversation, we get to know Him through reading His Word and bowing ourselves to Him in prayer.

As you go through each week of these devotions, may God bless you with renewed strength for your every trial. By God's mercy may you begin to know that He and His Word can be relied upon for every situation. May you begin to know today that your deepening relationship with Christ better equips you for what this world puts in your path.

spring

*Bloom into your
Life with Christ*

The Spring of life
Finds you filled with
Confidence and
filled with
encouragement.

God responds by
growing you
to His understandings.

———◆———

Through your self-growth
of changed attitudes
and life outlooks,
your very own garden
begins to bloom.

Spring

One step forward, two steps back.
The harder I try, the more I lack.

How did I get in the worldly maze?
Is this forever or just a phase?

The road ahead
He has firmly chosen.
Before this moment,
my path I had frozen.

By His Words, a blossom begins.
By His Love, confidence
and encouragement He sends.

Each of His days
grows strength and beauty.
All to me, He has freely given
and never attached any duty.

Kathleen J. Jones

He Gives Us Hope for Everyday

God has provided us a glimpse into church beginnings in Corinthians I and II. Paul was able to communicate with the Corinthians, through his letters, on their various needs. It is a wonderful thing to open an old letter and remind ourselves of the happenings of that time. We often remember good times and bad. The same is true for Paul's letters. We will find happy and sad, good and bad, things that need correcting and things for which God must be very proud. There was life in Corinth, just as there is life today in your city, town, or community.

Sunday   **II Corinthians 1:3 "Blessed be the God and Father of our Lord Jesus Christ, the Father of mercies and God of all comfort..."**

Start your week by lifting your arms and thoughts high to the Father of Jesus Christ and YOU. Praise Him with your words and thoughts today for tender mercies He has provided in the past and has set aside for your future. He is our greatest comfort in every situation. Thank Him that you don't have to look for anyone else because He is always there for you.

Reflections

Monday II Corinthians 1:4 "…who comforts us in all our tribulation, that we may be able to comfort those who are in any trouble with the comfort with which we ourselves are comforted by God."

In recent years, several movies carried the 'pass it on' theory. God is the author of this theory. He gives to us willingly whenever we are in need. First, thank Him for His comfort in all situations just because you call to Him. Second, "PASS IT ON." Find someone who needs comforting. Offer them your compassion; then offer them God's. If that person will allow, pray together to the Father to ask for His continued comfort. If your joint prayers are not wanted, find a secret place and pray to the Father for that person.

Reflections

Tuesday   II Corinthians 5:7 "For we walk by faith, not by sight…"

No matter your personality, walking by faith is not an easy task. It is a learned experience. Today, let us give Him thanks that we can confidently walk by faith. Let us confess to Him any time we might have questioned how far we had to walk before He gave us a definitive direction. Next, let's close our eyes, and imagine all the beautiful places walking with Him in faith can take us. Lastly, let us tell Him of His majesty and glory for deciding our walk and making the path(s).

Reflections

Wednesday II Corinthians 5:17 "Therefore, if anyone is in Christ, he is a new creation; old things have passed away; behold, all things have become new."

Ever had an article of clothing you just loved? You loved the way it fit, the colors, the style, just everything about it! Then it got old and very ragged looking because you wore it and washed it so often. Nothing could be done except throw it away. Life with Jesus Christ is nothing like life with that garment. We don't have to worry about too many wash and dry cycles. He is there for us NOW and TOMORROW. Ask Him to wash away all the dirtiness in your life. He will throw it into the ocean, never to be seen again. By calling to Him daily, our lives can be refreshed. He loves us so much; He makes our lives new each time we come to Him.

Reflections

Thursday   **I Corinthians 14:33 "For God is not the author of confusion but of peace, as in all the churches of saints."**

Our days are filled with decisions. Most choices are made without realizing we have made a judgment call. We often do not call upon the Lord because we feel He is too busy, or we are too busy and do not want to wait for the answer. For one day, call upon the Father for every decision. See if it doesn't release you and give you peace. Tell Him thank you for all the answers He is going to give you, even those for which you are not aware.

Reflections

_____
_____
_____
_____
_____
_____
_____
_____
_____
_____
_____
_____
_____
_____
_____
_____
_____
_____

Friday   **I Corinthians 14:40 "Let all things be done decently and in order."**

Usually our hope begins to wane when life just keeps coming at us. It seems we must deal with new trials daily. Confusion comes when we must add new trials to the old ones. But God is not a God of disorder. His creations are always orderly. Ask the Father today to restructure your plan or make you a new one. Let Him tell you what is important to get done today. Praise Him for setting up all your tomorrows. Let Him make all your lists and any timetables you feel must be met.

Reflections

Saturday   **II Corinthians 4:7 "But we have this treasure in earthen vessels, that the excellence of the power may be of God and not of us."**

We are clay pots. We will wear out and break and get old. But God never will! Cast all your hopes on Him. Let Him bear all your burdens. Sing praises to your Father in heaven, who will cover your every need, make all your decisions, hold you tight from every harm, and love you through each day with His promises. He was, He is, and He will always be your El Shadday, your God Almighty.

Reflections

Lips of Love

There are times we get together and have *'friendly'* discussions – oh we don't mean anything by what we are discussing, we are just being silly, or having private fun. But is it really private? If the truth be known, is it really fun or friendly? Satan makes sin appear simple, which is why we must be on our guard. Let's practice having Lips of Love this week as we learn what God's Word has to say about our friendly discussions.

Sunday   **Ephesians 4:29 "Let no corrupt communication proceed out of your mouth, but that, which is good to the use of edifying, that it may minister grace unto the hearers."**

The word 'corrupt' means evil, and evil means harmful. But if evil means harmful, ouch! How many times have we been sitting around and casually discussing someone? Could our words be construed as harmful? Could we be evil? Maybe the words we speak are true, but does that mean it is OK for us to discuss someone else, especially when that person is not present. Perhaps you're saying to yourself, "But I'd tell them to their face." Do you really mean that? This scripture does not qualify that our harmful conversations are true or false. It says let NO harmful communication proceed. What is harmful then? Suppose someone's child or parent heard what was being said. How would that person feel hearing your words, even if those words were truthful? The words could still cause harm. When we consider the definition of harmful, our communication can take on a whole new meaning. Begin today, and commit to the Lord that you will not let corrupt communication proceed out of your mouth.

Reflections

_____
_____
_____
_____
_____
_____
_____
_____
_____
_____

Monday   Ephesians 4:29 "Let no corrupt communication proceed out of your mouth, but that, which is good to the use of edifying, that it may minister grace unto the hearers."

The verse above tells us that what does proceed from our mouths is to be good to the use of edifying. Edifying means to instruct or improve. If our communications do not instruct or improve, then they are not to proceed out of our mouths.

Reflections

Tuesday **Ephesians 4:29 "Let no corrupt communication proceed out of your mouth, but that, which is good to the use of edifying, that it may minister grace unto the hearers."**

In this last section of the verse: "that it may minister grace unto the hearers." God's Word tells us our words should not be harmful, and they should edify, but also they are to minister grace to those that HEAR. Grace refers to a pleasing and admiring quality. How many times have our words gone awry? We may be disgruntled with a spouse, a child, another family member, a friend, a boss, or a co-worker. Our words do not often minister grace at those times. So let's stop and consider what others hear from us?

Reflections

Wednesday   Colossians 4:6a "**Let your speech be always with grace…**"

Our verse gives us the words 'always' and 'grace.' 'Always' tends to trip me up. God tells us we are to 'strive' for mastery over sin. God knows we are not perfect, but we should ask ourselves if we're really trying? The word 'grace' should remind us that Christ gave us eternity when we did not deserve it. Today, let's strive to fill our speech with grace.

Reflections

Thursday   Titus 3:2 "Speak evil of no man…"

This verse most definitely sums it all up. What else needs saying? Remember that evil means harmful, so if we desire to have Lips of Love, this verse has to reign in our hearts.

Reflections

Friday   **Hebrews 13:5a "…let your conversation be without covetousness…"**

When we consider our general conversations, let us not find that we covet. The Ten Commandments instruct us of this, and in this verse, we are told not to even discuss 'coveting' something or someone. The rest of the verse tells us to be content with what we have. WHY? Because Christ will never leave us or forsake us, He is all we need, so what does that leave to covet? Learning to totally rely on Jesus, can teach us the right conversation.

Reflections

Saturday   I Peter 3:1b "…be won by the conversation of the wives;"

I pray you can take this one-step farther, and see who we can 'win' by our conversation. The verse above shows us that our conversations can win others for Christ. I pray God's love and grace be in your heart and flow through your Lips of Love.

Reflections

Passion Week

Passion Week begins with Palm Sunday, the last week Jesus walked the earth as 'The Son of Man.' Our focus this week is on how God uses the Old Testament and the New Testament to tell us what He asked of His Son. Focus on each day's scripture and at the end of the week review Zechariah 9:9 for a weekly reflection.

Zechariah 9:9 "Rejoice greatly, O daughter of Zion! Shout, O daughter of Jerusalem! Behold, your King is coming to you; He is just and having salvation, lowly and riding on a donkey, a colt, the foal of a donkey."

Sunday Mark 11:1 – 2 "Now when they drew near Jerusalem, to Bethphage and Bethany, at the Mount of Olives, He sent two of His disciples; and He said to them, 'Go into the village opposite you; And as soon as you have entered it you will find a colt tied, on which no one has sat, Loose it and bring it.'"

Reflections

Monday   **Matthew 21:4 – 6** "All this was done that it might be fulfilled which was spoken by the prophet saying: 'Tell the daughter of Zion, behold, your King is coming to you, lowly, and sitting on a donkey, A colt, the foal of a donkey.' So the disciples went and did as Jesus commanded them."

Reflections

Tuesday Mark 11:8 – 10 "And many spread their clothes on the road, and others cut down leafy branches from the trees and spread them on the road, then those who went before and those who followed cried out, saying: 'Hosanna! Blessed is He who comes in the name of the Lord! Blessed is the kingdom of our father David that comes in the name of the Lord! Hosanna in the highest!'"

(Hosanna in the highest = Jesus our Messianic Deliverer)

Reflections

_____
_____
_____
_____
_____
_____
_____
_____
_____
_____
_____
_____
_____
_____
_____
_____
_____
_____
_____

Wednesday Psalm 118: 25 – 26 "Save now, I pray, O Lord; O Lord, I pray, send now prosperity, blessed is he who comes in the name of the Lord! We have blessed you from the house of the Lord."

Reflections

Thursday   Matthew 21:10 – 11 "And when He had come into Jerusalem, all the city was moved, saying, 'Who is this?' So the multitudes said, 'This is Jesus, the prophet from Nazareth of Galilee.'"

Reflections

_____
_____
_____
_____
_____
_____
_____
_____
_____
_____
_____
_____
_____
_____
_____
_____
_____
_____
_____
_____
_____
_____
_____
_____

24

Friday Luke 19:39 – 40 "And some of the Pharisees called to Him from the crowd, 'Teacher, rebuke Your disciples.' But He answered and said to them, 'I tell you that if these should keep silent, the stones would immediately cry out.'"

Reflections

Saturday — John 12:16 "His disciples did not understand these things at first: but when Jesus was glorified, then they remembered that these things were written about Him and that they had done these things to Him."

Reflections

Who is in Control?

Some of us think we need to be in control of what is going on around us. We work both inside and outside the home. If we can be all, we must be able to be in control of our own lives.

Sunday   **Genesis 15: 4"Then the word of the LORD came to him: 'This man will not be your heir, but a son coming from your own body will be your heir.'"**

Genesis 16:2 "so she said to Abram, 'The LORD has kept me from having children. Go, sleep with my maidservant; perhaps I can build a family through her.'"

Waiting - How many times have we received a word from God, but we felt, He was just taking too long to fulfill what He said He would do? We then decide, "I am going to go ahead and help Him achieve what He said." Sarai moved ahead, and it was not what God had in mind. To achieve HIS results, we must WAIT for HIM.

Reflections

_____
_____
_____
_____
_____
_____
_____
_____
_____
_____
_____
_____
_____
_____

Monday Genesis 17:1-2 "When Abram was ninety-nine years old, the LORD appeared to him and said, 'I am God Almighty; walk before me and be blameless. I will confirm my covenant between me and you and will greatly increase your numbers.'"

Waiting's Answer - God had a plan. Sarai thought she would help Him along with His plan. It did not turn out the way God had in mind. But God's real plan did. He planned to increase Abram's numbers greatly. All Sarai and Abram had to do was wait for God's plan to be fulfilled in God's time. Do not be a Sarai when you are given a word from God. His answer will come to pass. Wait on Him to fulfill HIS PLAN.

Reflections

Tuesday — Genesis 20:1b-2 "For a while he stayed in Gerar, and there Abraham said of his wife Sarah, 'She is my sister.' Then Abimelech King of Gerar sent for Sarah and took her."

Fear - Abraham had decided Abimelech would kill him and take Sarah. Abraham decided to take matters into his own hands by telling a lie. It was after all 'just a little lie.' She really was his sister. But even little lies show we are not trusting God. Fear feeds dishonesty.

Reflections

Wednesday — Genesis 20:4-5 "Now Abimelech had not gone near her, so he said, 'Lord, will you destroy an innocent nation? Did he not say to me, 'She is my sister,' and didn't she also say, 'He is my brother?' I have done this with a clear conscience and clean hands.'"

Trust instead of Fear - God knew what Abraham and Sarah had done. They did not trust God to keep them safe as they traveled. Trust and do not fear what may lie ahead. If we are following God's path, there is nothing to fear.

Reflections

Thursday **John 11:3** "So the sisters sent word to Jesus, 'Lord, the one you love is sick.'"

John 11:6 "Yet when he heard that Lazarus was sick, he stayed where he was two more days."

Timing - Mary and Martha called out for Jesus to come now saying, "Our brother is sick; he needs your healing hands." When we call to Jesus, do we demand his answer immediately? These verses tell us it is God's timing, and not ours, which Jesus follows.

Reflections

Friday — John 11:4 "When he heard this, Jesus said, 'This sickness will not end in death. No, it is for God's glory so that God's Son may be glorified through it.'"

Time for Glory - At times, we may think and feel that if God does not act at the very moment we ask, He is not who He says He is. When we ask and God answers immediately, who are we inclined to think was in control? We may tend to believe it was because 'we asked' that the answer was immediate; therefore, we were in control of when the answer was given. This scripture tells us that Jesus waited to answer because He was glorifying God. We, too, can give God glory by waiting for His answer.

Reflections

Saturday **Luke 23:23** "But with loud shouts they insistently demanded that he be crucified, and their shouts prevailed."

Luke 24:5b-7 "Why do you look for the living among the dead? He is not here; he has risen! Remember how he told you, while he was still with you in Galilee: 'The Son of Man must be delivered into the hands of sinful men, be crucified and on the third day be raised again.'"

Thankfully God is in Control - We need to allow God to be in control. The people thought they were in control of killing Jesus, but God was in control. Jesus was crucified, and He arose for us, according to God's plan. Let go of the control, and allow God to show the way.

Reflections

_____
_____
_____
_____
_____
_____
_____
_____
_____
_____
_____
_____
_____
_____

For Sale

In the paper, in the front yard, on the Internet, and registered with all the multiple listing services are houses waiting to be purchased by new owners. As I drove along, I noticed the signs and advertisements everywhere. "Why did they jump out at me so?" I asked. The Holy Spirit and I were in our normal 'ride home from the office conversation.' So, when the 'For Sale' signs continued to draw my attention, I simply had to ask myself, "Are YOU For Sale?" "Of course not", I answered! Then, as He always does, God gave me a closer look. He will do the same for you with this week's devotions.

Sunday   **I John 1:9 "If we confess our sins, he is faithful and just to forgive us our sins, and to cleanse us from all unrighteousness."**

Forgiveness - Are you 'on the market?' If you have Salvation, that is absolutely wonderful. But did you know that even with Salvation, we still sin? God's forgiveness is necessary everyday. Forgiveness should not be requested in generalities. We need to be specific as to our sins. And here is the clincher: you have to 'confess.' To be sure we do not allow ourselves even the appearance of being 'For Sale,' we must stay in a right relationship with Christ. Satan is going to have his 'realtors' searching for new property. Look at yourself this week. Have you asked for forgiveness? If not, ask Him today, and turn toward a right relationship with Him.

Reflections

Monday	Deuteronomy 30:19-20 "I call heaven and earth to record this day against you, that I have set before you life and death, blessing and cursing: therefore choose life, that both thou and thy seed may live: That thou mayest love the LORD thy God, and that thou mayest obey his voice, and that thou mayest cleave unto him: for he is thy life, and the length of thy days: that thou mayest dwell in the land which the LORD sware unto thy fathers, to Abraham, to Isaac, and to Jacob, to give them."

Obey - May I submit to you that unless we obey His voice, we will most definitely be putting ourselves 'on the market' for sin? Sin creeps up on us, little by little, piece by piece. Then, "BAM!" Sin is in our faces, and we are entering into a pre-contract. Hearing and obeying God's voice will keep us from signing on the dotted line of sin. Take some time today to read His Word and ***"cleave unto him: for He is thy life."***

Reflections

Tuesday **Psalm 51:10 "Create in me a clean heart, O God; and renew a right spirit within me."**

Renew -"My heart is clean," may be your first thought, and it's true. God created a clean heart for you, but could there be things that have shaded your heart to gray? Look deeper into this verse and to 'the spirit within.' God is not just about creating a clean heart. He wants to renew the spirit within you daily. He is asking today, "Are YOU For Sale"?

Reflections

Wednesday   **Ephesians 2:20b "…Jesus Christ himself being the chief corner stone;"**

Support - When purchasing a building, a major concern is the structural support. No matter the building material, the corner stone is the most important support. Put some blocks together. If the corner block is not secured, the blocks tumble down. Our lives are like that without 'the Chief corner stone.' We tumble, wobble, are out of line and not level. Let Christ be your CHIEF corner stone, and you will have sure support.

Reflections

Thursday   2 Peter 2:18b "…they allure through the lust of the flesh…."

Allure -To sell a piece of property requires taking pictures and writing ads that allure, so the property will attract buyers. To 'allure' is to exert a very powerful and often dangerous attraction on someone. Satan uses 'alluring' schemes. If we are not careful, we, too, will be allured by Satan's dangers. It happens when we hang out with wrong crowds, 'discuss' someone, watch the wrong programs and movies, listen to wrong music and wrong advise. II Peter 2 tells of false prophets and the results of listening to them. All of these are easy to do if we are denying the Lord our God. What is alluring you today?

Reflections

.iday   I John 4:8b "...God is love."

Love - When you find the right property, your heart and soul are filled as you exclaim, "Oh, I love it!" Today, think on the ONE that is love and how much HE loves you. Ask yourself, "Am I FOR SALE?" Look to the world, and say, "I am not for sale! God has purchased me, and He is a permanent resident in my life."

Reflections

Saturday   John 3:16 **"For God so loved the world, that he gave his only begotten Son, that whosoever believeth in him should not perish, but have everlasting life."**

Eternal - Yesterday we determined we have been purchased by a permanent resident and are NOT for sale. Today's verse tells us we have everlasting life. We have the Son of God in our hearts forever! He resides within, and Satan knows this. Satan tries to allure and cause us to forget WHO lives in our hearts. The God who is love gives us the strength to stand up and say, "NO WE ARE NOT FOR SALE!" Think on this as you pass those for sale signs in the future. Whisper a prayer of praise and thanksgiving. We have a permanent resident.

Reflections

Jesus and the Seven RE's of Us

Everybody wants a Re-do. Our God is a God of seconds, thirds, and even more chances. He allows us to make our mistakes, and if we desire, we can ask for a "re-do." In light of this, let's take words that begin with 'RE' to show our God of seconds.

Sunday   **Matthew 7:8 "For everyone that asks receives; he who seeks finds; and to him who knocks, the door will be opened."**

He receives us. He takes us from where we are and brings us back to Him. Jesus delivers us to The Father, and The Father receives us. Do you hear the knocking? He is waiting for you to open the door, so He can receive you.

Reflections

Monday   **Psalm 130:7- 8 "O Israel, put your hope in the LORD, for with the LORD is unfailing love and with him is full redemption. He himself will redeem Israel from all their sins."**

He redeems us. Redeem means to pay for the sins of humanity with death on the Cross. Christ paid the highest cost anyone could pay for us. To Him, we are worth the price of His death on the cross. Believe and know, that to Him, you are worthy of His death. Use your name in the place of Israel in the above verse. It will bring it home to you.

Reflections

Tuesday **Isaiah 1:18b** "Though your sins are like scarlet, they shall be as white as snow; though they are red as crimson, they shall be like wool."

He removes our sins. We become white as snow when He removes all our dirty and ugly spots. Every time we sin and then confess, our sins are taken away. We become white as snow. Allow HIM to remove your sins today. How glorious is His Word!

Reflections

Wednesday   **Isaiah 61:4 "They will rebuild the ancient ruins and restore the places long devastated; they will renew the ruined cities that have been devastated for generations."**

He restores us. Have you ever seen how an old piece of furniture is restored? With loving hands, the scratches are removed one by one. We can become like old furniture: scarred and broken, devastated by the trials of life. God will restore us with loving hands and give us a life renewed.

Reflections

Thursday   Isaiah 64:8 "Yet, O LORD, you are our Father. We are the clay, you are the potter; we are all the work of your hand."

He remolds us. We begin as children, and He remolds us into the most beautiful people we can become. His word tells us, "He is the potter, and we are the clay." Allow His hands to mold and remold you into the beautiful person He wants you to become.

Reflections

Friday   **Psalm 66:5 "Come and see what God has done, how awesome his works in man's behalf!"**

He refines us. Like the rock polished and buffed to reveal the jewel, God refines us. Look in the mirror, and see His awesome work. As we continue in the changing process, He continues the improving process: refining us in small ways, making us more pure. Through His refining, we become as a precious jewel.

Reflections

Saturday   **Revelation 22:12** "Behold, I am coming soon! My reward is with me, and I will give to everyone according to what he has done."

He rewards us. We do the wrong, and He does the cleaning--restoring us to the most beautiful people we can be. Accepting Him as our savior is all we must do to receive eternity with Him. We are given the re-dos and the rewards.

Reflections

Patience

I used to pray for patience. Then someone told me praying for patience is exactly what brings the tribulations we receive in life. God answers our prayers for patience by sending situations that demand it of us. I wasn't sure I believed exactly that; but I did quit praying for patience!

Instead, I went (where I should have gone in the first place) to God's Word(s) on patience. I pray you will use these scriptures daily. Contemplate them. Let God respond to you. Use your thought time this week to find how God wants you to increase your patience. I believe patience is one of the things God does want us to grow.

Sunday   **Galatians 5:22 "But the fruit of the spirit is love, joy, peace, long suffering, kindness, goodness, faithfulness."**

Long suffering = patience. Patience is a part of the Fruits of the Spirit, and according to medical science, we are to have three fruit servings per day for a healthy body. Is patience on your menu today?

Reflections

_____
_____
_____
_____
_____
_____
_____
_____
_____
_____
_____
_____
_____

Monday Lamentations 3:26 "It is good that one should hope and wait quietly for the salvation of the Lord."

Hope and wait quietly = patience. We are commanded to "wait quietly."

Reflections

Tuesday   **Ecclesiastes 7:9 "Do not hasten in your spirit to be angry, for anger rests in the bosom of fools."**

Many times our impatience brings us to the boiling point, making us (according to scripture) FOOLS.

Reflections

Wednesday   **Romans 15:4 "Whatever things were written before, were written for our learning, that we through the patience and comfort of the Scriptures might have hope."**

Four days into this particular devotional, and we have gained: Fruit of the Spirit, salvation of the Lord, (This salvation is for the things of daily life - this is not our salvation thru Jesus Christ), not being a Fool, and today, Hope. All of these are added just by gaining patience.

Reflections

Thursday   **Psalm 37:7 "Rest in the Lord, and wait patiently for Him; do not fret because of him who prospers in his way, because of the man who brings wicked schemes to pass."**

We are to be assured God will answer and in a timely manner. Our thoughts should be on Him and not our neighbors, who have perhaps achieved goals through wicked schemes. Remember, our time is not His time. He leads—We follow.

Reflections

Friday   Psalm 40:1 "I waited patiently for the Lord; and He inclined to me, and heard my cry."

The most important part of patience is WAITING ON THE LORD. By showing Him our patience, He will hear us and respond. If we can wait on the Lord, we have conquered patience.

Reflections

Saturday — **Romans 5:3-5** "We also glory in tribulations, knowing that tribulation produces perseverance; and perseverance, character; and character hope. Now hope does not disappoint, because the love of God has been poured out in our hearts by the Holy Spirit who was given to us."

And so we are back where we started. Praying for patience brings tribulation. So, let us not pray for patience, but instead, let us look to our Father to supply. He will not only supply the patience we need, but everything else as well. He has already given us patience by supplying us His Son, Jesus Christ. We just need to stop, and use (call on) the one Jesus left with us, the Holy Spirit.

Reflections

Speech

This week, let's look at what God's Word has to say about our 'speech.' What we say, how we say it, and the attitude in which we are speaking. Each of these, plus more, tells a lot about whom we are and our relationship with Christ. Pray each day that the Holy Spirit will touch you and help you have the 'speech' HE wants you to have.

Sunday   **Proverbs 7:21 "With her much fair speech she caused him to yield, with the flattering of her lips she forced him."**

To get the full effect of this verse you should read the entire seventh chapter. The speech of temptation is alluring, to be sure, but most often to our detriment. What about your speech? Do you sometimes adjust your speech to entice and get your desired result? Our speech is to be approved by God. Today, think on every word you speak – is what you say approved by God?

Reflections

_____
_____
_____
_____
_____
_____
_____
_____
_____
_____
_____
_____
_____
_____

Monday   **Psalm 17:6 "I have called upon thee, for thou wilt hear me, O God: incline thine ear unto me, and hear my speech."**

God wants to hear from you. In verse 3 of Psalm chapter 17, we are told that God proved the writers' heart, and God visited in the night. When you are awake in the wee hours, talk to God. He is listening to your speech.

Reflections

56

Tuesday   **Luke 1:22 "And when he came out, he could not speak unto them: and they perceived that he had seen a vision in the temple: for he beckoned unto them, and remained speechless."**

This verse tells of one that was rendered 'speechless' because of his unbelief. When you hear of something or see something that is seemingly unbelievable to our human selves, you are left speechless. But are there times we should remain speechless? Use this day to ponder the thought of 'When should I be speechless, Lord?' Trust God. He will tell you when to speak and when to be speechless.

Reflections

Wednesday   **2 Corinthians 7:4a "Great is my boldness of speech toward you, great is my glorying of you: I am filled with comfort…"**

In the verses of 2 Corinthians 7, Paul is excited and happy that his direct approach brought the people to repentance. Yes, it was painful, but the pain brought the hearer to salvation, and that is exciting and comforting. Being bold does not mean being rude or callous – it is giving the Word of God straight and direct to bring others to Him. How is your boldness? Do you even try? How about trying once today? Can you be BOLD?

Reflections

Thursday   Matthew 26:73 "And after a while came unto him they that stood by, and said to Peter, Surely thou also art one of them; for thy speech betrayeth thee."

We've discussed how our speech can tell others about us and about our relationship to Christ. Today's verse is a prime example. Even though Peter tried, he could not convince others he was not a follower of Christ. What a problem to have! Most often, the situation is reversed. Does your speech betray the real you? We all slip and fall, but the key is to get up, and go in God's direction. If you have slipped or fallen today, ask for forgiveness, and turn your speech around. Let others hear Christ in your speech.

Reflections

Friday — Colossians 4:6b "Let your speech be always with grace, seasoned with salt, that ye may know how ye ought to answer every man."

The key word here is 'always.' Even when we are tired, right in the middle of something, answering for the zillionth time, or at our limit, our speech is to be with grace.

Reflections

Saturday   **1 Kings 3:10 "And the speech pleased the LORD, that Solomon had asked this thing."**

A speech that pleased the LORD! Solomon had such a pure heart of prayer; he was given more than he asked. He was not thinking about what he could get or if his prayer was pure. He just pleased the Lord. As we end this week, let's strive to keep our speech pure before God and man.

Reflections

Our Mansion

John 14:1-4 "Let not your heart be troubled; ye believe in God, believe also in me. In my Father's house are many mansions: if it were not so, I would have told you. I go to prepare a place for you. And if I go and prepare a place for you, I will come again, and receive you unto myself; that where I am, there ye may be also. And whither I go ye know, and the way ye know."

Across our world, the size and style of homes range from a 'shanties', to 'estates,' to 'mansions.' While I drove to my home the other day I felt a twinge of envy, as some homes were very elaborate, including the landscaping. My home is in the "remodel state." The Holy Spirit reminded me I will be united with Christ in heaven, and His children will ALL have mansions. We will all live in true Equal Housing.

John 14:1-4 above tells us our mansions are already there – no additional construction! Jesus is preparing a place for us. I assure you, His preparations leave nothing to be desired. As you read and pray over the thoughts for each day, may I challenge you to look around as you drive to and fro? Let the Holy Spirit speak to you with the homes you see – then as He speaks, let His wonderful love fill your soul.

Sunday   NO MORE CONSTRUCTION
If you have ever remodeled or built a house, then you know the perils of construction. It is one mess after the other. Stress builds, and we become troubled within. This stress leads us to emotional anguish. The pains can be so intense; we could be convinced our hearts were about to explode. But, we do not have to cater to that anguish. Our scripture verses begin with, "Let not your heart be troubled." Our hearts can be calm. Believe in Jesus Christ. Trust Him with your every care. Pray to Him. He will calm your troubled heart. Look for construction sites as you are out today. When you gaze upon the 'site,' know this: YOUR MANSION IS already COMPLETE.

Reflections

Monday **IN MY FATHER'S HOUSE**

Living on our own, we are responsible for everything, such as: utilities, taxes, upkeep, food, and insurance. When we lived at home with our parents, they paid the bills, and we had need of nothing. God, Our Father in heaven, is waiting to care for us, just like that. Look to Him in whatever need you have. The stresses of life, financial issues, a problem child or two, and relationships can be given over to our Father. Enjoy being under His care, and bask in His love for you. Today, see how many homes you can find having the appearance of an expert's care. Our Father leaves nothing un-kept for us. Of that, we can be sure!

Reflections

Tuesday   **WE ARE NOT ALONE!**

I saw a nice farmhouse up on a hill all alone. The barn was quite a distance from the house, no garage or carport – just the house. I thought to myself, "Wow – wouldn't that be nice." Then I wondered, "Do the ones that live there ever get lonely?" When we go through a time of loneliness, it seems all too easy to let negativity and pain fester. However, when loneliness is gone, we actually see pressing forward to the love of God was what healed our hearts. We will not be lonely in the mansion God prepares for us. Our verse tells us there are many mansions. So, we won't be alone or lonely. We will all be absorbed in praising Christ.

Reflections

Wednesday   **HONESTY**

Absolute honesty is the only way. Shades of the truth are not the truth; they are shades of a lie! The Word of God tells us Jesus is truth. In our scripture verse, He says, "If it were not so, I would have told you." Jesus will forever be true. If we are to be like him, we should live the absolute truth. Allow the Holy Spirit to speak to your heart as you go through each day. Live the truth. Breathe the truth, and sleep the truth. As you pass homes today, pray and ask the Holy Spirit to help you keep your home truthful.

Reflections

_____

_____

_____

_____

_____

_____

_____

_____

_____

_____

_____

_____

_____

_____

_____

_____

_____

_____

_____

Thursday   **THE HOMESTEAD**

A homestead is the owner's fixed residence and in some states, is exempt from seizure and forced sale for the recovery of debts. Our home in heaven has been declared a homestead, as well. The Lamb of God was slain and prepared our homestead so we might enter into heaven pure and wearing robes of white as we meet our Father. Think of pulling into your driveway. Isn't it great to be home! Enjoy the thoughts of your eternal home each time you pull into the driveway of your earthly one.

Reflections

Friday   **COME AGAIN**

Do you enjoy having guests over? I love having family or friends come over to my home. It's fun to decorate or have a loved one over after you have freshly cleaned or remodeled. As we look over our verse today, note that Jesus tells us HE WILL COME AGAIN. Think about that as you close your door after each visitor, and know that Jesus will return. Praise Ye the Lord!

Reflections

Saturday   **THE WAY YE KNOW**

GPS - God's Positioning System. In today's world, we use a GPS to guide us from one point to another on the roadways. A voice will navigate instructions leading the way. If we make an incorrect turn, GPS corrects the path and points us to the corrected way. Our verse today tells us that we know the way. God's Word is our GPS for His way. While you are out driving your regular paths, think on the fact that God desires to show us His way. With Him, there are no wrong turns. Carry your new GPS everywhere! As His Word tells us, "hide it in your heart…"

Reflections

Wisdom

When we need to seek wisdom from God's Word, we often think we must look to the book of Proverbs. But God has provided us with a complete Bible filled with wisdom.

Sunday   **Psalm 57:1 "Have mercy on me, O God, have mercy on me, for in you my soul takes refuge. I will take refuge in the shadow of your wings until the disaster has passed."**

In times of trouble or pain, we know we can cry out to The Lord for mercy. He will take us in the refuge of His wings. Think about a mother bird covering her baby from the disaster that may be approaching. She covers her child with her wings so whatever is coming at them, will come at her and not the child. God does the same for us. Allow Him to cover you with His wings in times of trouble or pain.

Reflections

Monday   **1 Peter 5:5b "All of you, clothe yourselves with humility toward one another, because, God opposes the proud but gives grace to the humble."**

Do you have someone in your life you are holding a grudge against? Do you always want to be first to be noticed? Do you like receiving as opposed to giving? These all are thoughts of self-honoring. But God's Word tells us to be humble; let go of the grudge you hold against another, and forgive them. He also advises us to step back, and let another be recognized. Give without wanting to receive. He will give grace to the humble. Today, allow grace to come into your heart.

Reflections

Tuesday   **Hebrews 11:1 "Now faith is being sure of what we hope for and certain of what we do not see."**

Do you hope for a day filled with no rain clouds? At the end of the day, do you sit back and remember all the puddles you stepped in and think to yourself, "I just can not have a day filled with hope." When we see a cloud above us, we can be certain God is walking with us through the puddles below. Believe in Him for all your hopes, being certain of even what you do not see.

Reflections

Wednesday Isaiah 6:8 "Then I heard the voice of the Lord saying, 'Whom shall I send? And who will go for us?' And I said, 'Here am I. Send me!'"

Today, listen for the voice of The Lord asking you, "Who will go for us?" He may not be asking you to go to some distant land. He may be just calling for you to go wherever you go, with a heart open to Him. He will be at your side. Always go with an attitude of "Here am I; send me!"

Reflections

Thursday   Psalm 105:4 "Look to the LORD and his strength; seek his face always."

Begin each day seeking His strength. Looking to the Lord is our only way to get through each day. Allow His strength to be your strength for whatever comes.

Reflections

Friday   **Matthew 11:29 "Take my yoke upon you and learn from me, for I am gentle and humble in heart, and you will find rest for your soul."**

When we take His yoke upon us, we learn from Him. By learning from Him, we begin to follow His examples. But we cannot know His way without reading His Word. Staying in His Word daily gives us the examples we need and builds our relationship with Him.

Reflections

Saturday   **Luke 12:15 "Then he said to them, 'Watch out! Be on your guard against all kinds of greed; a man's life does not consist in the abundance of his possessions.'"**

What greed is in our lives today? Are we concerned with only our possessions? Or, do we count as our abundance the love of the Father, Son, and Holy Ghost? Giving our love and Christ's love to others is the abundance Christ wants us to possess.

Reflections

Righteous!

A few very popular movies out today use the word "righteous." When I looked righteous up in my thesaurus, I found words like: godly, upright, just, moral, good, and puritanical. Most of these words, I understood right away but I had to look farther for puritanical. It can mean strict, severe or rigid.

My Topical Bible lists over 34 pages of verses having to do in some way, with being and doing what is righteous. This week we are going to focus on the righteousness of Jesus and what that means to us.

Sunday   **II Corinthians 5:21 "He made Him who knew no sin to be sin for us, that we might become the righteousness of God in Him."**

Besides the physical pain of the cross, Jesus bore the mental and emotional pain of sin. Not because He was sinful, but because He knew we were, are, and are going to be. Multiply by 10,000 or more the pain you have felt when you knew you had sinned. That is what Jesus felt for you. He did it so you could "become the righteousness of God in Him." Thank Him once again for that.

Reflections

Monday I Corinthians 1:30 **"Of Him you are in Christ Jesus, who became for us wisdom from God—and righteousness and sanctification and redemption."**

We often think of and thank Jesus for being our redemption and Savior. But He is also our righteousness and our sanctification. Only through Him can we come to God with wisdom, righteousness, and sanctification. Lift our Lord Jesus in praise today to the Father who loves us all.

Reflections

Tuesday   **Philippians 3:9 (Being) "Found in Him, not having my own righteousness, which is from the law, but that which is through faith in Christ, the righteousness which is from God by faith."**

Try as hard as we might, we can never do or say enough right things to become righteous. We are who we are, and we cannot follow all the rules all the time. It just will not happen. Not to worry! Through faith in Jesus Christ, we already have all the righteousness we need. Praise the Father and the Son today for the righteousness freely given by faith.

Reflections

Wednesday   **Romans 4:5 "To him who does not work but believes on Him who justifies the ungodly, his faith is accounted for righteousness."**

If our faith accounts for our righteousness, maybe we should be building that faith on a daily basis. There are those who will tell you faith only grows by trial. While faith can grow by trial, it is not the only way faith grows. Our faith can grow by spending time with God in prayer, reading His Word, and by joining together with other believers. I pray fervently you will spend more time in each of these endeavors this week.

Reflections

_____
_____
_____
_____
_____
_____
_____
_____
_____
_____
_____
_____
_____
_____
_____
_____
_____
_____
_____
_____

Thursday Romans 8:3 "What the law could not do in that it was weak through the flesh, God did by sending His own Son in the likeness of sinful flesh, on account of sin:"

God was so good to give the Israelites His laws. He was showing them He knew whom they were and how they were going to react. He understood flesh is weak. We have a Savior who is stronger than both the law and our weak flesh. He wants to tell us today: Don't count on yourself. Count on Me! Praise and Glory go to Jesus Christ and our Father who sent Him.

Reflections

Friday   **Isaiah 32:17 "The work of righteousness will be peace; and the effect of righteousness, quietness and assurance forever."**

This world and most days are filled with commotion, loud sounds, and lots of confusion. But because we have righteousness through Jesus Christ, we can call on Him any time, anywhere, to fill our surroundings with quiet and confidence. He will give us peace when things are disruptive and non-sensical. Ask Him to fill our lives for today.

Reflections

Saturday — **Romans 10:10 "With the heart one believes unto righteousness, and with the mouth confession is made unto salvation."**

From our mind comes reasoning. From our heart comes belief. With our eyes, we see God's wonders. With our ears, we hear His directions. With our mouths, we confess who He is to us and for us. Confess to others what He means to you in your life and theirs.

Reflections

May 'Flower'

April showers bring May flowers, so what do May 'flowers' bring? Pilgrims! (A childhood joke from long ago.) The Pilgrim leaders set sail for North America because they were concerned with losing their cultural identity. These men arranged with English investors to establish a new colony in North America. They faced a multitude of challenges. As Christians, we have good reason to be concerned with losing our cultural identity. Consider this question as you go through your daily devotions: Is my identity being shaped by today's culture or a Christian culture?

Sunday 2 Timothy 2:15 "Study to shew thyself approved"

Study. Once out of school, I thought I would be finished with having to study. But as I grew into my adulthood, studying became a way of life. I wanted to learn more. God tells us to study His Word. In a world of self-pleasure, we can maintain our Christian identity, as well as leave a legacy, by knowing the Word of God. What identity will your legacy leave?

Reflections

Monday James 1:23-25 "For if any be a hearer of the word, and not a doer, he is like unto a man beholding his natural face in a glass: For he beholdeth himself, and goeth his way, and straightway forgetteth what manner of man he was. But whoso looketh into the perfect law of liberty, and continueth therein, he being not a forgetful hearer, but a doer of the work, this man shall be blessed in his deed."

Am I a 'Doer'? The Pilgrims were concerned for their identity so much they set sail. To be concerned is to be involved. The word concern also references self-concern. If you are not a doer of the Word, you may be self-concerned. Set sail today, and be a hearer and a doer.

Reflections

Tuesday Luke 15:8-10 "Either what woman having ten pieces of silver, if she lose one piece, doth not light a candle, and sweep the house, and seek diligently till she find it? And when she hath found it, she calleth her friends and her neighbours together, saying, 'Rejoice with me; for I have found the piece, which I had lost.' Likewise, I say unto you, there is joy in the presence of the angels of God over one sinner that repenteth."

Seek diligently. What would cause you to set sail and seek diligently? The pilgrims left their homeland to conserve their identity. They were concerned they were losing who they were and what they stood for in their homeland. In the verse today, the woman was so concerned over what she actually lost that she lit a candle and swept the house to search for it. Are you willing to seek diligently? Are you willing to give up a few of your personal pleasures to find your right relationship with Christ?

Reflections

Wednesday Luke 15:8 (see verse for Tuesday)

Sweep the House. I remember being a young girl and trying to sweep up sugar I had spilled. Needless to say, it was very time consuming. I had to go over the area several times, and even then, I was not convinced I got all the grains. So then, I used a damp cloth to wipe the area. Sweeping your spiritual house can be like my sugar experience. Your life is ever changing and getting all the grains together may take some time, even a damp cloth. Get alone with God today, and ask Him to help you sweep your house, so you may find that which was lost.

Reflections

___
___
___
___
___
___
___
___
___
___
___
___
___
___
___
___
___
___
___
___

Thursday — Mark 4:38b-40 "and they awake him, and say unto him, 'Master, carest thou not that we perish?' And he arose, and rebuked the wind, and said unto the sea, 'Peace, be still.' And the wind ceased, and there was a great calm. And he said unto them, 'Why are ye so fearful? How is it that ye have no faith?'"

Arrival to the New Land - The pilgrims originally set their site for the mouth of the Hudson River (modern day New York), but they arrived at the tip of Cape Cod (Massachusetts). On November 11, they dropped anchor, but did not leave the ship until March 21st (four additional months on the ship!) There are times we arrive at a location other than where we planned. Like the ship's course, our course can be altered by storms. Stay with the faith God gives, and allow Him to still the storm and guide you to a safe landing.

Reflections

Friday   Facing Challenges - Book of Job

The Mayflower began its voyage with 102 Pilgrims, plus crew, and ended with 53, including the crew. Challenges and death were real on their journey. They were real to Job and his family, too, but he stood fast. There are 42 chapters in the book of Job. Struggle after struggle, Job continued to face the challenges. The strength and faith he had in God carried him through. When we turn our backs on a challenge, the challenge does not go away. We just don't see it. Trust in God with each challenge. He will give you the strength for your journey.

Reflections

Saturday   **Zephaniah 3:17 "The LORD thy God in the midst of thee is mighty; he will save, he will rejoice over thee with joy; he will rest in his love, he will joy over thee with singing."**

God is in the Midst. The Pilgrims completed their voyage and disembarked the ship to begin their new lives. With the LORD thy God in your midst, you, too, can disembark, and begin your new life. Keep God in your midst, for He is mighty. Rest in His love today, and keep your Christian cultural identity alive. He "will joy over thee with singing!"

Reflections

Father's Day

With Fathers Day coming up, I thought it would be fun to use that time to talk about our Heavenly Father and how we can honor Him.

Sunday   **John 3:16 "For God so loved the world that He gave His one and only Son, that whoever believes in him shall not perish but have eternal life."**

Our Father gave His only Son, so we can be adopted into His family. Jesus died on the cross for our sins. When we accept Jesus as our Savior and ask His forgiveness, we are given eternal life in His kingdom.

Reflections

___
___
___
___
___
___
___
___
___
___
___
___
___
___
___
___
___
___
___

Monday   **Malachi 2:10a "Have we not all one Father? Did not one God create us?"**

F for Father, our creator - God is our origin and our beginning, yet we forget this as we go about our day.

Reflections

Tuesday   **Daniel 3:17 "If we are thrown into the blazing furnace, the God we serve is able to save us from it, and he will rescue us from your hand, O King."**

A for Able - He is able to save us from the 'blazing furnace,' which we can be thrown into, or we may walk into on our own. Not only is He able to save us, He does save us. He saved Shadrach, Meshach, and Abednego from the fiery furnace. He will save us from the fiery furnace, not only in our every day lives, but also from the fires of hell. All we have to do is ask. He will.

Reflections

Wednesday   **Psalm 22:4 "In you our fathers put their trust; they trusted and you delivered them."**

T for Trust - He is Trust. No matter what, we can know that we can trust in the One True God. Trust in Him to deliver you from any and every circumstance.

Reflections

Thursday   **Romans 10:17** "Consequently, faith comes from hearing the message, and the message is heard through the word of Christ."

H for Hear - How do we hear Him? We hear Him by: being in His Word, by having faith in Him, and by witnessing what He has done for us. Through these daily devotions, you are taking part in hearing what He says to you. Listen for His still small voice. He will have something wonderful to say.

Reflections

Friday   Psalm 119:142 "Your righteousness is everlasting and your law is true."

E for Everlasting – His righteousness and truth are everlasting. The laws He gave Moses are as true today as they were when Moses received them. If we ask Him to be our Savior, He is everlastingly and ever present with us. He will abide in us until we meet Him in heaven. We cannot be without Him.

Reflections

Saturday   Revelation 19:6 "Then I heard what sounded like a great multitude, like the roar of rushing waters and like loud peals of thunder, shouting: Hallelujah! For our God Reigns."

R for Reigns – This verse brings to mind the sound of thunder from a recent storm. The feeling of the 'thunder' seemed to be in my back yard. That loudness was crying out "Our God Reigns" and thrilled my heart and magnified my soul. The next time you hear thunder, shout from your soul, "Our God Reigns."

Reflections

Summer

Let an All-powerful God REFRESH
your hot dry Spirit!

Wearing many hats,
we become hot
and flustered.
We begin to drown
in our own sweat.

―◆―

Through
Summer's devotions,
we find
God's Word cools
the hot dry spirit.

Summer

Daughter, sister, mother, wife
And now there's a salaried
position in my life.

Each day I run to and fro,
Sustaining ME has met a new low.

I ponder the words,
"He has Risen" and know for me,
ALL He has given.

Daily I search
throughout His teachings
For His answers to my beseeching.

All my hats I wear at one time
Because it is His cross
I bear and not mine.

Kathleen J. Jones

Elohim
(e-lo-HEEM)
Creator

This week, we are going to discuss "Praying" a name of God. Hopefully, we can create a habit of addressing God with one of His Holy names. As you complete each of the daily devotions, try to use Elohim specifically in your prayer. Get to know your Father in a deeper way, as each day passes.

Sunday — Genesis 1:1 **"In the beginning God created the heavens and the earth."**

This verse is so short; we often just slip by it without thinking it through. In ten short words we are told there is nothing we see, touch, smell, hear or air we breathe that He did not create. Take the day, and notice everything around you, everything you use in your day, and everything your mind conceives. Then thank Elohim for it all.

Reflections

Monday — **Genesis 1:3** **"Then God said let there be light; and there was light."**

Ever been in a terrible storm late at night and all the electricity went out? This storm took all the lights in your entire area. What did it feel like? It happened to me, and I was scarred to death. I couldn't see well enough to find the candles. I was alone; it was dark, and there was no moon or stars, just dark and wind and rain. Praise Elohim today for ALL the light He provides in those dark times and every day.

Reflections

Tuesday   **Genesis 1:26 "Then God said, "Let Us make man in Our image, according to Our likeness…"**

God loves you so much; even from the beginning, He wanted you in His image and according to the likeness of Jesus, the Holy Spirit, and all His angels. He has so much confidence in you; He never questioned making you in His image. He just made His decision, loved you, and 'made away.' We, then, become accountable for the choices we make in our life. God does not force us to 'live' in His image and likeness. Confess to Elohim today your responsibility for being made in His image and likeness. Lift praises to Him for His loving you so much.

Reflections

Wednesday — **Genesis 1:27 "So God created man in His own image; in the image of God He created him; male and female He created them."**

I was once told if God said something more than once, it must be important. Two verses next to one another state the same thought. I hope you have considered what being in God's image means to you. If you have not considered that, then do it today. If you have considered being in God's image, then ask yourself and Elohim if there are any changes you need to make in your daily living, so others can see you in His image.

Reflections

Thursday   Genesis 1:28(a)   "Then God blessed them…"

So, let me get this straight: God did all the work, and then He blessed man and woman. This picture is so backwards to our world today. Most everyone wants a pat on the back before they have finished the job, and they definitely want all the blessing for any work they may or may not have done. Maybe I'm wrong on that thought! But I'm not wrong in that God has not changed. He blesses us for work He has done. Now that is our God of gods.

Reflections

Friday — **Genesis 1:28b "…fill the earth and subdue it; have dominion over the fish of the sea, over the birds of the air, and over every living thing that moves on the earth."**

Ok—so not only does He bless man and woman, but He gives us dominion (authority) over all He has created. When is the last time you know of someone who created something from nothing and then handed control over to someone else? Let me think--never. Now that is confidence in ones creation! It is also evidence of His love. Lift up your voice today to Elohim for His confidence in you and all His creations. Take a moment to sing His praises using His name Elohim.

Reflections

Saturday   **Genesis 2:3 "Then God blessed the seventh day and sanctified it, because in it He rested from all his work which God had created and made."**

As I have noted before, to sanctify is to make holy. God made the seventh day holy, and He rested from all His work. We, as Christians, use Sunday (the first day) to call holy and rest. The reason we do that is because Sunday is the day of the week Jesus rose from the grave. Actually, I believe each day God has made is Holy. But the scripture tells us to use the day for holiness and rest. How many of us rest on that Holy day? If God did it, shouldn't we? I do understand we have so much to do in our human lives. So are we saying God did less in His Holy life? (Not a fair question? Or do you just not like the answer?) Remember to rest tomorrow, and while you do, give Elohim one more day to hear from your heart how glorious He is.

Reflections

His Refreshing Preparations

Psalm 23:5 "Thou preparest a table before me in the presence of my enemies; Thou anoints my head with oil; My cup runs over."

SUNDAY   "THOU PREPARE"

An invitation has arrived for dinner with friends. Of course you accept: no cooking, no cleaning, and no menu you have to think up. Plus, "they are your friends." But when you arrive, five minutes prior to the invitations noted time, you notice there is no aroma coming from the kitchen. The table isn't set, and the hosts aren't even finished dressing. Verse 5 promises "God prepares." He sets a date, a time, a place, and sends you an invitation. When you step to His door, the menu has been set; food assembled and cooked. The presentation is elegant and everything is at the correct serving temperature. All you have to do is sit down, and enjoy what He has prepared.

Reflections

Monday "A TABLE BEFORE ME"

When you arrived, your friend's dinner table was stacked with books, toys, and weekly papers. Before you could sit down, you not only had to clear the mess, ready the table with eating utensils, but you also had to find a chair. God's table has the most elegant cloth you can imagine, with matching napkins. You instantly notice each place setting is of the finest china and stemware. Eating utensils are, of course, gold. Serving dishes are all of crystal. The chair He offers reminds you of a throne. It is clear His table is complete.

Reflections

Tuesday "IN THE PRESENCE OF MY ENEMIES"

God has not only planned and prepared for you, He has also placed you on a throne. In addition, He does all of this for all to see. Our verse says "in the presence of my enemies." An enemy can be a rival, someone who has caused us pain, or someone who just makes us uncomfortable. The Lord wants everyone to know how much He loves us and wants to provide for us. He wants even our worst foes to be told in the boldest of ways how important we are as His children.

Reflections

Wednesday "THOU ANOINT MY HEAD"

In biblical time, only leaders, the very important, and/or rich were anointed. The anointing had very important and significant reasonings. David was anointed by Samuel, the priest of priests, in the presence of His father and brothers. I Samuel 16:13a tells us the Spirit of the Lord came upon David from that day forward.

Our verse tells us God anoints our head. We are anointed by the one true God, our Lord, Master, and Savior. We are that important to Him. All we have to do is let Him do the anointing.

Reflections

Thursday "WITH OIL"

Then and now, oil is very precious and costly. These fragrant oils were prepared according to a recipe given by God at the time the Israelites left Egypt, making them rare and considered Holy.

Today, we use fragrant oils to sooth our skin in winter and to soothe our temperaments. We use specific oils to heal burns and cuts. Take all of these properties, and know God has additives we haven't even considered. He offers healings we cannot understand. He fills our senses with fragrances we have never experienced. His oil is the oil of everlasting salvation. We only have to offer our Head for His anointing oil.

Reflections

Friday   "MY CUP"

Almost everyone has a favorite cup or glass from which they prefer to drink their favorite beverage. As time elapses, you have to refill the cup each time you want to enjoy your beverage. It is a manual, continuous process. You fill it; it fills you. Consider the beverage is a need, a hurt, an illness, a loved one for whom you are concerned. You are the cup. You are filled with this beverage. But aren't we really empty? There just isn't anymore of you to give or do. Ask God to fill your cup with His beverage, and it will be filled. Let God provide a cup kept by Him.

Reflections

Saturday   "RUNS OVER"

Ever been out to eat and the server only filled your cup half full? Or the server poured your first cup full but never came back to ask if you needed more? Did it make you want to ask, "Hey, are you running out of coffee back there?"

When God is your server, your cup is never half full. Our scripture tells us God supplies our needs to overflowing. He remains at our table to fill our cup continually. Call upon the Lord to be your server, and allow Him to fill you with His goodness and mercy the rest of your days.

Reflections

Songs

Worshiping the Lord comes in many forms. One of the ways is in song. We have favorite songs or lyrics that really bring us into a worship mode. This week, we are going to take different verses in the Bible where song is mentioned or God's people rose up in song to worship. As you go through this week, keep a song in your heart for God. You can worship Him with His words. It does not have to be a song you hear on the radio. Just take His words, and sing them back to Him.

Sunday **Zephaniah 3:14 "Sing O Daughter of Zion; shout aloud, O Israel! Be glad and rejoice with all your heart."**

Sing O Daughter - This scripture says it all! Sing aloud to God today. Shout to him, and be glad, for He has set you free. Rejoice in Him today with all your heart. There is no other that 'can do' or 'will do' what He has done and will do for you. So Sing!

Reflections

Monday   **Ephesians 5:19 "…Sing and make music in your heart to the Lord,"**

Beautiful Music with your Heart - Continue to praise Him in song today. Bring the music from your heart. Allow your praise to come from within. The music will be beautiful sounds to Our Father in Heaven. All around you will enjoy the sound, as they hear Him being praised.

Reflections

Tuesday　　1Corinthians 14:15 "...I will sing with my spirit, but I will also sing with my mind."

Mind and Spirit - So far this week, we have shouted to The Lord and sung with our heart. Now let us sing with our mind and our spirit. Give it all to Him. Praise Him with all you have. Let there be nothing left of you that is not praising Him today.

Reflections

Wednesday Isaiah 5:1 "I will sing for the one I love…"

The One you Love - We hear many songs of love: some about the Lord and some about people we love. Today, give your song only to Him. No other can love you the way He does, and today, give it back to Him in song. Show Him how much you love Him by singing just to Him.

Reflections

Thursday Psalm 33:3 "Sing to him a new song…"

Sing a new Song - Take anything you have today that will make music. It may be a pencil you tap on your leg. It makes music when you are praising Your Lord. Sing to Him: words you feel, words you think about Him. It is a new song to Him. Let Him hear your music.

Reflections

Friday   **Judges 5:3 "Hear this, you kings! Listen, you rulers! I will sing to the Lord, I will sing; I will make music to the Lord, the God of Israel."**

Sing only to Him - This song is the beginning of the 'Song of Deborah' when God gave the Israelites victory. Sing with Deborah as she sang praises to God for the victory she was given. Remember the victories you have been given by God. Let the rulers and the kings of the times you were chained, hear you praising the One who set you free and gave you victory.

Reflections

Saturday Revelation 5:13 **"Then I heard every creature in heaven and on earth and under the earth and the sea and all that is in them, singing;"**

Hear Everyone Sing - They are singing, "Worthy is the Lamb." Close this week in song, telling Him and all you know, He is worthy. He was slain for you. Praise Him for all He has done. As Deborah sang, you also sing, for the victory He has given. Raise your hands as you sing, "You Are Worthy! Worthy is the Lamb!"

Reflections

What Waiting Can Bring

Sunday — **Acts 1:4 "And being assembled together with them, He commanded them not to depart from Jerusalem, but to wait for the Promise of the Father, 'which', He said, 'You have heard from me;'"**

Jesus was with His disciples just before He ascended to His Father in heaven. Before leaving, He did two things: he instructed them to <u>wait</u> and reminded them of a <u>promise</u> given. Waiting is always hard, especially if what we wait for is significant. The disciples were waiting for the largest gift ever to be given. The only gift any bigger was Jesus' death on the cross. Jesus told them previously of this promise, but it was so important, He mentioned it again. If Christ has asked you to wait at any time, the outcome must be huge. So wait with His patience, His love, and His expectations.

Reflections

Monday   **Acts 1:5 "for John truly baptized with water, but you shall be baptized with the Holy Spirit not many days from now."**

To be baptized is to be immersed. John immersed with water. But now, not only has Christ promised the Holy Spirit, but also He promised the disciples would be immersed with the Holy Spirit. This same promise belongs to each of us. When we accept Jesus as our personal savior, we are immersed with the Holy Spirit. This means the Holy Spirit covers us from head to toe, inside and out. He covers our thoughts, what we see, hear, and breathe. He covers our bodies, so everything we touch is also touched by the Holy Spirit. These are the reasons we are to stay holy. We should not be responsible for putting the Holy Spirit in or on anything, which can be deemed unholy. Remember your immersion today.

Reflections

Tuesday **Acts 1:6** "Therefore, when they had come together, they asked Him, saying, 'Lord, will You at this time restore the kingdom to Israel?'"

When I read today's verses, the question that comes immediately to mind is, "Did you hear what He is giving you?" As soon as I ask, I am reminded of the times I have been waiting so very long, and my mind goes back to things I wanted in the past, and yet they still have not come to fruition. The disciples were also stuck on what they wanted from the past. But instead of being stuck in the past, we should stay on tract with what Jesus wants for us now. Remind yourself today what He wants for you today and the future.

Reflections

Wednesday   Acts 1:7 "And He said to them, 'It is not for you to know times or seasons which the Father has put in His own authority.'"

I feel like I hear a little frustration in Jesus when He speaks the above passage. But, it is just my interpretation. Scripture tells us He is patient beyond our comprehension. Frustrated or not, Jesus was emphatic: "It is not for you to know!" The word 'surprise' indicates something that is unexpected, and yet it is our human nature to want to know ahead of schedule. But Jesus says, "Trust in me, in the Father." Know He has the perfect time and season for all things. Wait for His surprise today. He will follow through.

Reflections

Thursday   **Acts 1:7 "And He said to them, 'It is not for you to know times or seasons which the Father has put in His own authority.'"**

Some of us, by nature, take all the authority others will let us have. Some of us want others to take the authority. For those who do not care to be authoritative, following this scripture is a little easier. For those of us who want all authority, this scripture should be memorized and repeated daily. It is God Himself who has put authority under His power. This is authority over all things, including when to answer prayers: immediately or later or perhaps not in the way we expect. Life has taught me, I do not have the experience to know what is best and when is best. God, in His infinite wisdom and love, knows and delivers when the time is exactly right for all concerned. Remember this day answers affect all those around us, and God looks out for all.

Reflections

Friday — **Acts 1: 8a** **"But you shall receive power when the Holy Spirit has come upon you;"**

Take a moment, and think about something you prayed for, but you had to wait to receive. When God answered, did it not leave you with a powerful feeling? The Holy Spirit is powerful. By Him and through Him, we can accomplish anything. God's Word promises us that. We often do not call upon this power, but that does not mean it is not there. This power is not to be used foolishly or selfishly, but we are called to use it. Today use the power of the Holy Spirit to witness in a new way to someone you love or just someone you know.

Reflections

Saturday — **Acts 1:8b "and you shall be witnesses to Me in Jerusalem, and in all Judea and Samaria, and to the end of the earth."**

This is the day we have waited for, the day of our witness for Him. Matter of fact, this is the day He has waited for, the day we would call upon Him to become the witnesses He deserves. We have all waited long enough. Pull out all the stops! Call upon the Holy Spirit you have been immersed in, and witness in your work place, your city, your state, and throughout the world.

Reflections

Church of Philadelphia

Revelation 3:7-13 "And to the angel of the church in Philadelphia write; These things saith he that is holy, he that is true, he that hath the key of David, he that openeth, and no man shutteth; and shutteth, and no man openeth; I know thy works: behold, I have set before thee an open door, and no man can shut it: for thou hast a little strength, and hast kept my word, and hast not denied my name. Behold, I will make them of the synagogue of Satan, which say they are Jews, and are not, but do lie; behold, I will make them to come and worship before thy feet, and to know that I have loved thee. Because thou hast kept the word of my patience, I also will keep thee from the hour of temptation, which shall come upon all the world, to try them that dwell upon the earth. Behold, I come quickly: hold that fast which thou hast, that no man take thy crown. Him that overcometh will I make a pillar in the temple of my God, and he shall go no more out: and I will write upon him the name of my God, and the name of the city of my God, which is new Jerusalem, which cometh down out of heaven from my God: and I will write upon him my new name. He that hath an ear, let him hear what the Spirit saith unto the churches."

Sunday   "An Open Door that no man can shut"

To think that our God will set an open door before us that no man can shut is amazing. Being a loser of keys, I have been locked out a time or two. Trying to find a way inside is exasperating. God will give us an open door to be a witness for Him. In the United States of America, we have an open door to follow Him. Do you follow Him? We can say a lot with our mouths, but what are we saying with our actions? Watch for the open doors He gives you?

Reflections

_____

_____

_____

_____

_____

_____

_____

Monday   "Little Strength"

How strong are you? God's Word tells us we are fighting a spiritual battle. Our strength is little. We are made strong through Christ. Rely on His strength to make you strong.

Reflections

Tuesday "Kept God's Word"

Can you imagine meeting God face to face and hearing Him say to you, "You kept my Word"? The Church of Philadelphia is definitely special. How were they able to hear these words from God? You may say to yourself, "I can not keep all His Word. I am not perfect. Even God tells us we are not perfect." You are right; we are not perfect, which is why we cannot keep His entire Word. However, when we repent, we keep His Word. You see, part of His Word also tells us to repent. How can you keep His Word unless you know it? Make a renewed commitment today to learn God's Word and keep it.

Reflections

Wednesday **"Did not deny God's name"**

Deny – what a word! Have you ever been in denial: when things around you are not what you would like them to be, or maybe you are not what you want to be? Whatever the situation, being in denial is not accepting the truth. God is truth. This church did not deny his name. They accepted God and accepted Him for who HE is. Do you accept God for all He is? Let's be like the church of Philadelphia: accept God and do not deny His name.

Reflections

Thursday   **"Keep thee from the hour of temptation"**

Satan and his demons come to us in hoards at times, fighting with everything they can and in every way they can. God tells us He will not allow us to be tempted above that which we are able to bear. The choice is ours! God keeps the door open for us. What will our choice be when we are tempted? He can and will keep us from temptation. But, we must ask. Do you ask?

Reflections

Friday   "Hold fast"

Is there a consequence to not holding fast to God's Word? Yes, we can lose a reward. I am reminded of the first time my husband held our firstborn. Our child was so tiny, and my husband did not want to drop him. As I watched while he held our little boy, I noticed the baby's leg was a light shade of blue. His father was holding fast! That is the way we are to hold on to the things of God: with a strong tight grip.

Reflections

Saturday   **"Him that overcometh will I make a pillar."**

When you have times that the word 'overcome' does not fit into your vocabulary, remember this verse. God tells us He will make us a pillar. Pillars are the MAJOR support in any building. We can overcome, and when we do, we are able to be a MAJOR support for others. What a joy to know we can actually be a helper to someone else. Oh, I know there are times you can not even help yourself, let alone another, but isn't that what we are here for: to be able to be a support for each other when we can? To Him that overcometh, I will make a pillar! Be an 'over-comer.'

Reflections

"Our Father"

Sunday   **Psalm 68:5**   "A Father to the fatherless, and a defender of the widow, is God in His holy habitation."

If you had an earthly father who was very attentive to you growing up, it isn't hard to imagine or understand what it means to call our Lord "Our Father." Words that describe this position in life consist of: protector, provider, teacher, trainer, fixer, patient, strong, and decision maker, just to name a few. Take time today to think on these titles. Even if your earthly father did not meet these names, your Heavenly Father does.

Reflections

Monday   Isaiah 64:8   **"But now, O' Lord, You are our Father; We are the clay, and You our potter; And all we are the work of Your Hand."**

Ever feel like your life is spinning out of control? The only way to make clay into a perfect "pot" is to spin it on a wheel as it is being shaped. The best part of our life of clay, is that Jesus Christ our Savior, Lord, and Father, is the one pressing the feed for the spin. His hands shape our "pot." These are steady hands, never wavering, never pressing too tightly or lightly. His touch is always one of perfection.

Reflections

Tuesday — **Isaiah 63:16 "Doubtless You are our Father, Though Abraham was ignorant of us, And Israel does not acknowledge us. You, O LORD, are our Father; Our Redeemer from Everlasting is Your name."**

From the very beginning, to the everlasting of time, the "point" is: The Lord Jesus Christ is our Father, our Redeemer. Even those who came before us and had no knowledge of us or those within our midst today who refuse to admit we belong to the Lord, do not matter. The only true "point" is the Lord our Father. Isaiah says, it does not matter whom or when, no one can argue this "point." Remind yourself of this point several times today.

Reflections

Wednesday   **Matthew 12:50**   **"For who ever does the will of My Father in heaven is my brother and sister and mother."**

Jesus calls the Lord, His Father. He tells us many times, if we obey or follow the wishes of His Father, we become His sister(s)/brother(s). This can only mean His Father becomes our Father. The only stipulation for this equation is that we must do the will of the Father. What is His will for you today? Today is all you need to think about. His will for you is so finely planned; you only have to follow one day at a time. Ask forgiveness where you failed yesterday. Follow Him today. Tomorrow has been settled by the Father.

Reflections

Thursday **Mark 11:25** **"And whenever you stand praying, if you have anything against anyone, forgive him, that your Father in heaven may also forgive you your trespasses."**

We are told at least twice in God's Word we must forgive those that trespass against us. That is the only way God will forgive us. Scripture says "anything against anyone." Anything! Anyone! Pretty big area! But guess what? This also includes YOU. Yep, you must forgive you. So dig down today, and confess that torment you have been carrying as baggage. Confess it to yourself. Now that it is confessed, forgive yourself. It is over. Gone FINISHED. You belong to the Father. He forgives you, too.

Reflections

Friday   John 6:44 "No one can come to me unless the Father who sent me draws him; and I will raise him up at the last day."

Jesus states in order for us to get to Him, our Father must first have called us or drawn us to Him. So, our Father not only forgives us, but calls us. Do you have a memory of your earthly father calling you as a child? If you do not remember your earthly father then someone else?

This calling for you must have been important. Think it through. The person calling you had to stop what they were doing, walk to the porch or another room, decide words to use, adjust their voice to the appropriate level so you could hear, and then the caller had to engage the brain to speak. Even though calling out is something we do every day, it is a process. Our Heavenly Father is responsible for calling us to Our Savior. It is a process. Think on that today. Then thank Him, (Our Father).

Reflections

Saturday   **John 5:19 "Then Jesus answered and said to them 'Most assuredly, I say to you, the Son can do nothing of Himself, but what He sees the Father do; for whatever He does, the Son also does in like manner.'"**

Jesus knew what to do, only because He saw the Father do it. How is it we expect ourselves to do anything without seeing our Father do it? There is only one way we can "see our Father" do anything. We have to read His Word, contemplate His Word, pray His Word, and then do His Word. All our steps and happenings are in His Word. Our only responsibilities are to see, to watch, and to do, in like manner.

Reflections

You Are God's Specialty

We can all be known for running the gambit of emotions in a very short time span. God made us this way, and He has a plan for us to follow, no matter in which seat of the emotional roller coaster we sit.

Sunday　　**II Chronicles 5:14 "so that the priests could not continue ministering because of the cloud; for the glory of the Lord filled the house of God."**

　　　　　　Matthew 5:4 "Blessed are those who mourn, for they shall inherit the earth."

Day one, you wake up feeling really good and upbeat. You know you have issues that must be dealt with, but it is 'all good,' and God will supply. Then, you receive information that literally leaves you gasping for breath in your lungs and heart.

Reflections

Monday **I Corinthians 14:33** "For God is not the author of confusion but of peace, as in all the churches of the saints."

Deuteronomy 1:30 "The Lord your God, who goes before you, He will fight for you according to all He did for you in Egypt before your eyes."

Day two, you wake up in a daze. You try to reprocess yesterday's information, but you just cannot get any of it to make sense. You are totally confused for yourself and your loved ones. Then, you become protective toward those you love. Your mind races to what questions they will have. Can you answer their questions, and will they worry needlessly?

Reflections

Tuesday   **Jeremiah 29:11 "For I know the thoughts that I think toward you, says the Lord, thoughts of peace and not of evil, to give you a future and a hope."**

James 4:7 "Therefore submit to God. Resist the devil and he will flee from you."

Day three, the moment your eyes open, the scriptures begin to flood your mind. They are reassuring scriptures, full of love and hope. Then, almost immediately, your mind becomes confused because you cannot find any logical reasoning about your information.

Reflections

_____
_____
_____
_____
_____
_____
_____
_____
_____
_____
_____
_____
_____
_____
_____
_____
_____

Wednesday   **Proverbs 16:32 "He who is slow to anger is better than the mighty, and he who rules his spirit than he who takes a city."**

II Timothy 1:7 "For God has not given us a spirit of fear, but of Power and of love and of a sound mind."

Day four, you spend most of the day replaying the last three days. You begin to feel angry. You are angry at yourself, angry at the information, and angry that even on the Internet, there are no explanations. Then, you call a friend and discuss the information and just how you feel. You confess you really do not know how you feel. You are so confused. All confidence in what you thought you knew is gone.

Reflections

Thursday **Hebrews 10:35-36** "Therefore do not cast away your confidence, which has great reward. For you have need of endurance, so that after you have done the will of God, you may receive the promise...."

Romans 8:1 "There is therefore now no condemnation to those who are In Christ Jesus, who do not walk according to the flesh, But according to the Spirit."

Day five, some explanations for your information have suddenly come through. It all seems so simple. Why, you ask yourself, was the information not given in this manner in the beginning? Then, you audibly berate yourself by softly speaking, "Oh ye of little faith."

Reflections

Friday — Hebrews 13:5 "Let your conduct be without covetousness; be content with such things as you have, For He Himself has said, 'I will never leave you nor forsake you.'"

I John 3:2 "Beloved, now we are children of God; and it has not yet been revealed what we shall be, but we know that when He is revealed, we shall be like Him, for we shall see Him as He is."

Day six, you awaken knowing there are issues to deal with, but God will supply.

Reflections

_____
_____
_____
_____
_____
_____
_____
_____
_____
_____
_____
_____
_____
_____
_____
_____
_____
_____
_____
_____

Saturday   Psalm 34:1 "I will bless the Lord at all times; His praise shall continually be in my mouth."

Psalm 92:1 "It is good to give thanks to the Lord, and to sing praises to Your name, O Most High."

Psalm 96:4 "The Lord is great and greatly to be praised; He is to be feared above all gods."

Day seven, your heart, mind, and soul are full of praise and the desire to never stop the thanksgiving and bringing honor to His glory.

Reflections

_____
_____
_____
_____
_____
_____
_____
_____
_____
_____
_____
_____
_____
_____
_____
_____
_____
_____
_____
_____

Letting Go and Letting God

At times, I find myself in a pool of my very own "needing to let go" and wondering if I am going under for the last time. To illustrate my point: I recently saw a chipmunk caught in the middle of a backyard swimming pool. How long had he been in there? With the strength he had left, he paddled his feet as fast as he could, struggling with all his might to stay afloat. As I stood and watched out for him, my friend ran to get the pool net. I could see him fighting for what seemed to be his last breath. Several jerks of his head told me in no uncertain terms we had to help and quick. With one scoop of the net he was safe. His breathing was faint, and we could tell he was so tired. He lay there for some time. Then after gaining just enough strength to muster his escape, he was off, and I knew he went to find his safe place.

Letting go and letting God is not as easy as it sounds. Sometimes we find ourselves treading water in pools of our own making or a pool someone else has made. Truly letting go and letting God can be possible. Through the devotions this week, I pray the Holy Spirit will guide you and help you out of your pool. I pray He will scoop you up into His net of safety. There you can breathe the fresh air of Jesus Christ. Open your heart to Him. He will NOT let you drown.

Sunday   **I Peter 5:7 "Casting all your care on Him; for he careth for you."**

In this verse, we are told to CAST (throw with force). And we are told what we are to cast – CARE – How much? ALL! Whose? OURS! I thought I was to cast 'the thing' on Him. But, we are to cast our 'care' on Him. One definition of 'care' is 'a troubled state of mind.' Throw with force our troubled state of mind on Jesus. Do that today. Go fly fishing, and do some 'casting.'

Reflections

Monday Matthew 13:47 "Again, the kingdom of heaven is like unto a net, which was cast into the sea, and gathered the good into vessels, but cast the bad away."

A net gave the chipmunk his life again. God's net is ready to rescue us too. Far too many times, I have felt my head jerking so as to not go under. This verse shows me that we can be rescued. Think of the vastness of the sea. Then think of the net of God being 'cast' into that vastness to rescue you. In the mist of the sea, we are as a speck of sand. Praise God His net is woven tight enough that we will not fall out. We don't have to struggle. All we need to do is trust in Christ

Reflections

Tuesday   **Psalm 88:4 "I am counted with them that go down into the pit: I am as a man that hath no strength…."**

The chipmunk tried with all of his strength to live and not drown. But what it really took was the strength of another to scoop him into the net and set him on his own feet. The same is true for us. We need only allow the Lord to scoop us up and set us on our feet.

Reflections

___
___
___
___
___
___
___
___
___
___
___
___
___
___
___
___

Wednesday   Psalm 18:1-3 "…The LORD is my rock, and my fortress, and my deliverer; my God, my strength, in whom I will trust; my buckler, and the horn of my salvation, and my high tower. I will call upon the LORD, who is worthy to be praised: so shall I be saved from mine enemies."

As the chipmunk began to jerk his head, it was as if his feet just could not go anymore. We are like that when we are trying on our own. We get to a point that we cannot go on (the point where Satan wants us). Try as he might, this chipmunk's strength was failing. In Psalm 18 we are told twice that God is our strength. Refer to the last section, 'saved from mine enemies'. Satan would have us drown and drown in a big way, but this verse tells us that we can CALL ON THE LORD, and be rescued.

Reflections

Thursday II Corinthians 10:5 "...bringing into captivity every thought to the obedience of Christ..."

When we are held captive by the waters in the mist of the pool, we are unable to swim to the edge and climb out by ourselves. At times, I feel I am a captive in my own world. I am being held captive by the indecisiveness of my heart and mind. I paddle with whatever strength I can muster. However, we can bring our thoughts into captivity through His Word, and we can determine in our hearts and minds that we will obey Christ.

Reflections

Friday   I Corinthians 9:24b "... so, run that ye may obtain."

Hebrews 12:1 "...let us run with patience the race that is set before us,"

Just as the chipmunk ran once his strength returned, we too should run that we may obtain. We must run the race that is set before us, and we each have a different race to run. The pool drained the strength from the chipmunk, but once out, he was able to continue his race. We, too, must continue our race.

Reflections

Saturday   **Psalms 4:8 "I will both lay me down in peace, and sleep: for thou, LORD, only makest me dwell in safety."**

The chipmunk was off to safety, even though danger continued to lurk ahead. Our danger continues as well. Satan will not stop his attacks against us until our earthly life is over. We can dwell in the Lord's safety and lay down in peace and sleep. Stay in your 'SAFE' place. Let go, and let GOD.

Reflections

Faith

We show faith to this world each day when we: open the closet door, flip the light switch, or turn the key in the ignition to start the car. How do you show your faith to your Father in Heaven? Since faith is a noun we cannot 'do' faith. We must 'do' an action to show Him our faith. You showed faith when you: opened the closet door to find something there to wear, flipped the light switch trusting in the electricity, or turned the key in the ignition faithfully believing the car would start.

Sunday   **Hebrews 11:6 "But without faith it is impossible to please Him, for he who comes to God must believe that He is, and that He is a rewarder of those who diligently seek Him."**

Just how do we diligently seek Him? Here are a few ideas. We can pray or talk to Him often through out the day. We can read His words given to us divinely in the Bible. We can serve Him daily by looking for those who need Him in various ways. Bow and ask the Lord Jesus Christ to open your eyes to an action that will show Him your faith. Be ready to act. This is one prayer He will answer quickly.

Reflections

_____

_____

_____

_____

_____

_____

_____

_____

_____

_____

_____

_____

Monday Hebrews 11:8 "By faith Abraham obeyed when he was called to go out to the place which he would receive as an inheritance. And he went out, not knowing where he was going."

If you don't know the story of Abraham, go to Genesis 12 and read it. It is a story you can use to get you started on this road of faith. Here was a man comfortable in his way of life. God told him, "Get out of your country." Sounds a little more than scary! But Abraham did not resist. With wife, nephew, and other family members in tow, he showed his faith and obeyed God. Ask God to show you something you can do for Him today. Then obey.

Reflections

Tuesday Hebrews 11:9 "By faith he dwelt in the land of promise as in a foreign country, dwelling in tents with Isaac and Jacob, the heirs with him of the same promise;"

Sometimes our daily life puts us in a foreign land. You know the one, the place where, from the moment you awoke, nothing felt real or normal. No matter how hard you tried, you couldn't get back home, where everything is right and goes according to plan or at least to your expectations. But this day, the day you are awake in that foreign place, everything from putting butter on your toast, to answering your bosses' twentieth question, has left you feeling alone. Dwell there today, but ask God to join you. The problem with a foreign land is you feel alone. God never leaves us alone. He is always there for us to call upon. The best part is: He wants you to call.

Reflections

Wednesday — **Hebrews 11:11 "By faith Sarah herself also received strength to conceive seed, and she bore a child when she was past the age, because she judged Him faithful who had promised."**

God had promised Sarah a child. Sarah bore that child because of her faith in God's promise, a child that was very important in the line of Jesus our Savior. God is no less faithful to us than He was to Sarah. He has made us countless promises in the Bible. Take hold of them. Judge Him to be faithful in all our needs and wants. Hold to those truths. By holding to those truths, we will be strong and able to receive His benefits today and tomorrow. Praise Him today for: the strength He has given you, His faithfulness, and His love for you.

Reflections

Thursday   **Hebrews 11:30 "By faith the walls of Jericho fell down after they were encircled for seven days."**

Jericho was a walled city in the land given to Joshua and the Israelites. The story is in Joshua starting Chapter 6. Joshua had no idea how to fight these mighty men and this walled city. He and the Israelites had just barely entered the Promise Land. They were not warriors. We so very often have walls that need to come down, walls that hold a myriad of mighty foes. God didn't leave Joshua to bring down the walls alone. Read Joshua 5:13-15, and see how God sent help. He will do the same for you. Pick any wall you have. Pray and ask God to help you encircle the wall and blow your trumpet. It might take seven days, it might take longer, but God will be with you every day the wall is still up. Only by His strength can the wall come down. Only by your faith will God bring the wall down.

Reflections

Friday　　Hebrews 11:31 "By faith the harlot Rahab did not perish with those who did not believe, when she had received the spies with peace."

When the spies came to Rahab's door, she could have turned them away. She could have told the city leaders the spies had visited her and what the spies told her. She could have done a lot of things, but what she did was 'believe.' She had faith God would save her and her family from the planned destruction of the city. It is by our faith we are saved through Jesus Christ, who died on the cross and rose again. If you have not accepted Him as your personal Savior, ask Him today. Ask Him to forgive your sins and become your Adoni (Lord and Master). He loves you and wants you to spend eternity with Him. Do not perish with others, but have eternal life through Jesus Christ.

Reflections

Saturday — **Hebrews 12:2 "…looking unto Jesus, the author and finisher of our faith, who for the joy that was set before Him endured the cross, despising the shame and has sat down at the right hand of the throne of God."**

Because He loves you so much, Jesus endured the cross with joy. He is now at the right hand of God, His Father and yours. By our faith, we will join Him, who authored and finished your faith. Sing His praises this day for bearing the shame of the cross and being the author and finisher of our faith.

Reflections

Unquenchable Love

Sunday   **Song of Solomon 8:7 "Many waters cannot quench love, neither can the floods drown it: if a man would give all the substance of his house for love, it would utterly be condemned."**

The Song of Solomon is a wonderful book of love and everything love encompasses. I fell in love with this book while a very young preacher spoke the words with much passion. I could not help but be captivated. I realized God's love in a wonderful and exciting new way. I challenge you to take your bible, and read the entire Song of Solomon. Read it with the love and passion of God. Let His Unquenchable Love encompass your whole being.

Reflections

Monday — **John 15:13 "Greater love hath no man than this, that a man lay down his life for his friends."**

John is considered a friend of God. Can you imagine what that is like? Are you a friend of God? You can be. God showed His unquenchable love by giving His Son for our sins. If you miss a friend or loved one, cuddle up to The Heavenly Father. "Greater love hath no man…"

Reflections

Tuesday   **Proverbs 27:6 "Faithful are the wounds of a friend; but the kisses of an enemy are deceitful."**

How do you feel about friendly criticism? Do we enjoy having others tell us what they consider wrong about us, about our actions, or for that matter, anything to do with 'us'? Today's verse tells us a wound of a friend is 'faithful.' If you are the friend to "inflict the wound," I am sure you hurt as well. Let Jesus help you. He is faithful. Pray, and ask Him. On the flip side, if you are the one that "receives the wound," call on Jesus. He will guide you through the healing process. I pray your wounds will heal to make you a stronger friend of God.

Reflections

Wednesday Hebrews 3:13 **"But exhort one another daily, while it is called Today; lest any of you be hardened through the deceitfulness of sin."**

I heard a message on the radio about spiritual lethargy. (To hear the entire radio message, go to http://www.harvest.org/radio/, and check out the radio archives for the week of June 10 – 15). Let me see if I can paraphrase to you in a few sentences what the message was. There were ten virgins at the wedding feast: five prepared and five not prepared. Here is the spin that is not normally preached. If the five were so prepared, why didn't they address the fact that the other five were not? They were all part of the 'wedding party.' Should not they have been a help to others? Here is a point made in the sermon: When we have a really good meal and eat too much, we may desire sleep and even take a nap. Have we done this, as Christian's? Are we taking a nap and forgetting that today will only be called today, once. When it is over, it becomes yesterday. Unquenchable love is a love that refuses to be put out or subdued. If we are not exhorting one another, what are we doing? This verse says if we are not exhorting then we better be careful because being hardened by deceitfulness of sin is just around the corner. While to exhort can be to lift up or spur on, it can also mean to warn or to admonish. Let's go out there, and exhort one another TODAY!

Reflections

Thursday   1 John 3:17 "But whoso hath this world's good, and seeth his brother have need, and shutteth up his bowels of compassion from him, how dwelleth the love of God in him?"

Take care to note this verse begins with 'but whoso hath.' You cannot give what you do not have. I know this verse says the 'world's good,' but think of it this way: if we have something, anything of value, including the gospel of Christ, we are to share it with others in need. How can we shut up our compassion and not give to the need of others. So many are hurting, ask for strength and compassion from Jesus. Be a witness for Him TODAY.

Reflections

Friday   **Ephesians 3:19**   "**And to know the love of Christ, which passeth knowledge, that ye might be filled with all the fullness of God.**"

Being filled with all the fullness of God might seem impossible on earth; nevertheless, this verse tells us that we can know the love of Christ. Knowing the love of Christ, we will be filled with His unquenchable love. Praise Him, and feel His unquenchable love deep within your soul. Know the reality of Romans 8:39: "Nor height, nor depth, nor any other creature, shall be able to separate us from the love of God, which is in Christ Jesus our Lord."

Reflections

Saturday Ephesians 5:1-2 "Be ye therefore followers of God, as dear children; And walk in love, as Christ also hath loved us, and hath given himself for us an offering and a sacrifice to God for a sweet-smelling savor."

Saturday represents the end of a workweek for most of us. Our spiritual workweek will end with our trip to heaven. At the end of my lifetime, I want to be known by God as a follower of God. Walk in God's Unquenchable Love. As you go forward in your life, I pray you remember the Song of Solomon, Chapter 8, verse 7: "an unquenchable love."

Reflections

Know

The word 'know' is defined as "information firmly in the mind, firm belief in the truth of something, and to recognize differences." Throughout God's Word, we are told we can know some things. Ezekiel 37 tells of "The Valley of Dry Bones." In verse 13 and 14 of Ezekiel, the once very dry bones are told they "shall know." This week, we will see a variety of verses in which we can "be firm" in our knowledge. We CAN KNOW God's Word.

Sunday   **Exodus 6:7**   **"And I will take you to me for a people, and I will be to you a God: and ye shall know that I am the LORD your God, which bringeth you out from under the burdens of the Egyptians."**

As we rest in Jesus today, let Him bring us out from under the burdens in our lives and in our hearts. We can live free and act on our freedom. Try this: replace each 'you' and 'ye' with your name, then replace the word 'Egyptian' with each of your burdens (name them all) – God waits to bring you out of bondage.

Reflections

Monday   John 8:32 "And ye shall know the truth, and the truth shall make you free."

This chapter of John began with a desire to trick. However, Jesus turned the trick into a chance to show His real purpose. The Pharisees and scribes did not want the real truth. But Jesus is the real truth. No matter what is going on in our lives today, we can be sure Jesus is our truth, and He will set us free: spiritually free, emotionally free, and mentally free. Jesus is there for us. Know His truth, and be free.

Reflections

Tuesday **James 4:14** "**Whereas ye know not what shall be on the morrow. For what is your life? It is even a vapour, that appeareth for a little time, and then vanisheth away.**"

May I suggest you read the entire chapter of James 4? Drawing close to God will give you the security your heart desires. Our flesh will try to use that desire for evil and enticements. God is the only one that knows our tomorrows. Let us pray, and leave those tomorrows in His most capable hands. Plan your future in Christ, and He will direct your path in all your tomorrows.

Reflections

Wednesday — Joshua 3:10 "And Joshua said, Hereby ye shall know that the living God is among you."

Everyday, every moment, and every space, our living God is among us. How comforting to know He wants to be among us. When we are: at our lows, excited and happy, doing laundry, or shopping, He is there. If we have accepted Christ as our Savior, then He is always among us. That is something HE wants us to KNOW.

Reflections

Thursday   Matthew 7:20 **"Wherefore by their fruits ye shall know them."**

Some people just seem to constantly be judging others in how they look, what they wear, where they live, what they drive, and how they speak (just to name a few instances). Matthew, Chapter 7, tells us that we do not need to be concerned with those things. If we want to know if a person is in the family of God, we are to look at their fruits. What 'fruits' are you bearing today? Can others look at you and see an orchard of wonderful fruits? Or do they see barren trees? Perhaps there is a drought going on in your life, in your orchard. Make a change today, and let others see your basket full of bountiful fruit.

Reflections

Friday   Joshua 4:22   **"Then ye shall let your children know."**

Children are a blessing from God. Can our children look at our lives and 'really' know we have a relationship with Christ? Can they know we trust our future to God? This chapter tells of leaving a 'reminder' for the children, so they will ask, and then they can be told how God brought the Israelites out from bondage. What reminder do our children see in us? You may not have a child, but this applies to you as well. Children look at all adults. Let them KNOW the Christ that lives within you.

Reflections

Saturday   **Isaiah 43:10**   "**Ye are my witnesses, saith the LORD, and my servant whom I have chosen: that ye may know and believe me, and understand that I am he: before me there was no God formed, neither shall there be after me.**"

In this verse, God tells us we can know and believe Him. He also says we can understand that He is God. He chose us. We are His witnesses, and it is our responsibility to be a witness for Him. When you have no strength and feel no life within, let God breathe His spirit and life into your soul. Rest in Him, and know that He is the Lord.

Reflections

Sleep

I am a very light sleeper, but sleep is something our bodies require. This week, let's take a look at sleep from God's Word. Join me, and let the Holy Spirit guide you.

Sunday — **Genesis 2:21 "And the LORD caused a deep sleep to fall upon Adam, and he slept: and he took one of his ribs, and closed up the flesh instead thereof…"**

Deep/Restful Sleep: A comforting restful sleep knowing you are where God wants you to be. The Lord caused Adam's deep sleep. When we live in a close relationship with Christ, we, too, can have "deep restful sleep." Trust in Him each day, and you can be sure your sleep will be restful.

Reflections

Monday   **Genesis 15:12** "And when the sun was going down, a deep sleep fell upon Abram; and lo, an horror of great darkness fell upon him…"

Horror Sleep and Troubled dreams: God had told Abram what was on the horizon. He told Abram in his dream that his seed was going to be afflicted for 400 years. How sad to know your relatives were going to be servants/slaves for 400 years. What pain Abram must have felt. We may be sleeping, but the troubling knowledge of the future does now allow us to have 'Sunday's' sleep. We can trust God throughout our troubling times, and He will give us the sleep our bodies need.

Reflections

Tuesday   **Genesis 31:40** "Thus I was; in the day the drought consumed me, and the frost by night, and my sleep departed from mine eyes."

Troubled and No Sleep: Consumed by your 'issue'? We can allow problems, concerns, or life issues to consume us, and we become a Jacob, without sleep. When we turn our problems, concerns, and real life issues to Christ, we become as Adam. Our body and soul are healed through our restful sleep.

Reflections

Wednesday   Ezekiel 34:24-26 "And I the LORD will be their God, and my servant David a prince among them; I the LORD have spoken it. And I will make with them a covenant of peace, and will cause the evil beasts to cease out of the land: and they shall dwell safely in the wilderness, and sleep in the woods. And I will make them and the places round about my hill a blessing; and I will cause the shower to come down in his season; there shall be showers of blessing."

Restful Sleep in the Woods: Blessings while in the wilderness of life's trials. I am not a camper. Sleeping in the woods is not a happy time for me. But this verse tells us having the Lord as our God, we can dwell safely in the wilderness and actually SLEEP in the woods. We can have this same safety and sleep in the wilderness of life's trials. Let the LORD be your God.

Reflections

Thursday   **Proverbs 6:9 "How long wilt thou sleep, O sluggard? When wilt thou arise out of thy sleep?"**

Arise out of Sleep: Time to WAKE UP. A sluggard is sluggish, slow, and almost lethargic. When we neglect reading our bible and praying one day at a time, we are at risk of becoming a sluggard. Proverbs tells us it is time to wake up, and ARISE OUT of our sleep. Use the energy God gives you, and press forward with His strength.

Reflections

Friday   **Proverbs 3:24** **"When thou liest down, thou shalt not be afraid: yea, thou shalt lie down, and thy sleep shall be sweet."**

Sweet Sleep: Lie down with a smile. Alone on a dark and dreary night with only the quite of nature can be scary to some. There are people who might consider courage to mean we are never afraid. We can have the courage of Christ. When we have His courage, we will not be afraid. We can lie down and have a wonderful sweet sleep. Our sleep can resemble our favorite 'sweet treat' Accept the courage of Christ. Lie down, and wake up with a sweet smile on your face.

Reflections

Saturday   **Genesis 28:16 "And Jacob awaked out of his sleep, and he said, 'Surely the LORD is in this place; and I knew it not.'"**

Awaken out of Sleep: Jacob had been sent out by his father to find a bride. It was a long journey, and Jacob found a place to lay his head. He struggled all night long and woke to realize the LORD was with him. We go through our days and nights with trials, tribulations, questions, and concerns. We can struggle and fight, but struggling and fighting will be to no avail. Lay your needs and desires in the almighty hand of God. Awaken out of your sleep, and trust in Him today. HE WILL perform that which He desires in you.

Reflections

Ultimate Sacrifice

John 15:13 "**Greater love hath no man than this, that a man lay down his life for his friends.**" We have several Federal holidays to remember our military. Men and women have given their lives for the freedom of the United States of America, as well as protecting around the globe. Christ made the ultimate sacrifice for all. His life was given to pay the sin debt for all. Sacrifice is to give up something of value. Let's consider our sacrifice this week

Sunday   **Exodus 8:27 "We will go three days' journey into the wilderness, and sacrifice to the LORD our God, as he shall command us."**

Can I sacrifice? Sacrifice as a noun means 'an act of offering to a deity.' Sacrifice as a verb means 'to make or perform.' Moses pled with Pharaoh to sacrifice to the LORD. He would not give in to Pharaoh and sacrifice within the Egyptians' homeland. He would not compromise the instruction the Lord had given him. We can sacrifice as the children of Israel did. We can leave the bondage of our Egypt. Take time today, and ask God to help you stand strong and not compromise the instructions He gives to you.

Reflections

Monday   **John 15:12**   **"This is my commandment, that ye love one another, as I have loved you."**

Time and Personal Desire: Having a friend is very special. When we are a friend, we are charged with a very serious responsibility. What are our motives as a friend? Do we have time for our friends? Do we sacrifice our personal desires for the needs of our friends? Through the strength and guidance of the Holy Spirit, we can be a true friend and love as He loves us.

Reflections

Tuesday   **I Timothy 2:1 "I exhort therefore, that, first of all, supplications, prayers, intercessions, and giving of thanks, be made for all men."**

Prayer and Supplication: Jesus called us 'friend' throughout the New Testament. We have the privilege of 'prayer and supplication.' Jesus spent many hours in prayer. Take time today to follow His example and sacrifice some of your time in prayer for your friends and family. Making a list is a good way to stay on focus during your prayer time.

Reflections

Wednesday   **I Chronicles 16:11-1 b2**   **"Seek the LORD and his strength, seek his face continually. Remember his marvelous works that he hath done, his wonders, and the judgments of his mouth…"**

Marvelous Works: Here we are at mid-week, and for many, this is considered 'hump day.' (The day we have reached the top of the hill.) We are on the tip of the hump and ready for a downhill slide. This can signify a time of ease. During our 'time of ease,' remember His marvelous works, His wonders, and the wonderful judgments of His mouth! Let Him love you to a pleasant calm of heart.

Reflections

Thursday   **Hebrews 12:1** "Wherefore seeing we also are compassed about with so great a cloud of witnesses, let us lay aside every weight, and the sin which doth so easily best us, and let us run with patience the race that is set before us."

Lay aside the weight: Men and women of the military are quick to learn they must follow orders. They must also lay aside every weight that may cause them or their squad harm. Their focus must be on the situation at hand. As Christians, we, too, must learn to lay aside those weights and even the sin that plagues our very soul. We can run WITH PATIENCE the race that is set before us! God has a plan for your life. Run the race that is set before you.

Reflections

Friday   **Hebrews 12:2 "Looking unto Jesus the author and finisher of our faith; who for the joy that was set before him endured the cross, despising the shame, and is set down at the right hand of the throne of God."**

Endure: Sometimes, we feel as if we cannot endure our situation. This verse shows us that the ultimate endurance was made by the author and finisher of our faith: Jesus Christ. Once the ultimate sacrifice was made, Jesus was set down at the right hand of the throne of God.

Reflections

_____

_____

_____

_____

_____

_____

_____

_____

_____

_____

_____

_____

_____

_____

_____

_____

_____

Saturday   **John 15:13 "Greater love hath no man than this, that a man lay down his life for his friends."**

John 3:16 "For God so loved the world that he gave his only begotten son, that whosoever believeth in him should not perish, but have everlasting life."

The Ultimate Sacrifice: The Ultimate Sacrifice was made by Jesus Christ. He gave his life for his friends. Join me in pledging today to follow Christ and strive to show others they too can have everlasting life with Him.

Reflections

_____
_____
_____
_____
_____
_____
_____
_____
_____
_____
_____
_____
_____
_____
_____
_____
_____
_____
_____
_____
_____
_____
_____
_____

Autumn

Life's changing colors are revealed
using God's Plan.

Colorful trials span
throughout the lives
of the young teen
to the busy co-ed,
from the unwed mother
to the career traveler,
and from the newly wed
through to the great-grandmother.
These trials can cause women
to dwell on the negatives of life.

◆

Colors come to life
as we rely on God's Word.
Relax and enjoy each new day,
as Autumn's devotions
bring you
to a closer relationship
with Christ.

AUTUMN

A coolness in the breeze
tells of changes in the air.;
just what trials may abound,
and do I care?

Colors surround me as do needs.
All becomes shades of grey
and my depression it feeds.

He holds my tether full of hope.
By His Word I find my rope.

His grasp on me is ever tight.
He received all of me
when he fought that fight.

As years have passed, I love Him more.
Thinking often of the Cross He bore.

From dusk till dawn, I will sing His praise
Because it was for me, from death He raised.

Kathleen J. Jones

Adoration of Our Holy Father

Adoration can mean affection, love, passion, worship, devotion, or idolatry. When the negatives of life seem to engulf your very soul, let this weeks devotions bring the 'Adoration of your Holy Father' to fruition. Lift your voice and hands in praise.

Sunday   **Psalm 37:4 "Delight yourself also in the Lord, and He shall give you the desires of your heart."**

Has God told us He will give us anything we want in today's scripture? Yes and No! Yes, if we delight ourselves in the Lord. Our desires change if our focus is on God. We become more in tune to his desires for us. The more often we seek him by our prayers and reading his word, the more closely we listen to what is right and what fits into his plan. Show Him your true affection today by lifting your voice to him. Listen for his response, and then go forward.

Reflections

Monday   **Joshua 23:11 "Therefore take careful heed to yourselves that you love the Lord your God."**

When we truly love someone, our actions show it. We try to make life easier for them in every way. We listen to their advice. We accept their knowledge of a particular experience. We more readily accept their help in certain areas of our life. The same is true with your love for your Holy Father. The more you love Him the more closely you will listen to His advice. He has made a plan for you. Ask him to show you His plan, and then respond to it.

Reflections

Tuesday   **Philippians 2:8** "**And being found in appearance as a man, He humbled Himself and became obedient to the point of death, even the death of the cross.**"

What are you passionate about? Does chocolate, coffee, children, spouse, or shopping come to mind? Would you die for your passion? Jesus did. He had only one passion. That passion included leaving heaven, becoming a man, and following the will of His Father to die on the cross. Because Jesus followed His passion, He now sits at the right hand of God. Make your passion the Holy Father and His will for you. Your rewards will be incomprehensible.

Reflections

Wednesday — **Exodus 34:8 "So Moses made haste and bowed his head toward the earth and worshipped."**

Bowing our head is a good place to begin when worshiping the Lord. To carry the journey forward, we must set our hearts toward our destinations. Having a right heart will change our attitude. Turning our attitudes, we will replace old actions with new ones. Actions show our true worship of the Father. Bow your head today. Move your heart; navigate your attitude, and act upon your Lord's wishes.

Reflections

Thursday Matthew 26:33 "Peter answered and said to Him, 'Even if all are made to stumble because of You, I will never be made to stumble.'"

And yet, we know Peter did stumble. But his devotion to Christ was always deep within. Jesus knew what was about to happen and cautioned Peter about the events. When the Roman guards came for Jesus, Peter panicked and went the way of everyone else. After Jesus rose again, he went personally to Peter and forgave him. We, like Peter, sometimes let our 'happenings' get in front of our devotion to Christ. Ask His forgiveness today for any time you may have failed to let your devotion to Him control all your 'happenings.'

Reflections

Friday   Exodus 20:3 "You shall have no other gods before me."

This is the first commandment given to Moses. It is our first commandment today. But some of the 'gods' we bow to today are: television, jobs, comforts we enjoy, children, or husbands. Though we owe Him everything from life itself to the everlasting life with Him, we still put other things before Him. Spend time today putting aside all those 'gods' and put Him first in all you do or say.

Reflections

Saturday**Deuteronomy 6:5** "You shall love the Lord your God with all your heart, with all your soul, and with all your strength."

Loving the Lord your God with heart, soul, and strength is to put Him first in every thought and deed. To do this you must first offer Him your independence. Ask Him to direct all your paths, speech, and thoughts. Give Him your Adoration with your deeds and your words.

Reflections

Prosperity

When you hear the words "prosperity" or "prosperous," does your mind automatically think MONEY? We can be prosperous in many ways, only one of which includes our money. In reading God's Word, we will find ways He is the God of Prosperity. We will also find what He expects us to do with the prosperity He brings us.

Sunday — **Genesis 33:11 "'Please take my blessing that is brought to you, because God has dealt graciously with me, and because I have enough.' So he urged him and he took it."**

These are words spoken by Jacob to Esau upon Jacob's return to his homeland. Remember, Jacob had fled after having taken Esau's blessing deceitfully. While away, Jacob had become very rich. He was rich in money, wives, flocks, and his relationship with God. God had blessed him substantially. When Jacob returned, he gave Esau a sizable portion of his money, flocks, and household goods. Take stock of all you have this week. Is there a portion you might share?

Reflections

Monday   **Psalm 127:1 "Unless the Lord builds the house, they labor in vein who build it, unless the Lord guards the city, the watchman stays awake in vain."**

Are you trying to build your prosperity without God? His words cannot be any plainer. If you are trying to do anything without His blessings it just won't work out the way it should. I agree, there are those very prosperous that have nothing to do with God, but if we were allowed a close look into their daily lives, we might not find things so 'happily ever after.' Include the Father in your plans for prosperity, whether those plans be building a house or guarding all you currently have.

Reflections

Tuesday   **Ecclesiastes 7:14 "In the day of prosperity be joyful, but in the day of adversity consider: Surely God has appointed the one as well as the other, so that man can find out nothing that will come after him."**

By God's design, we have prosperity and adversity. Which ever you are in the midst of at this time, know the other will occur. God set it up that way. There have been times I have been in the midst of both at the same time. Maybe my money was doing great, but my family or friendship life was so out of whack I wondered if I would make it through. We have so many facets to our lives; it is imperative we consider each facet before deciding if He has placed us in a waste and or if He has set us on the mountaintop.

Reflections

Wednesday — **Hosea 4:7 "The more they increased, the more they sinned against ME; I will change their glory into shame."**

One reason God may not have increased our prosperity to its full potential is the verse above. The more God gave the Israelites, the more they sinned against His will. Check yourself on just how you are responding to the prosperity God has brought you. If you are sure there is NO prosperity in your life, ask yourself, "How have I responded to God in the past?"

Reflections

Thursday   **Hosea 13:6**   **"When they had pasture they were filled; they were filled and their heart was exalted; therefore they forgot ME."**

A very real danger in prosperity is that it can lead us to abandon our relationship with Christ. We get so busy in the "more and more" business, we do not take the time to build our prosperity in our relationship with God. Our time becomes filled more and more with work, family, and friends and whatever we can find to take time away from the one who really loves us. Set aside time today and every day to make your relationship with the Father and Son prosperous.

Reflections

Friday   **II Chronicles 12:1 "Now it came to pass, when Rehoboam had established the kingdom and had strengthened himself, that he forsook the law of the Lord, and all Israel along with him."**

When we get so sure of where we are and how we are doing, it isn't just ourselves that can be pulled away from God and what He has for us. We all hold some kind of leadership: maybe as parent or worker or spouse. Others are watching what and how we do. Don't become a Rehoboam and take the entire country down with you! Lift your attitude toward your prosperity to Christ today--let Him help you.

Reflections

Saturday   **II Chronicles 26:16 "But when he was strong his heart was lifted up, to his destruction, for he transgressed against the Lord his God by entering the temple of the Lord to burn incense on the altar of incense."**

Uzziah became king at the age of 16. He did many great things for more than just Israel. He was so well known, kings from other lands brought him gifts. Remember the scripture "pride goeth before the fall?" Uzziah became so prosperous in all areas but one, his relationship with God, he felt equal to perform what God had commanded only the high priest could do. Be careful with your pride. Always remember where all prosperity comes from!Go with God and His Son Jesus Christ this week, and fill your bowls full of prosperity.

Reflections

Directions

There are times we want to know exactly how to get from A to Z. We are now in the technology age where we can pull up maps on the Internet or possibly we have a GPS in our cars. For those of us that do not know what a GPS is: Basically, it is a small computer showing the best way to get from A to Z. However, we have always had our **GPS, *'God Paved Streets'*.** We are going to spend this week looking at the directions God has given us to travel 'His' paved streets.

Sunday   Jeremiah 29:11 "For I know the plans I have for you declares the Lord…"

We begin this week knowing He has already set our directions in place. His word tells us, He knows His plans for us. They are not the same plans for all. We each have our own streets we are to take. They are paved by God. Today, pray for Him to show you the direction He wants you to go.

Reflections

Monday   **Genesis 11:27 "the Lord had said to Abram 'Leave your country, your people and your father's household and go to the land I will show you.'"**

Sometimes our directions are not complete. We must take each step one at a time. God did not give Abram the complete path he was to take all at one time. He said, "Go where I show you." We must use our faith to follow the paved street because we know who paved this street.

Reflections

Tuesday **Jonah 1:1-3a** "The word of the Lord came to Jonah son of Amittal; 'Go to the great city of Nineveh and preach against it, because its wickedness has come up before me.' But Jonah ran away from the Lord and headed for Tarshish…"

Sometimes we know exactly where we are to go. He has given us the complete direction, each and every street, every turn and even what we are to do once we get there. But we disobey. We run from Him. We are afraid of what we must do, or like Jonah, we disagree with why or what He has planned for us. Do not be afraid to follow His Street. Have faith in God. He knows much more about our capabilities than we do.

Reflections

Wednesday Joshua 1:2 "Moses my servant is dead. Now then, you and all these people get ready to cross the Jordan River into the land I am about to give to them -- to the Israelites."

Be clear in the direction God is sending you. Get ready to go, and do what He is telling you to do. Make certain you understand where, when, and how you are to take your step. Ask Him for the plan. He may only give you the first part, but that is the beginning, and that may be all you need for that moment.

Reflections

Thursday   Joshua 1:9 "Have I not commanded you? Be strong and courageous. Do not be terrified; do not be discouraged for the Lord your God will be with you wherever you go."

Be confident that wherever God is sending you, you will be able to fulfill His plan. He has created you with abilities you need, and He will be with you. He has not given you these abilities to waste. Use them for His Glory. You will be glad you did.

Reflections

Friday Joshua 1:8 **"Do not let this book of the law depart from your mouth; meditate on it day and night, so that you may be careful to do everything written in it. Then you will be prosperous and successful."**

There are times we will want to take a turn away from God's path. Be aware of the stop signs and turns calling out to you. Avoid them by knowing and being in His Word daily. He will help you avoid the pit falls. Following God's path brings prosperity and success.

Reflections

Saturday   Joshua 1:11b **"Get your supplies ready. Three days from now you will cross the Jordan here to go in and take possession of the land the Lord your God is giving you for your own."**

Get ready and go. Pick up what you need to take, and commit yourself to the work God has for you. He is waiting for you to accept His plan for your life. Begin traveling on 'God Paved Streets.'

Reflections

Words

There are some words we use everyday, but what do they really mean to our Lord and us. Day Light Savings brings changes to our outside world. But this could be a time we should be looking toward making changes to our inside world. We will take words we use in our 'outside world' and see what our 'inside world' (the Holy Spirit within us) has to say about the real meanings.

Sunday   **Romans 6:16 "Don't you know that when you offer yourselves to someone to obey him as slaves, you are slaves to the one whom you obey-whether you are slaves to sin which leads to death, or to obedience which leads to righteousness?"**

Obedience - A dictionary defines obedience as the act or practice of following instructions, complying with rules or regulations, or submitting to someone's authority. Referring to the scripture above, to whose authority are we submitting ourselves? Are we submitting ourselves to the regulations or rules of the world outside, or are we allowing the Holy Spirit to give us instructions? Do we take the instructions and comply, or do we take the easy way and go with the world? Today, before you make a decision small or large, ask the Holy Spirit to guide you. Allow Him to give you instruction and comply with His authority. He knows where the decision will lead.

Reflections

_____
_____
_____
_____
_____
_____
_____
_____
_____

Monday   **Psalm 37:5-6 "Commit your way to the Lord; trust in Him and He will do this; He will make your righteousness shine like the dawn, the justice of your cause like the noonday sun."**

Commitment - Commitment is loyalty, devotion or dedication. Commitment to the Lord has its rewards, as does a commitment to the outside world. Committing our way to the Father will allow the righteousness within us to shine like the morning dawn. This is a brightness that allows a new beginning each day, no matter what the day before may have hidden. His justice shines like the noonday sun. He went to the cross for us, so we would not live in darkness. Today, commit all of yourself to The Lord not just your heart, but all of your ways…your complete life. He will shine through you today no matter what darkness lurks around you.

Reflections

Tuesday   Psalm 74:16-17   "The day is Yours, and Yours also the night; You established the sun and moon. It was You who set all the boundaries of the earth; You made both summer and winter."

Boundaries - Boundaries are limits: the point at which something ends or beyond, when it becomes something else. Have you set your own limits, or do you allow God to set them for you? Are you living in your own comfortable land, or are you stepping out in faith? He set the boundaries of this world. Our scripture tells us He established the sun and the moon. He knows whether you can survive the cold winter, and He also made the heat of the summer. Allow Him to set your limits. Step out in faith today, and cross over the boundaries you have drawn. He will keep you in the warmth of His winter and the cool of His summer.

Reflections

Wednesday I Chronicles 29:18 "O Lord, God of our fathers Abraham, Isaac and Israel, keep this desire in the hearts of your people forever, and keep their hearts loyal to you."

Loyalty - Loyalty is a feeling of devotion. As you read the words "a feeling of devotion," do they create a desire in your heart to jump up and praise The Lord? The writer is appealing to the Lord to keep the yearning for Him in the hearts of his people forever. The appeal includes to be ever devoted to Him and to ever serve Him. Do you yearn for this desire? Take time, and ask Our Father to put this desire in your heart. Be steadfast, dedicated, and faithful to Him who is always faithful to you.

Reflections

Thursday   Romans 12:8   "...if it is leadership let him govern diligently..."

Leadership - Leadership is the ability to guide, direct, or influence people. To be diligent is to show persistent and hard-working effort in doing something. We may not think of ourselves as leaders, but God knows when He wants us to lead. This scripture speaks of the gift of leadership. There are times when God gives you the leadership ability to show others His ways and direct them to Him. Just as we spoke of boundaries yesterday, the time may be right for you to direct the path of a loved one to Him. Ask Him today to show you if this is that moment in time. If now is the time, He will give you this ability. Then go for it with diligence for The Lord.

Reflections

Friday 2 Timothy 4:2 "…be prepared in season and out of season…"

Prepared – Being prepared is to be ready beforehand or to put together in advance. Yesterday, we spoke of leadership; today know He has prepared this day for you. He knows where this day will lead. Allow Him to prepare you for each event that will take place today. You will be allowed to experience a day of learning and growing as you have never before. Remember, He set the day beforehand. He made it ready for you. Now allow Him to ready you.

Reflections

Saturday   **Deuteronomy 33:12 "…Let the beloved of the LORD rest secure in him, for he shields him all day long, and the one the LORD loves rests between his shoulders."**

Security - Security is the state or feeling of being safe and protected, freedom from worries. Do you rest in the security of The Lord? Do you feel safe and protected or free from the worries of each day? Today, give those worries to Him; allow Him to shield you all day long. Relax, and know you are the beloved of The Father, and rest between HIS shoulders.

Reflections

A Week of Thanksgiving

There are times in our lives when the only thing to do is lift praise and thanksgiving to our Lord Jesus Christ. Often, we feel inept at just what to say to get our feelings across. I have found the best way to say what I want to say is to turn to the scriptures, and pray them to God. For this week, take each scripture, and write it on a card or a piece of paper, and carry it with you. During any lull in your day, pull out the scripture, and say it allowed in an attitude of prayer. Remember to write your first thoughts of the scripture in the reflection section of the book. Praise Him often and honestly.

Sunday   **Psalm 9:1 – 2**   "**I will praise You, O Lord, with my whole heart; I will tell of all Your marvelous works. I will be glad and rejoice in You; I will sing praise to Your name, O Most High.**"

Reflections

_____
_____
_____
_____
_____
_____
_____
_____
_____
_____
_____
_____
_____
_____
_____

Monday — Psalm 13:6 "I will sing to the Lord, because He has dealt bountifully with me."

Reflections

Tuesday   **Psalm 26:7 – 8** "That I may proclaim with the voice of thanksgiving, and tell of all Your wondrous works, Lord. I have loved the habitation of Your house, and the place where Your glory dwells."

Reflections

Wednesday   **Psalm 40:5** "Many, O Lord my God, are Your wonderful works which You have done; and Your thoughts toward us cannot be recounted to You in order; if I would declare and speak of them, they are more than can be numbered…"

Reflections

Thursday   Psalm 92:1, 2, 4   "It is good to give thanks to the Lord, and to sing praises to Your name, O Most High; to declare Your loving-kindness in the morning, and Your faithfulness every night… For You, Lord, have made me glad through Your work; I will triumph in the works of Your hands."

Reflections

Friday   **Psalm 98:1** "Oh, sing to the Lord a new song! For He has done marvelous things; His right hand and His holy arm have gained Him the victory."

Reflections

Saturday   **Psalm 136: 1 – 3**   **"Oh, give thanks to the Lord, for He is good! For His mercy endures forever. Oh, give thanks to the God of gods! For His mercy endures forever. Oh, give thanks to the Lord of lords! For His mercy endures forever:"**

Reflections

Hezekiah – Added Days

2 Kings 20:1-7 "In those days was Hezekiah sick unto death. And the prophet Isaiah the son of Amoz came to him, and said unto him, 'Thus saith the LORD, Set thine house in order; for thou shalt die, and not live.' Then he turned his face to the wall, and prayed unto the LORD, saying, I beseech thee, O LORD, remember now how I have walked before thee in truth and with a perfect heart, and have done that which is good in thy sight. And Hezekiah wept sore. And it came to pass, afore Isaiah was gone out into the middle court, that the word of the LORD came to him, saying, Turn again, and tell Hezekiah the captain of my people, Thus saith the LORD, the God of David thy father, 'I have heard thy prayer, I have seen thy tears: behold, I will heal thee: on the third day thou shalt go up unto the house of the LORD. And I will add unto thy days fifteen years; and I will deliver thee and this city out of the hand of the king of Assyria; and I will defend this city for mine own sake, and for my servant David's sake.' And Isaiah said, 'Take a lump of figs. And they took and laid it on the boil, and he recovered.'"

Sunday   "set thine house in order"

There comes a time when order is necessary. As a compulsive list maker, order is part of my everyday life. But I have friends, who never have order show up at their doorsteps. The order in this scripture was directed by God to Hezekiah. He was sick unto death, as the word comes from Isaiah, and Hezekiah knew this was serious. We can live every day with our house in order. Talk to God about your house (physical and emotional as well as your 'household.') HE will help you, and direct you to set your house in order today.

Reflections

_____

_____

_____

_____

_____

_____

_____

Monday   **"and Hezekiah wept sore"**

Nights and days pass; weeping seems as if it will never subside. Then one day, you feel the presence of God, and you are able to dry some of those tears and freshen up. Hezekiah knew the right person to pray to. Verse 3 says it all: "I beseech thee, O LORD." It is important that we know whom to beseech. Loved ones can be a great help because they are there in the flesh, but when we are deep in pain, we need the supernatural help that only God can give. Call on Him today for yourself or a loved one.

Reflections

Tuesday   "have walked – have done"

When Hezekiah prayed to God, he reminded God of what he 'had' done and how he 'had' acted. I cannot help but wonder how God really felt about the 'have' done. God has such a wonderful love for us that I am sure He smiled and remembered the joy He felt while Hezekiah walked in the truth, had a perfect heart, and even did well in the sight of God. That pleasantry must have caused God to smile, and thus, He 'added the days.' We, too, can make God smile. Everyday be a part of God's smile.

Reflections

Wednesday "I have heard thy prayer"

Here is one example of proof that God will hear our prayers. Hezekiah prayed unto the Lord, and Isaiah did not even have time to leave the courtyard before God told him to turn around, and go back to tell Hezekiah the Lord heard him. Amazing! Maybe our prayers don't always get answered that fast, but they can be. Rest in the knowledge that God wants to hear our prayers. Go to HIM today. Let Him say to you, "I have heard thy prayer."

Reflections

Thursday   "I have seen thy tears"

I have had my fair share of tear-filled nights that NO one saw or knew. How did I get through? Because I knew God saw my tears. I knew God cared about every tear that seeped from my eyes. When I had cried so much that tears refused to come, God still saw my tears. He will see your tears, too. The pain in your soul can only be healed by our wonderful God. Don't be afraid to let HIM see. He already knows and wants to comfort you.

Reflections

Friday   **"I will heal thee"**

Let an all knowing, all-powerful God heal you. Times can seem so very hard. We need emotional healing, physical healing, and spiritual healing. No one can heal like our Savior. Hezekiah was sick unto DEATH. In whatever way you relate to Hezekiah's situation, ALLOW GOD TO HEAL YOU.

Reflections

Saturday   Why did God heal Hezekiah?

Besides the fact that he heard his prayer and saw his tears, why did God heal Hezekiah, as well as deliver him? Check out verse 6, God wants us to see and know HIS MAJESTY! He says, "for mine own sake, and for my servant David's sake." God made a promise, and HE keeps HIS promises. If you read the rest of this story, you will see that Hezekiah became very selfish in his thinking, and God knew that, yet He still healed him. This gives me the thought that it really wasn't for Hezekiah's sake that God healed him. It was to show God's own Majesty. We are not here for 'us.' Although we are God's children, and He loves us, this whole earthly experience is about God and God showing HIS MAJESTY. Be a part of that showing, and tell others about HIM.

**Let others see God in your EVERDAY life.
And every 'added day' you have, Live for Christ**

Reflections

A Way of Life

For this week, we are going to Matthew, chapter 5, and dig deep about what Jesus had to say about our every day life. Of course, Jesus was talking in ancient times, but all He ever said is relevant today. His truths were relevant then; they are relevant today, and they will be relevant as long as He allows us to have tomorrows.

Sunday   **Matthew 5:18 "For assuredly, I say to you, till heaven and earth pass away, one jot or one tittle will by no means pass from the law till all is fulfilled."**

Thousands of people protest living under the law. There are laws of nature, laws of man, and laws of God. Think for a moment what life would be like if we had no laws.

Did your mind refuse to go any further when you got to the first mass chaos? Mine did. Jesus is telling us we can change anything anytime, but all God has previously said will come true. Praise God today for His laws and all His promises of fulfillment.

Reflections

Monday   Matthew 5:22a   "But I say to you that whoever is angry with his brother without a cause shall be in danger of the judgment."

Know someone with a habit that just pricks you every time you are around them? Maybe it is an action, or maybe a sound they make, or maybe something they say. It could be something you believe they should change in their life, but instead they just keep complaining about it. But it doesn't matter what the prick to you is. Jesus says if we are angry with our brother (or sister) for just being who they are, it is to our detriment. Bow today, and ask the Father to forgive you. Then go, and ask your brother or sister for their forgiveness. Chances are they didn't even realize they were bothering you.

Reflections

Tuesday   **Matthew 5:28**   **"But I say to you that whoever looks at a woman to lust for her has already committed adultery with her in his heart."**

Jesus addressed how men were looking at women, but this door swings both ways. If a female has seen some hunk and wondered what he would be like in the sack, then you are as guilty as the men of which Jesus spoke. There are other lusts we must control, too. Sometimes, we lust for jewelry, a large home, a new vehicle, lots of money, or closets full of clothes. All these lusts can bring destruction. They may cause us to lie and cheat in ways we would never have considered before. Watch where and on what you set your mind to thinking. Kneel, and ask Jesus for forgiveness. Then ask Him to put your thoughts on Him.

Reflections

Wednesday — **Matthew 5:32** **"But I say to you that whoever divorces his wife for any reason except sexual immorality causes her to commit adultery; and whoever marries a woman who is divorced commits adultery."**

Divorce is thought to be a way of life in today's society. But that is not how God planned it. If this is something that has happened to you, I am truly sorry. There never has been a "good" divorce. It hurts to the deepest core. And it hurts our Father in heaven even more deeply. But our heavenly Father can heal you and make you well. He can and will choose your next partner. Give yourself time to heal and time for Him to point you in the right direction. Spend your waiting time in His word with His people. Thank Him today for bringing you through.

Reflections

Thursday   **Matthew 5:37**   **"But let your 'Yes' be 'Yes' and your 'No' be 'No.' For whatever is more than these is from the evil one."**

Wouldn't it be wonderful in this life if we could trust one another so much we could do away with contracts and courts? But of course, we cannot. There are those in this world who will cheat just because they can. But you don't have to be one of them. If you say you will do something, do it. Take the responsibility of keeping your word. Both yes and no hold responsibility. You just have to figure out which one is the right one for the moment. Ask our Father before you answer with yes or no. He will give you the correct reply for every situation. He knows your tomorrows, and only He knows which things you can and cannot do.

Reflections

Friday — **Matthew 5:42 "Give to him who asks you, and from him who wants to borrow from you do not turn away."**

There are those of us who are especially good at giving. Then, there are those of us who always think twice before we let go. Jesus says give to those who ask, and do not turn away those who want to borrow. The truth is we cannot out give Jesus. If we will just let go and give what others might need, He will provide more than we need. He will fill our cup to overflowing. It is one of His many promises to us. So let go today, and give to someone who asks, and do not turn away. Thank Jesus for the opportunity to show His love to someone else.

Reflections

Saturday   **Matthew 5:44 "But I say to you, love your enemies, bless those who curse you, do good to those who hate you, and pray for those who spitefully use you and persecute you."**

This may be the hardest of Jesus' teachings to perform on a day-by-day basis. When we have been hurt, either physically or emotionally, it is difficult to lift the person who hurt us to the Lord. But that is exactly what Jesus tells us to do. If we can do this, there is a two-fold blessing for us. First, lifting that person up just may be the thing that brings him or her to the saving power of Jesus Christ. That person will not understand your reaction to the pain caused and could very well ask you why you reacted the way you did. If so, you have the perfect opportunity to speak of our Savior. Second, by lifting that person up to God and forgiving the injustice done to you, God provides a salve to you. He is our balm. He will heal the hurt and draw us closer to Him.

Reflections

From The Cross

From the beginning, Jesus' total concern has been for us. The cross was His darkest hour, and His most glorious hour (until His second coming). This week, we will spend our time learning from Him how to spend our most 'wanting' moments.

Sunday   Luke 23:34 **"Father, forgive them for they do not know what they do. And they divided His garments and cast lots."**

Forgiveness - Jesus was not just physically in pain on the cross, but from His words, we can believe His heart was breaking over what He knew was coming for this human race. Jesus saw the deepest hurts people would cause and where those causes would lead. In dividing His garments, the soldiers removed every symbol of His life as a man. Bit amidst their evil deeds, Jesus opened the door to their salvation. Should there be people you know who are doing their best to bring their lives to ruin, pray God will forgive them for what they do not know they do.

Reflections

Monday Luke 23:43 "I tell you the truth, today you will be with Me in paradise."

Paradise - Those who hung on crosses next to Jesus were definitely sinners. We cannot say they deserved the cross or even that they deserved to die, but they did deserve punishment. They were at their weakest moment on their crosses, too. Jesus knew who and what they had done; yet His provision was mercy to the point of paradise. So even if we are in the midst of punishment, Jesus will provide the mercy we need for His paradise.

Reflections

Tuesday — John 19:26b-27a "...He said to His mother, 'Woman, behold your son!' Then He said to the disciple, 'Behold your mother!'"

Provision - The loss of someone we love often causes us to focus on the negatives. Jesus knew focusing on the negative is not in our best interest. He provided an opportunity for His mother and His disciple to focus on something they could and would respond to for each other. If you have been handed a loss or know someone who has, provide a positive for him or her or yourself to focus on for a while.

Reflections

Wednesday Matthew 27:46 "Eloi, Eloi, lama sabachthani? That is, 'My God, My God, why have you forsaken me?'"

Forsaken - God is supremely holy and will never be in the midst of sin. Because Jesus took on all our sins, God had no choice but to turn His back on him. Jesus did what His Father requested, but He still had to bare the pain of our sins, which is separation from His Holy Father. When we have sinned, we are separated from our Holy Father. But because Jesus was forsaken on the cross, all we have to do is confess our sin, and we are again in God's presence.

Reflections

Thursday Luke 23:46b "...He said, 'Father, into Your hands, I commit my spirit.'"

Commitment - Jesus so trusted His Father that even in His darkest moment, He remained committed to God's desires. We, too, must commit to our Father in all our circumstances, and trust in His outcome.

Reflections

Friday John 19:30b "…He said, 'It is finished!' And bowing His head, He gave up His spirit."

Finished - Jesus freely gave all, including, His life, for us. At the moment He gave up His spirit, He made it possible for us to spend eternity with Him. If you have not given your life and spirit to Jesus, do it today. Ask Him now to forgive your sins, and tell Him you trust Him to be your Savior and Lord. Amen. It, too, is finished for you.

Reflections

Saturday   Luke 24:6-7   "He is not here, but is raised! Remember how He spoke to you when He was still in Galilee, saying, 'The Son of Man must be delivered into the hands of sinful men, be crucified and on the third day be risen.'"

Risen This is our testament for the proof that He lives today. If Jesus had not been raised from the dead, all He told us would be for naught. It all would have been a lie. If the truth is not in His resurrection, then the truth is not in the Bible. The truth is: He did rise and is coming again.

Reflections

Prayer of Jabez

I Chronicles 4:9-10 "And Jabez was more honourable than his brethren: and his mother called his name Jabez, saying, Because I bare him with sorrow. And Jabez called on the God of Israel, saying, Oh that thou wouldest bless me indeed, and enlarge my coast, and that thine hand might be with me, and that thou wouldest keep me from evil, that it may not grieve me! And God granted him that which he requested."

When December comes we wonder, "Where did the year go?" And we think, "What did I do with MY life this year?" With January around the corner, we start thinking about resolutions and how we can change ourselves for the better. This week's devotions center on a man who is remembered for his prayer—a prayer some may think selfish. But if we are to better ourselves, then don't we need to look at ourselves? After all it is ourselves we are trying to change. And change will come if we dedicate ourselves to this type of prayer. The change will come, and you will be thrilled.

Sunday   **"More honourable" "His mother bare him in sorrow"**

Finding these two phrases together confused me until I prayed. My own view on this is that Jabez's mother had already born several 'boys.' Life was hard on her, and then bam! She was pregnant again. Perhaps, it was a hard pregnancy, but the bible uses the word 'sorrow' not pain. Therefore, I believe she felt within herself something to the effect of, "Another child! Lord, you know my heart is heavy with my children now. How can I deal with yet another child?" But she did. And praise God because that child's name ended up in the bible in the mist of a lot of lineage detail where other names are left out. Do you wonder why? First phrase: "More honourable." We can look to our God and go through whatever he lays before us, and we can know that God will be in control, if we allow it. If you are in sorrow today, give it over to God. He will make your sorrow yield results, 'More honourable.'

Reflections

_____
_____
_____
_____
_____

Monday   **"And Jabez called on the God of Israel, saying…"**

Did you pray the prayer today? The recording of this awesome prayer begins with 'And Jabez was more honourable than his brethren…' I am sure he was not haughty or high-minded about this because then he wouldn't really have been 'honorable.' We can be honorable, and we can be MORE honorable. How? Do as Jabez, and call on God. He will keep us honorable. There is a lot the word honorable encompasses, so check out your dictionary. I think you will be amazed. For now, call on God.

Reflections

Tuesday   **"...Oh that thou wouldest bless me indeed,"**

Here is Jabez, whose name means pain, coming right out and asking God to bless him. He goes a step farther and adds the 'indeed.' I looked that word up. 'Indeed' actually goes back to a previous word used to give it 'more,' to give it 'strength,' or to add 'emphasis.' Think about this today. Jabez did not just ask for the Lord to bless him. He asked the Lord to BLESS HIM AND BLESS HIM INDEED. Again, my rendition: pour it on me Lord, not just a little, but really flood me with your blessing. We are NOT being selfish to ask God for His blessings. God wants to bless us. Ask Him today. "Oh that thou wouldest bless me indeed."

Reflections

Wednesday "and enlarge my coast,"

We have to go to a word study to get the meat of this request. Coast is not just a shoreline. My wonderful friend 'Webster' also gives the word 'frontier' as a definition for 'coast.' "It is a border between two countries, a stronghold – a region that forms the margin of settled or developed territory – the farthermost limits of knowledge or achievement in a particular subject."

Jabez asked for his 'stronghold,' his 'margin' to be enlarged. Pray this prayer today: "Jesus, enlarge the territory that is settled within me. Allow the limits to stretch and grow. Make the line that divides the calm and the raging within me to move, and make way for more calm in my soul." Yes, Jabez looked to God to enlarge his coast, and so can we.

Reflections

Thursday   **"...and that thine hand might be with me,"**

Jabez knew that in order for him to 'live up to' this prayer request, he could NOT be the one in control. The control must come from God and God alone. I looked up the word 'hand,' and in one simple definition, I found the reason for Jabez asking for God's 'hand' to be with him. Think about this: 'the hands are the chief organs for physically manipulating the environment, using the roughest to the finest motor skills (wilding a club; threading a needle). And since the fingertips contain some of the densest areas of nerve endings on the human body, they are also the richest source of tactile feedback, so that the sense of touch is intimately associated with human hands.' **Wikipedia The free Encyclopedia

This is God's hand that is with you, the hand that truly has the power to 'manipulate' the environment. Praise Him today knowing HIS HAND keeps you safe and secure.

Reflections

Friday   "…that thou wouldest keep me from evil, that it may not grieve me!"

It may seem as if this is a selfish request, but we should consider the complete picture of this prayer. Jabez wanted to live for God, and he wanted to do a work for God. This may be one of the most powerful requests that can be made. Satan tries to slither into our lives in a very subtle way, which brings us ever so slightly into evil. Jabez had the exact right prayer. Being in evil (however slightly), does make a child of God grieve. We are not effective if we are grieving. We can become sad, despondent, and even depressed at our failure to stay away from evil. This is a prayer request that we NEED. Yes God, keep me from evil, that it may not grieve me!

Reflections

Saturday "…and God granted him that which he requested."

Have you ever been in a situation in which you needed (in your mind) an answer to your prayer, and you needed it NOW or 'yesterday,' if you know what I mean? Of course, we all have. We have needed, wanted, and even pined for our petition to be granted. Then we are told to wait… When we read this verse, we can see that God does in fact grant our request, and we do not always have to wait. The key to remember is that God GRANTED the request.

Reflections

Designing Us

Some of you may remember the TV show 'Designing Women.' It came to mind a few days ago. The show was based on four women designing rooms for clients. In a sense, we are clients of God, and He is designing us to be the most beautiful Christian we can be. He works from the inside bringing His design to the outside.

Sunday   **Genesis 1: 27 "So God created man in his own image, in the image of God he created him; male and female he created them."**

Created by God – The verse today uses the word 'created' three times. This must be important for us to know. Every design begins with the basics. God's basis for His creation for us began with His image. Think of this today; and know that He created you in His image.

Reflections

Monday　　Psalm 139:13-14a　"For you created my inmost being; you knit me together in my mother's womb, I praise you because I am fearfully and wonderfully made…"

Created My Inmost Being - God created us in our mother's womb. He knew what he was creating before our earthly parents knew. Our minds, bodies, and souls were created in His image: fearfully and wonderfully.

Reflections

Tuesday — Jeremiah 1:5 "Before I formed you in the womb I knew you, before you were born I set you apart; I appointed you as a prophet to the nations."

Set Apart for a Purpose - God created us for a purpose. He knew us and set us apart to be His. Take today, and spend time with Christ asking: "For what purpose has He set me apart?"

Reflections

Wednesday   **Acts 17:26** "From one man he made every nation of men, that they should inhabit the whole earth; and he determined the times set for them and the exact places where they should live."

Determined a Time - God determined your time and this place exactly. No matter today's situation, what will you do with what He has given you?

Reflections

Thursday   **Isaiah 64:8**   **"Yet, O LORD, you are our Father. We are the clay, you are the potter; we are all the work of your hand."**

We are the Clay - We are the work of God's hands. He forms us until He is finished. Today, allow Him to work you, as a potter works the clay.

Reflections

Friday   Jeremiah 18:4 "But the pot he was shaping from the clay was marred in his hands; so the potter formed it into another pot, shaping it as seemed best to him."

His Design - God knows the design He has set for us. He desires to shape us to that design. Spend time today with Him, so you may become His design.

Reflections

Saturday   Matthews 9:17 "Neither do men pour new wine into old wineskins. If they do, the skins will burst, the wine will run out and the wineskins will be ruined. No, they pour new wine into new wineskins, and both are preserved."

New Wine in New Wineskins - Each day is a new day. Continuing in our old habits is like putting new wine into old wineskins. We are sure to burst! Spend time with God everyday to become new wine in a new wineskin.

Reflections

His Teaching Continues

Sunday	Matthew 27: 57-60 "Now when evening had come, there came a rich man from Arimathea, named Joseph, who himself had also become a disciple of Jesus. This man went to Pilate and asked for the body of Jesus. Then Pilate commanded the body to be given to him. When Joseph had taken the body, he wrapped it in a clean linen cloth and laid it in the new tomb which he had hewn out of the rock; and he rolled a large stone against the door of the tomb and departed."

God's provisions for us are never ending, just as they were for Jesus. His physical body had taken all the punishment it could withstand. The time had passed for His physical body to be of use. But God still had work for Jesus to do in the way of witnessing to all. No matter your circumstance, God intends for you to be a witness for Him.

Reflections

Monday   Matthew 27: 5 - 6   **"But the angel answered and said" ... 'Do not be afraid, for I know that you seek Jesus who was crucified. He is not here; for He is risen, as He said. Come, see the place where the Lord lay.'"**

Sometimes we are naturally aware of God's miracles. Then there are times we must be shown these miracles, so we know exactly what God has provided. Open your heart today. Ask God to take you to His place and let you see what He has laid for you.

Reflections

Tuesday   **John 20:19 "then the same day at evening, being the first day of the week, when the doors were shut where the disciples were assembled, for fear of the Jews, Jesus came and stood in the midst, and said to them, 'Peace be with you.'"**

Jesus always comes to us in peace. Our circumstances may have left us in fear, or weariness, or indecision. The darkness or light in your day does not matter call to Him! He will approach with love, peace, and understanding.

Reflections

Wednesday   **John 20:21**   **"So Jesus said to them again, 'Peace to you! As the Father has sent Me, I also send you.'"**

When Jesus spoke these words, He had just shown the disciples the scars left by His crucifixion, not to bring trembling and fear, but to get their attention, so they would know who was standing in their presence. It was important for Him to tell the disciples one more time, of the plans He had for them. He fully understood their hiding out, but it was important for them to remember what all the past three years had really been about. The same is true for us today! He knows where we are, and He wants to send us out!

Reflections

Thursday   **John 20:29**   **"Jesus said to him, 'Thomas because you have seen Me, you have believed. Blessed are those who have not seen and yet have believed.'"**

We cannot see, nor have we seen, Jesus in His physical body. But we can see His works daily. He offers to us special blessings because we continue to love and serve Him without being able to touch Him physically, as Thomas required.

Reflections

Friday — **John 20:22 - 23** "**And when He had said this, He breathed on them and said to them, 'Receive the Holy Spirit, If you forgive the sins of any, they are forgiven them; if you retain the sins of any, they are retained.'**"

Here, Jesus tries to emphasize to the disciples, the responsibilities of their position. If we call ourselves Christians, we have the same responsibilities today. If we cannot forgive, have we set in motion an event that we cannot control? Allowing our hearts to harden because of a hurt can cause just such an event! Look into your heart today, and see if forgiveness needs to be given.

Reflections

Saturday   Acts 1:4 - 5   "And being assembled together with them, He commanded them not to depart from Jerusalem, but to wait for the Promise of the Father, 'which,' He said, 'you have heard from Me; for John truly baptized with water, but you shall be baptized with the Holy spirit not many days from now.'"

More than anything, it is important we are where Jesus wants us to be when He wants us to be there. We may be confused at His timing or His place. Our reliance on His judgments for perfection is what He is asking. He will provide all that is needed, no matter where we are at the moment.

Reflections

The Beginning

When we are in a new year, we see ourselves at a new beginning. With that in mind, the devotions this week will be on Genesis 1. It was a time of beginning. We will look at how God began our world and how we can use this knowledge to focus our new beginning.

Sunday   **Genesis 1: 1-2a "In the beginning God created the heavens and the earth. Now the earth was formless and empty..."**

God began by taking nothing and creating this world and His Heavens. As we begin this week, let's first praise Him for what He has done. Next let's meditate on how there was nothing, then there was something--His creation. This something was not just anything... it was the world! If He can do this, then surely He can take the nothings that we believe we have and create them into something. Spend time with Him today telling Him about your nothings and asking Him to create them into the something He can use.

Reflections

Monday   Genesis 1:3   "God said, "Let there be light," and there was light."

Do you feel you are walking in darkness and cannot or do not know where your next step should be? Call upon Our Father. He is the creator of light. He will bring the light into focus for you. He will light your path and show you where your foot is to step. He created the light, and He is the light for us to follow. Today, call upon Him to light your path.

Reflections

Tuesday Genesis 1:6-8 "And God said, 'Let there be an expanse between the waters to separate water from water.' So God made the expanse and separated the water under the expanse from the water above it. And it was so. God called the expanse 'sky', and there was evening and there was morning, -- the second day"

Sometimes we wake up from a sleep and say, "Oh, another morning to go and do all that I must do." Instead of doing that, today let's begin by praising Him for the day He has given us. He knows all that will come and go. Allow Him to show you your day and be a part of your day.

Reflections

Wednesday Genesis 1:11 "Then God said, 'Let the land produce vegetation; seed-bearing plants and trees on the land that bear fruit with seed in it, according to their various kinds,' and it was so."

Vegetation, plants, and trees—they are beautiful to look at, and they also provide for us. They delight our eyes and our stomachs. Only a God like ours could have created something that would delight us in more than one way. As you go on your way to work or even just step outside your door today, praise Him for what He has given us. He is feeding us with nutrition to our brains and bodies. Thank Him today, all day long.

Reflections

Thursday **Genesis 1:16-18a** "**God made two great lights--the greater light to govern the day and the lesser light to govern the night. He also made the stars. God set them in the expanse of the sky to give light on the earth, to govern the day and the night, and to separate light from darkness.**"

God is still giving us light to show us the way. The light of the day brings us warmth. The warmth comforts us when we are cold or feeling down. A sunny day can lift our spirits, sometimes when nothing else can. The moon and stars at night can be so relaxing after a long day. We can gaze upon them and know The One who put them there. Take this day to mediate on all He did when He created the sun, the moon, and the stars.

Reflections

Friday — **Genesis 1:21-22a** "So God created the great creatures of the sea and every living and moving thing with which the water teems, and according to their kinds, and every winged bird according to its kind…God blessed them…"

God created the birds, the fish, and all the animals of this world. Then He blessed them. He thinks enough of these creations to bless them. The knowledge of His blessings helps us to realize what a gracious God we have. Praise Him today for His graciousness.

Reflections

Saturday   Genesis 1:26a-27 "Then God said, 'Let us make man in our image, in our likeness'…So God created man in his own image, in the image of God he created him; male and female he created them."

To make something is to assemble something, but to create means to bring something into existence. God created us. He brought us into existence, into beings. Today ask God what He means for you to be. You are His, so allow Him to make you into the one He desires for you to be.

Reflections

Freedom From the Laws of Sin

Ever hear someone say, "I'd become a Christian, but there are just too many rules?" This is one of Satan's biggest lies and often used in today's society. People today talk incessantly about "their freedoms" and all the encroachments being put upon those freedoms. Laws and rules are given for protection and guidance. Satan takes truth and freedom and turns them into lies and captivity.

Here are at least seven truths from God. Because we belong to him and have chosen to follow Jesus Christ, we gain these freedoms and more.

Sunday   **Romans 8:1 "There is therefore now no condemnation to those who are in Christ Jesus, who do not walk according to the flesh, but according to the Spirit."**

The scripture tells us if we are leading our lives to follow Jesus Christ, we cannot be condemned. It doesn't say "maybe" we will make it to righteousness. It says "now NO condemnation." Does this mean we will never make mistakes? NO! Jesus Christ died on the cross for all our sins. So when we give ourselves over to HIM, we cannot be condemned. This includes the sins of yesterday, today, and tomorrow.

Reflections

Monday — **Romans 8:6 "For to be carnally minded is death, but to be spiritually minded is life and peace."**

To be carnally minded is to be thinking and doing as the world sees fit. As in the days of Noah, everyone was doing what was right in their own eyes - Matthew 24:38. Being spiritually minded is following the ways of Jesus Christ. Learning the ways of the Holy Spirit, we become spiritually minded, and we are given life and peace--a peace our non-Christians friends cannot claim. When was the last time you could say one of those friends had true peace? Take a moment, and pray for them today.

Reflections

Tuesday   **Romans 8:9**   **"But you are not in the flesh but in the Spirit, if indeed the Spirit of God dwells in you. Now if anyone does not have the Spirit of Christ, he is not His."**

If the Spirit of God is in you, you will think and act like Jesus Christ. If you do not have the Spirit of Christ, you do not belong to Him. We demonstrate we possess the spirit or live in the flesh every time we speak or act. If you are unsure you posses the Spirit, ask God. Ask His forgiveness for your sins. Tell him of your trust in Jesus Christ. Allow Him to lead, guide, and direct every aspect of your life from this moment forward.

Reflections

Wednesday   **Romans 8:10** "And if Christ is in you, the body is dead because of sin, but the Spirit is life because of righteousness."

If you belong to Christ, though your body may die, your spirit will have life. Because Jesus died on the cross and rose again, you can have a Spirit of righteousness. This is God's promise. Claiming God's promise by accepting Jesus as your personal savior gives you the Spirit of righteousness.

Reflections

Thursday   **Romans 8:14**   **"For as many as are led by the Spirit of God, these are sons of God."**

If we have received salvation and are led by the Spirit we are now called sons of God. There are no additional "rules" to follow. There are no additional strings attached. So when you hear someone say, "I'd become a Christian, but there are too many rules," you can now respond by claiming your freedoms: No condemnations, No contentions, No carnal mind – you are FREE.

Reflections

Friday   **Romans 8:15**   **"For you did not receive the spirit of bondage again to fear, but you received the Spirit of adoption, by whom we cry out, 'Abba, Father'".**

Once we have accepted Christ Jesus as our Savior and Lord, we have given up any bondage. We have also been given freedom from fear. As children, we look to our parent(s) in fearful situations. By receiving the Spirit of adoption, we can now call upon our Holy Father in all circumstances. Cry out to your 'Abba Father,' and let Him be in control.

Reflections

Saturday   Romans 8:26 "Likewise the Spirit also helps in our weaknesses. For we do not know what we should pray for as we ought, but the Spirit Himself makes intercession for us with groanings which cannot be uttered."

We can now confidentially say as Christians, we do not have a set of earthly rules to follow. In addition, even at our weakest points, we can ask our Father for his care. If we are unsure or cannot find the words to use, the Holy Spirit will step in with utterances we cannot understand and intercede to the Father. Ask your non-Christian friends which column below, they might choose:

Freedom	Laws of Sin
Follow Christ	Follow the World
Life	Death
Righteousness	Sin
Let all be in God's control	Try to take control
Let the Spirit plead our cause	Work it out as best we can

**There is definitely a choice to be made.
Seems like an easy choice; but maybe not.**

Reflections

Winter

You are not left out in the cold
by your Savior.

Winter can bring
ice storms, blizzards,
and cold rain.

Step into these pages, and
enjoy a crisp new day
filled with
God's PEACE, LOVE, and JOY.

———◆———

These scriptures and devotions will
give you HOPE
and fill your soul
with LOVE
from the Father above.

Winter

There is a veil upon me;
It feels wet and cold.
I want to feel easy and free,
But instead the veil
has too tight a hold.

This breeze began soft and low;
now the stroke is so severe.
I begin to hear my Father;
He calls me, "One so dear."

The Words He speaks
gently upon me rest.
I am comforted to know
My future He has filled
with only His best.

Kathleen J. Jones

'IF'

If? This small little word can plague our hearts and minds. It is a little word, but it packs a big punch. We can dwell on our lives wondering things like: "What if I had done…, "What if I changed…," "What if I did not…," or "If only…." Wondering and dwelling on these questions will not give us the answers. This week, that little word will bring us to the Christ that answered these questions for all mankind.

Sunday   **Psalm 124:1-2**   "**If it had not been the LORD who was on our side, now may Israel say; If it had not been the LORD who was on our side, when men rose up against us:**"

Like it or not, we are on a side. When all is said and done, there are only two sides. Both sides answer to the True and Living God. Whatever we are going through today, we can win if the LORD is on our side. Read and pray this verse today. We have strength in HIM.

Reflection

Monday — **Exodus 18:23** **"If thou wilt do this thing, and GOD command thee so, then thou shalt be able to endure..."**

Our lives are full of choices. Those choices bring consequences and a variety of results. Exodus 18:23 tells us if we but do as God commands, we can endure. When we listen to our own commands, we yield zero endurance. If we can do as He commands we WILL endure. Muse on that today.

Reflection

Tuesday   **I Kings 11:38** "And it shall be, if thou will hearken to all that I command thee…; that I will be with thee, and build thee a sure house.…"

Listening to God's commands not only allows us to endure as we learned yesterday, but also, we now see that God will be with us and will build us a sure house. We can read His Word and know when everything seems to be crumbling around us, our foundation is sure.

Reflections

Wednesday   **Matthew 16:24**   **"Then Jesus said unto his disciples, if any man will come after me let him deny himself, and take up his cross, and follow me."**

Today's society speaks of the lack of equality. I wonder at times what equality is, and is it real. God's Word shows us in this verse that according to God 'ANY' one can come to Him. We do not have to pass a test, be a certain race, or even have a specific social level. We are all equal in His eyes. We have only to deny ourselves, take up our crosses, and following Jesus.

Reflections

Thursday I John 4:11 "Beloved, if God so loved us, we ought to love one another."

While driving down the highway or shopping in a store, it is rare to see the love of God in or coming from our fellow man. It is hard to put this verse into our everyday lives when others are not kind to us. We become filled with negative emotions and respond to others in a like manner. But we are not told to treat others as they treat us. We are told to love one another. Dig deep within yourself today, and show the love of God is abundant and alive.

Reflections

Friday — **Revelation 13:9 "If any man hath an ear, let him hear."**

Have you ever talked to someone and felt they weren't really listening? Maybe they seemed to be in another zone and not focusing on the conversation. God says if we have an ear, then let us hear. Focus upon Jesus and listen intently to His onversation. Everyone is invited to hear Him. The choice to hear is ours.

Reflections

Saturday   **Romans 10:9 "If thou shalt confess with thy mouth the Lord Jesus, and shalt believe in thine heart that God hath raised Him from the dead, thou shalt be saved.**

Friday we ended with 'the choice is ours.' Today's verse reveals that Christ is the only answer to the 'if' question. Receive the 'if' answer today. Maybe you are already a child of God? If so, go out, and help others receive the answer of 'if,' and come to Christ today. 'If' you will, they can.

Reflections

Micah

When school begins, some may be reluctant to have their little ones go off for the first time. For those parents, my heart goes out. I remember sending my eldest child off for his first time. I was in the military, and as I stood outside the door, tears filled my eyes and overflowed down my cheeks. An officer walked by, and I struggled to salute. He was gracious and must have understood or at least felt compassion for a very young mother because he gave the 'at ease' quickly and made conversation which 'eased' my aching heart.

Take time to read each chapter in Micah this week. I pray you, too, will see a God that feels compassion and gives us the 'at ease.' He will show through His Word that WE have a CHOICE in how we live our life.

Sunday   **Micah 1:1, 16 "The word of the LORD that came to Micah…concerning Samaria and Jerusalem…Make thee bald, enlarge thy baldness as the eagle…."**

We can be sure when the word of the LORD comes concerning our sin, we will receive judgment. This chapter tells us of the transgression and sins of the house of Samaria and Jerusalem and shows that HE discovered their foundation. Evil and transgression was found. We are told to enlarge our baldness (if someone is bald they can not hide anything on their head – we see all). Open up to God today. Reveal your transgressions to Him.

Reflections

_____

_____

_____

_____

_____

_____

_____

_____

_____

Monday   **Micah 2:1** "Woe to them that devise iniquity…this time is evil."

Today's chapter is a hard one to grasp. The world we live in today is evil. Think about the crime alone. I chose this verse because we have a responsibility as Christians to show the love of Christ to an evil world. Ask God to tell you how to show His love today.

Reflections

Tuesday **Micah 3:7b** "...they shall all cover their lips; for there is no answer of God."

Have you ever been so shocked that your mouth dropped open, and you covered your lips? I have, and it is usually not a 'good' shock. This chapter begins with the question, "Is it not for you to know judgment?" It seems to ask, "Do you think you will not be judged?" Can you answer that question with a clear heart?

Reflections

Wednesday   Micah 4:2b "…he will teach us his ways, and we will walk in His paths…"

It is mid-week, and what a great day to read this chapter and know that the Lord will redeem us from the hand of our enemies. Even though the trials of life bring pain 'as a woman in childbirth,' we are told to gather together to "Arise and thresh."

Reflections

Thursday   Micah 5:15b   "…such as they have not heard."

This week's subject is the compassion of God. In this chapter, we learn God is on target and is preparing to take action. The false prophets and soothsayers mentioned here should have been concerned, but sadly they probably were not then and are not even today. God is in protection mode for those of us that have agreed to 'walk in his paths.' If you have not agreed to 'walk in his paths,' won't you do that now?

Reflections

Friday   Micah 6:3   "O my people, what have I done unto thee?"

As a mother, I can just feel God's painful heart. When my child acted unruly, it pained my heart. I had to ask my child, "Why? What have I done to you that would make you go against my rules? Breaking the rules does not leave you feeling full or satisfied." We know that sin does not satisfy. God's love and compassion is the only true satisfaction.

Reflections

Saturday   **Micah 7:19**   "**He will turn again, he will have compassion upon us; he will subdue our iniquities; and thou wilt cast all their sins into the depths of the sea.**"

The reality of God's compassion is upon us. Through this entire book, we have seen God's children listen to the 'wrong crowd'. Then they returned to the God of compassion. It is true that God will have compassion upon us, and He will subdue our iniquities…we must but ask in Jesus name. Let's show others the compassion of Christ. Be a witness today.

Reflections

_____
_____
_____
_____
_____
_____
_____
_____
_____
_____
_____
_____
_____
_____
_____
_____
_____
_____

Senses

Have you ever thought about your senses being in the Bible? Well why not? After all, God did give them to us? We are said to have only five senses, but to finish the week, let's consider that we have two more: knowing and admitting.

Sunday　　　　**Psalm 146:8 "the Lord gives sight to the blind…"**

Sight: Many times we are blinded by what we do not want to see. We know the truth, but deep down, we do not want to admit it. Let's focus on His truth today. Focus on the knowing and admitting. Let HIS LIGHT shine, so you may fully focus on Him.

Reflections

| Monday | Rev. 1:3 "…blessed are those who hear it and take to heart what is written…" |

Hearing: Sometimes when we hear something we wonder, "Is that really what God meant?" Just listening to others speak His word is not the best way to know His truth. He can fill our hearts by what others speak, but He would rather fill our hearts directly. Pray and ask for His understandings as you read His word today.

Reflections

Tuesday Psalm 34:8 "Taste and see that the Lord is good."

Taste: Does just thinking about your favorite food give your mouth a good feeling? The Lord is just like that favorite food, only better. Daily tasting what He has to say is better than any food we could ever put to our tongues. This day may not be one of the best chunks of our favorite food, but The Lord will add a topping we cannot resist. Just give this day to Him for the frosting.

Reflections

Wednesday   **II Corinthians 2:15**   **"For we are to God the aroma of Christ…"**

Smell (Aroma): When you light candles then walk out of the room; do you come back in to smell the sweet aroma? God's Word tells us we are the aroma of Christ to God. What better smell can there be than Christ? Today, thank the Lord for dying on the cross, so you could be the aroma of Him to your Father in heaven.

Reflections

Thursday Mark 5:28 "…she thought, "If I could just touch his cloak…"

Touch: This woman knew that she could be healed by just touching Christ's garment. What faith! Do you ever think about what it would have been like to touch His garment? We cannot physically touch His cloak, but we can touch His Word to know Him. We can know Him through prayer and study. He will touch our hearts and heal us.

Reflections

Friday   Romans 3:23   **"For all have sinned and fall short of the glory of God.**

Knowing: You may be thinking, "That is not a sense." But we use many of our senses to commit sin. Sin is part of us as human beings. We can use these same senses to stop our sinfulness. We cannot be perfect, but we do know the One who is. Ask for His forgiveness, and use your senses for His glory.

Reflections

Saturday   **Titus 3:7 "...having been justified by his grace, we should become heirs..."**

Grace: We are justified by His Grace. We are sinners, but we are forgiven sinners. God gave His Son, so we might have grace. His Grace allows us to be heirs in the kingdom of God. This grace allows us to be siblings in Christ. Praise to Our Father. He has given us what no one else could or ever will be able to give us.

Reflections

Phrases We Often Use

Sunday   **Luke 18:27 "Jesus replied, "What is impossible with men is possible with God."**

It is Impossible

We say, "It is impossible." Try as we might, even with hundreds assisting, sometimes we just cannot get 'it' done. The scripture says we are right. It may be impossible for man, but if God is involved, it is possible. You need to have just the right people to get a job done. Asking God is always the 'right people.' Put your trust in Him, and He will make it possible.

Reflections

Monday — John 3:16 "For God so loved the world that he gave his one and only Son, that whoever believes in him shall not perish but have eternal life."

No One Really Loves Me

We may all have said or felt like there were times when nobody really loved us. But there is one who knows what love is and loves us every moment. Do you know: if you were the only person on this earth, Christ would still have died on the cross for you? We may not have a spouse, boyfriend, or even a really good friend whom we feel loves us enough, especially if they knew everything about us. But, God knew about us before we were born, and He still sent His Son to die on the cross for us.

Reflections

Tuesday   Hebrews 13:5b "…because God has said, 'Never will I leave you; never will I forsake you.'"

I Feel All Alone

When we feel alone, we should remember His Word says He will never leave us. Therefore, we are never alone. We always have Him to go to with our prayers. The word 'forsake' means to abandon or to give up. Our earthly loved ones may give up on or abandon us, but He never will. Even if we try to walk away from Him, He will continue to be there for us.

Reflections

Wednesday   **Colossians 1:9 "For this reason, since the day we heard about you, we have not stopped praying for you and asking God to fill you with the knowledge of His will, through spiritual wisdom and understanding."**

I Am Not Smart

"I am not smart," we might say to ourselves. But, His Word tells us He will fill us with knowledge, wisdom, and understanding. This wisdom is not the wisdom as the world defines wisdom. It is His wisdom, and His understanding. His wisdom and understanding comes from the beginning of time—something the world does not have. We become wise in Him and His ways when we spend time with Him in prayer and reading His Word. This makes us so much more than 'smart.'

Reflections

Thursday 2 Timothy 1:17 **"For God did not give us a spirit of timidity, but a spirit of power, of love and of self-discipline."**

I Am Afraid

Do you ever feel afraid? God gives us the power to 'not' be afraid. He says, "I give you a spirit of power." Jesus left us with the Holy Spirit. It is that Spirit which allows us to not be afraid, to love with the agapé love, and even to discipline ourselves for His work.

Reflections

Friday II Corinthians 12:9 **"My grace is sufficient for you, for my power is made perfect in weakness."**

I Can Not Go On

When we feel weak and we think we cannot go on, we should put our trust in Him. Hardships of this world can make us feel this kind of weakness. We must allow Him to help us when we are down. Our weaknesses are made perfect in His power. Even if we hold power in our grasp or hold a powerful position it is not perfect power. We can go on, even in our weakest moments because the perfections of His power are more than sufficient.

Reflections

Saturday — **Proverbs 3:5-6** "Trust in the Lord with all your heart and lean not on your own understanding; in all your ways acknowledge Him, and He will make your paths straight."

I Can Not Figure This Out

When we feel confused and cannot figure things out, scripture tells us that is exactly where the Lord wants us. We are to lean on His understandings and He will guide us, walk with us, and make the crooked ways become straight for us. When we are not sure what path to take, we must call on Him and acknowledge who He is. He will straighten our path and take away any confusion we might be experiencing.

Reflections

Is it 'Worth' it?

In the struggle through the wilderness the children of Israel murmured, "Would to God we would have stayed in Egypt" (as captives and not free). They were promised a land flowing with milk and honey. Yet, they could not focus on the promise of God. They were told the outcome and chose to murmur and complain instead of enjoying the fact that 'ONE DAY' they would reap the benefits; their suffering would be worth it! What about us? We have been told the outcome. Are our present struggles worth it?

Just because we know the outcome does not mean getting there won't hurt. What we go through is nothing compared to the pain God felt on the day His Son died. God knew Jesus would be raised from the dead; yet, He (God) had to turn his back on his very own Son, and let him suffer. God hurt for Jesus when Jesus died on the cross. God also knew by Jesus' death, we could have redemption and live eternally with Him.

Sunday   **Exodus 1:13-14a "And the Egyptians made the children of Israel to serve with rigour; And they made their lives bitter with hard bondage…."**

"Slaves"

We can become slaves in our own lives without realizing we are falling into captivity. Captivity happens one choice at a time, and pretty soon making choices without seeking our precious Father becomes a way of life. And so there we are – slaves. Take today, and choose to seek your Father in heaven in every aspect of your life.

Reflections

_____

_____

_____

_____

_____

_____

_____

Monday	Exodus 2:24a "And God heard their groaning, and God remembered his covenant with Abraham, with Isaac, and with Jacob."

"The Promise"

Agreements today are broken as quickly as they are made, but not so with God! Even in the people's groaning, He remembered and acted on His promises. In our groaning, He hears us, too. We can be confident today and everyday that God will remember and will take action. The promises from so long ago are ours still. Trust Him to take action for you.

Reflections

Tuesday Exodus 12:31 "…rise up and get ye forth...and go, serve the Lord."

"Get Up and Go"

Trials come and go. However, there are times we must live in our choices. No matter the situations we are in, we can look at this verse, grab our boot straps, and then rise up and get! It is hard; I know first hand. Trust me, your relationship with Christ will be so amazing you will forget the pain you felt. So, come on – let's get UP and GO – Serve the Lord with gladness.

Reflections

Wednesday — **Exodus 14:22** "**And the children of Israel went into the midst of the sea upon the dry ground...**"

"Crossing the Red Sea"

I am sure the Israelites were scared, tired, and their emotions rolling. Yet, in this impossible situation, GOD made a way for them, and He dried up the ground! No mud holes to sink into and slow them down. He will do this for us also. Consider the 'Red Seas' we must cross. If we seek Him before we step into that water, he will dry the 'land' for our safe passage.

Reflections

Thursday   **Numbers 11:6. "But now our soul is dried away: there is nothing at all, besides this manna, before our eyes."**

"The Wilderness"

We encourage you to take some time to read Exodus 15-Numbers 12. God's people were a long time in the wilderness! A lot happened there –the good with the bad - obedience and disobedience. But God always PROVIDED the peoples' NEEDS. The problem was they wanted Him to provide their 'wants.' God had a lot for them to learn and knew they needed time. Some lessons take us longer to learn than others, but throughout our 'wilderness,' God will provide for us.

Reflections

Friday Numbers 13:25 "And they returned from searching of the new land after forty days."

"Spying out the new land"

Finally, it was time for the Israelites to come to their new land. They had been in the wilderness so long, they thought they would all die and never reach the Promised Land. So, some disobeyed to the limit that they did not enjoy the bounty. How many times did the Israelites wonder, "Is there ever going to be any release?" Today, we see that God directed them right to the Promised Land. He continued to let them choose their course. This is so important for us to see. While Satan clouds our judgment in a way that we are confused to the max, God will gently guide us and let us be the final decision maker. Satan does not do that. He will set the decision in such confusion and 'pretty words' that we rush to make our choices. Let God direct you. Allow Him to lead you to the new land. He will let you 'spy it out' before you dwell there. That is the beauty of an intimate relationship with God–you will be able to know the right thing to do!

Reflections

Saturday **Numbers 13:30** "And Caleb stilled the people before Moses, and said 'Let us go up at once, and possess it; for we are well able to overcome it.'"

"One Believed"

Our devotion title this week is "Is it worth it?" Looking back on an extremely trying situation and knowing the beauty and awe of the outcome, the question comes to us: Was it worth it? Before we see the end result, we often ask ourselves, "Is it worth it?" Caleb saw the magnificence of this new land. He was assured and confident in the Lord and told the people they were WELL ABLE TO OVERCOME the trials and tribulations they faced. It was all worth it to him. The trials and tribulations we go through may seem to be a horrid wilderness while we are in the midst of them, but if we can be ONE THAT BELIEVES, we, too, can look the situation in the face – eye to eye – and report, "Let us go Up AT ONCE, and possess it, for WE ARE WELL ABLE TO OVERCOME IT!" A more intimate relationship with Christ is absolutely worth it. Believe today and everyday!

Reflections

Defining You

Sunday **Genesis 1:27** "So God created man in his own image, in the image of God he created him male and female, He created them."

You Are…God's Creation

You were created by God not just something that came along. You were created to be someone special. You have been created in God's image, and that alone makes you special.

Reflections

Monday   Psalm 139:15   "My frame was not hidden from 'You' when I was made in the secret place."

You Are…an Individual.

When God created you, you were individually made. This means you are an individual and not from a cookie cutter. He individually made each of us precisely, to His measurements, for His work.

Reflections

_____
_____
_____
_____
_____
_____
_____
_____
_____
_____
_____
_____
_____
_____
_____
_____
_____
_____
_____
_____

Tuesday **Luke 11:9** "So I say to you; 'ask and it will be given to you; seek and you will find; knock and the door will be opened to you.'"

You Are...a Seeker.

You are to seek Him in all ways. Seek to know Him more by reading His word, by praying to Him, and by worshiping Him all through out the day.

Reflections

Wednesday   Proverbs 3:5 "**Trust in the Lord with all your heart and lean not on your own understanding.**"

You Are…Trusting in Him.

Because you seek Him, you are able to trust in Him more each day. Each time you seek Him anew, you have shown Him a new trust. Each time your trust grows for Him, so does your love.

Reflections

Thursday Psalm 119:50 "My comfort in my suffering is this; Your promise preserves my life."

You Are…Assured by Him.

You are assured by His promise to be with Him in eternity. That promise will strengthen you as you endure life's daily bumps. When you suffer and need His assurances, call on your Savior for His promise. He is listening and waiting to hear from you. Go ahead call - on Him today.

Reflections

Friday   **Proverbs 4:18** "The path of the righteous is like the first glean of dawn shining ever brighter till the full light of day."

You Are…Made Righteous by Him.

You were made righteous the moment you asked Him to be your Lord. It is through Him your righteousness will shine like the first of the dawn. Your righteousness will grow ever brighter with each day. Learn from Him, and let His light shine through you, so that you will light the way for others to see Him.

Reflections

Saturday — **Proverb 7:4** "Say to wisdom, 'You are my sister,' and call understanding your kinsman."

You Are…Wise by Him.

God's children have wisdom and understanding as family members. Wisdom and understanding do not stand in the forest waiting for us to find them. God gave us wisdom and understanding through Christ. His wisdom includes information for yesterday, today, and tomorrow. Our understanding is complete in Christ. No more wondering if we have all the facts to make a decision. Call on Christ for any decision and there in lies your wisdom and understanding.

Reflections

Patience for Coming Events

At this time, some of you will have your Christmas shopping done, wrapped and under the tree. Then there are those of us who will have just begun and those who are thinking about getting started. In all of those scenarios, there is one thing that will challenge all of us. That thing is Patience! We all have it, but at this time of year, it is usually worn to within an inch of its life and ours. Come with me this week, and give it over to God.

Sunday   **Psalm 9:1-2 "I will praise You, O Lord, with my whole heart; I will tell of all Your marvelous works. I will be glad and rejoice in You; I will sing praise to Your name, O Most High."**

Sometimes patience is a hard thing to come by. If in those moments, we can turn our thoughts to our Heavenly Father we can transform our minds, and thereby our actions, to being patient. Our thought processes really do control our actions. When you find yourself at an impatient moment, think on God with your whole heart. Remind yourself of Him and all His wonders. Rejoice in His presence.

Reflections

Monday — Psalm 13:6 **"I will sing to the Lord, because He has dealt bountifully with me."**

Impatient moments usually come at a time when we have no time. We are full up with to-dos, and the list is getting longer. Seems as though no matter how many items we check off, there have been three more added. Take today, and sing to our Father all He has provided to you. These provisions should include not just the worldly things we must have to live, but also the love we have for others and their love returning to us.

Reflections

Tuesday Psalm 26:7-8 "That I may proclaim with the voice of thanksgiving, and tell of all Your wondrous works, Lord. I have loved the habitation of Your house, and the place where Your glory dwells."

By proclaiming out loud God's works in our lives we have brought glory to our Father and peacefulness to our mind. It only takes a few seconds to say out loud, "Thank you!" for His love toward us in every way. Take a moment; it will do you good.

Reflections

Wednesday   **Psalm 40:5**   "**Many, O Lord my God, are Your wonderful works which You have done; and Your thoughts toward us cannot be recounted to You in order; if I would declare and speak of them, they are more than can be numbered.**"

What God provides is unnumbered and cannot be counted. But we can make a small list. Take some time today, and write a list of what He provides for you each and every day. Then add to that list, things that have been out of the ordinary. Put your list in your billfold or something you carry with you at all times. When stress hits and you patience wanes, pull your list out, and read it aloud.

Reflections

Thursday — Psalm 92:1, 2, 4 "It is good to give thanks to the Lord, and to sing praises to Your name, O Most High; to declare Your loving-kindness in the morning, and Your faithfulness every night... For You, Lord, have made me glad through Your work; I will triumph in the works of Your hands."

Try this for seven days without missing a day: Before you put your feet on the floor from last nights sleep, tell God thank you. You can either be specific about something or just say a general thank you. Say it out loud, so you actually hear yourself. It does not have to be loud, just verbal. See if it doesn't change your perspective for the coming day's happenings.

Reflections

Friday   **Psalm 98:1**   "Oh, sing to the Lord a new song! For He has done marvelous things; His right hand and His holy arm have gained Him the victory."

Know any gospel songs by heart? Doesn't matter, make your own. God loves to hear us singing to Him. Your words don't have to rhyme; they just have to be honest. He loves a melody. Your singing to Him will never be out of tune, so don't worry if your bucket isn't near by. Sing His praises and your questions.

Reflections

_____
_____
_____
_____
_____
_____
_____
_____
_____
_____
_____
_____
_____
_____
_____
_____
_____
_____
_____
_____
_____

Saturday — Psalm 136: 1 – 3 "Oh, give thanks to the Lord, for He is good! For His mercy endures forever. Oh, give thanks to the God of gods! For His mercy endures forever. Oh, give thanks to the Lord of lords! For His mercy endures forever:"

Mercy is one of God's strong points. Thank Him for that today, and include asking forgiveness for the times you have not been merciful to yourself. Our Lord positively loves to forgive us when we ask Him. His mercy endures forever. It only requires our asking.

Reflections

Flowers in December

December is a month filled with dichotomy. It is a fun month, but also busy. The weather can be freezing or sunshine all around. It may be filled with family and friends get-togethers, or it can have some very lonesome days and nights. As I took a few moments to enjoy some silence, I looked out my back window and saw a rose blooming in the middle of December. My first thought was, "I cannot be seeing what I think I see." As I walked to the rose garden, God touched my heart to say, "Yes, no matter what your surroundings, my daughter, I will grow you a beautiful flower."

Sunday   **Psalm 46:7 "The Lord of hosts is with us; the God of Jacob is our refuge.**

In our December of stress, He grows the flower of refuge. Stress is what we bring on ourselves by overloading our bodies with work or our minds with concerns. God promises peace to us if we but breathe His name. Go ahead; today, breathe to Him your stress.

Reflections

_____
_____
_____
_____
_____
_____
_____
_____
_____
_____
_____
_____
_____

Monday	**Isaiah 26:3** "You will keep him in perfect peace, whose mind is stayed on You, because he trusts in You."

In our December of <u>worry</u>, He grows the flower of <u>serenity</u>.

Today's generations are the champions of worry. The majority of us have enough money, housing, and food. We have friends and loved ones, but we still have maximum worries. Take today and give them all to God. His shoulders can carry all of them.

Reflections

Tuesday   **John 14:27**   "**Peace I leave with you, my peace I give to you; not as the world gives do I give to you. Let not your heart be troubled, neither let it be afraid.**"

In our December of <u>frustration</u>, He grows the flower of <u>peace</u>.

Frustration comes about when our plans or hopes have gone a different direction than we wanted. In the middle of being frustrated, it really does not matter the why of its misdirection. What matters is, it is not working out! Today, ask God to correct your slightest frustration. He will.

Reflections

Wednesday   Luke 10:19 "Behold, I give you the authority to trample on serpents and scorpions, and over all the power of the enemy, and nothing shall by any means hurt you."

In our December of <u>fatigue</u>, He grows the flower of <u>energy</u>.

Fatigue is not just tired. It the last step before collapse. It is physical, mental, and emotional shut down. Now is the season! Again, we are mostly responsible for doing it to ourselves, but Jesus gives us power over fatigue of any kind.

Reflections

Thursday **Psalm 37:8** "Cease from anger, and forsake wrath; do not fret, it only causes harm."
I Corinthians 13:8a "Love never fails."

In our December of <u>anger,</u> He grows the flower of <u>love</u>.

Some of us are very good at not showing our outward anger. This does not mean we do not get angry; it just means we seethe inside. We can get so good at it, we find ourselves physically sick with ulcers or even on our way to a stroke. But if we keep our hearts in a mode of love, we just cannot get very angry for very long.

Reflections

Friday Isaiah 43:2-3a "When you pass through the waters, I will be with you; and through the rivers, they shall not overflow you. When you walk through the fire, you shall not be burned, nor shall the flame scorch you. For I am the Lord your God the Holy One of Israel, your Savior;"

In our December of <u>weakness</u>, He grows the flower of <u>strength</u>.

Our weakness may be physical or spiritual. The Lord will handle them all. The trick is to ask Him to help, to turn our weakness over to Him, and to leave it with Him.

Reflections

Saturday	Philippians 4:8 "Finally, brethren, whatever things are true, whatever things are noble, whatever things are just, whatever things are pure, whatever things are lovely, whatever things are of good report, if there is any virtue and if there is anything praiseworthy, meditate on these things."

In our December of <u>depression</u>, He grows the flower of <u>joy</u>.

Depression can hit hard and fast. It can cause and be caused by anger, fatigue, frustration, stress, worry, and weakness. It can consist of mental abnormalities and physical pain. Dear One, Jesus can change all of this and make you free and joyous once again.

Reflections

Love & Hate--War & Peace

God's Word has a lot to say on these four words. To tell the truth, I knew I would find love, war, and peace in the Bible, but I was totally shocked at how much the Bible had to say about hate. I just didn't remember the Bible using the word hate that often - wrong again "Oh one of non-remembrance."

Sunday **Proverbs 26:24 "He who hates, disguises it with his lips, and lays up deceit within himself;"**

Romans 5:8 "But God demonstrates His own love toward us, in that while we were still sinners, Christ died for us."

Today's world is filled with deceit. I just never considered deceit equivalent to hating or even the action of hate. To be deceitful, we have to tell a lie or at least not tell all the truth. Either of those cannot be considered love, so we are actually showing hate or disdain to the individual to whom we have not been honest. God would not; nor has He ever, lied to us. We might not like all He tells us, but it is the truth. He shows us His love even while we are sinners. He tells us of His love in truth by sending His only Son to die on the cross.

Reflections

Monday   **Leviticus 19:17 "You shall not hate your brother in your heart. You shall surely rebuke your neighbor, and not bear sin because of him."**

Jeremiah 31:3 "The lord has appeared of old to me, saying: 'Yes, I have loved you with an everlasting love; therefore with loving kindness I have drawn you.'"

Sometimes it is very hard to love our brothers and sisters. One of the ways we do not show our love for both brothers and sisters is by not sharing our love of God and Jesus Christ with them. But God has told us He loves us so much He draws us to Him with loving kindness. Choose someone today to whom you can show loving kindness. By getting closer to them, you can tell them how much God loves them and wants to draw near.

Reflections

Tuesday — **Proverbs 10:12** **"Hatred stirs up strife. But love covers all sins."**

John 3:16 "For Go so loved the world that He gave His only begotten Son, that whoever believes in Him should not perish but have everlasting life."

How is it we have not figured out, on our own, that we cause all kinds of problems by hating? Our struggles (strife) today manifest themselves by making us physically, emotionally and mentally ill. Strife shows up when we argue and struggle with individuals or objects in our everyday lives. The only cure for hate or strife is love like our Father (God) loves us. If He could give away His Son so we could have everlasting life. What are we willing to give to spend eternity with Him?

Reflections

Wednesday **Deuteronomy 1:30** "The Lord your God, who goes before you, He will fight for you, according to all He did for you in Egypt before your eyes."

Romans 16:20 "And the God of peace will crush Satan under your feet shortly. The grace of our Lord Jesus Christ be with you. Amen."

How do we reconcile a God of peace who fights for us? That is definitely a question we can ask, but I believe the thought we should focus on with these scriptures is that God is a God of peace. Because He loves us so much, He will put His peacefulness aside to fight (war) all our battles. We cannot control the war, but He can. All our plans and strategies do not compare to what He will do in our war. We cannot battle Satan without God. Let Him do your battles today and every day. Call out to your seven-star General, Jesus Christ.

Reflections

Thursday **Deuteronomy 3:22** "You must not fear them, for the Lord your God Himself fights for you."

Isaiah 26:3 "You will keep him in perfect peace, whose mind is stayed on You, because he trusts in You."

Deuteronomy is the Lord speaking to Joshua and the battles he is about to do for the Promised Land. I believe God supplied this scripture for our battles, too. We are not to keep our minds (and hearts) on the battles, but instead, on God.

Reflections

Friday   Psalm 68:30b "Scatter the peoples who delight in war."

Colossians 3:15 "And let the peace of God rule in your hearts, to which also you were called in one body; and be thankful."

If we delight in war (disruption), God says we are to be scattered (be away from Him). If we delight in Him and His peace, we will be called into His body of believers, and we will be thankful. That sounds pretty easy to understand. Yet in today's world, there is so much strife going on, it is "work" to keep our minds "stayed" on Him. That is one reason to stay in constant contact with God. It is only through daily reading of His word and constant prayer that we can let our hearts be ruled with the peace of God.

Reflections

Saturday — **Psalm 120:6-7** "My soul has dwelt too long with one who hates peace. I am for peace; but when I speak, they are for war."

Is there someone in your daily life that thrives on causing disruption? If so, begin praying for them today and continue to pray for them. God can and will change them. We have no way to know someone's situation(s) in life. We cannot change them or even their situations. We can pray for them. We can give them positives where only negatives abide. Ask God to help you each time you are put in their path. He will tell you what to say and how to respond to anything they say or do.

Reflections

God's Provision in Your Wilderness

The devotions this week will show when we are in the wilderness, God is with us. He will provide. Take each step with Him, do not run ahead or even lag behind. Allow Him to be your guide.

Sunday — **Exodus 13:21-22** "**By day the LORD went ahead of them in a pillar of cloud to guide them on their way and by night in a pillar of fire to give them light, so that they could travel by day or night. Neither the pillar of cloud by day nor the pillar of fire by night left its place in front of the people.**"

You may be in a wilderness experience right now. God should be your guide. Spend time each day with Him in prayer. He will guide you day and night with His light. He is there at all times no matter how dark your wilderness. Look for His light and His light alone.

Reflections

Monday   **Exodus 14:13a, 16 "Do not be afraid. Stand firm and you will see the deliverance the LORD will bring you today. (16) Raise your staff and stretch out your hand over the sea to divide the water so the Israelites can go through the sea on dry ground."**

You may be at a point where you feel your wilderness is swallowing you. Believe the One guiding you will make a path to take you out. He knows where you are. He divided the waters for the Israelites, and He can bring you out of your wilderness. Stretch out your staff (your heart) to Him and follow on dry ground.

Reflections

Tuesday   Exodus15: 24-25a "So the people grumbled against Moses, saying, 'What are we to drink?' Then Moses cried out to the LORD and the LORD showed him a piece of wood, he threw it into the water and the water became sweet.'"

If you are at a point in your wilderness where your thirst cannot be quenched, drink of His sweet water. You will never be thirsty if you drink of Him. Today, throw the wood (His Word) into the water and drink. Allow Him to quench your thirst today and every day.

Reflections

Wednesday   **Exodus 16:4a "Then the Lord said to Moses, 'I will rain down bread from heaven for you. The people are to go out each day and gather enough for that day....'"**

God gives us enough to make it through the wilderness day by day, but we should not take more than He offers. He knows our needs. Ask Him for today's portion. He will rain it down on you as you need it.

Reflections

Thursday Exodus 16:11-12 "The LORD said to Moses, 'I have heard the grumbling of the Israelites. Tell them, At twilight you will eat meat, and in the morning you will be filled with bread. Then you will know that I am the LORD your God.'"

He provides our needs (bread) each day to survive the wilderness. He also makes provisions for our wants (meat). Everyday He rains down the bread and brings the meat to us. Remember; only gather the amount needed for that day to continue your path out of the wilderness.

Reflections

Friday — **Numbers 13:1-2, 26b, 28** "The LORD said to Moses, 'Send some men to explore the land of Canaan, which I am giving to the Israelites...'" (26b) "...There they reported to them and to the whole assembly and showed them the fruit of the land." (28a.) "But the people who live there are powerful, and the cities are fortified and very large."

Do not, as the Israelites did, doubt the fruit He is providing for you. They doubted the Lord and focused on the negatives. Today know He has wonders for you in the new land. Trust Him; walk into the new land He gives you.

Reflections

Saturday   **Joshua 3:3-4a "…giving orders to the people: 'When you see the ark of the covenant of the LORD your God, and the priests who are Levites, carrying it, you are to move out from your positions and follow it. Then you will know which way to go, since you have never been this way before…'"**

At the end of your wilderness, watch for Him to lead you out. Since you have not been on this path, let Him show you a land filled with fruits you cannot imagine. Believe and follow Him today to your new life.

Reflections

Keeping Resolutions

It is coming rather we want it to or not: The New Year. Yikes! Where did the last year go? The usual thing at this time of year is to make some New Year resolutions. Granted, very few are kept by the end of January, but let's look at how we can be resolution keepers all year long and all the years to come.

Sunday   **Psalm 119:105 "Your word is a lamp to my feet and a light to my path."**

It is very hard to see in the dark. If we cannot see the path, how can we make sure we are following the same path day after day? God's word is all the light we ever need. He gives us every answer to all questions. We only need to ask, believe, and wait for His time to answer. Many of the questions we have can be answered by simply opening His word and reading His answer.

Reflections

Monday   **Psalm 119:11 "Your word I have hidden in my heart that I might not sin against You."**

One of the quickest ways to answer some of our questions is to have God's word stored in our memory banks for recall any time. Memorizing God's word is not just for making sure we do not sin, but also can be used for the pleasure of assisting others. Sometimes just one of God's loving verses will lift our spirit for a week or even longer. Find a verse this week and memorize it, even if it is one just for you.

Reflections

Tuesday   **II Peter 1:2, 4 "Grace and peace be multiplied to you in the knowledge of God and of Jesus our Lord; (4) by which have been given to us exceedingly great and precious promises, that through these you may be partakers of the divine nature, having escaped the corruption that is in the world through lust."**

Only through the knowledge of God and Jesus can we have peace and it be multiplied. Only by their knowledge and peace should we make our resolutions (changes) for the coming years. Our knowledge of God and Jesus comes from His word (Holy Bible) and our personal relationship with them. Think on it this way: how many close friends do you have that you have no knowledge of their convictions or/and with whom you do not have a personal relationship? Bet that answer is none! Begin your resolutions for the year with a conviction to <u>know</u> the Father and the Son.

Reflections

Wednesday   John 8:31-32   "Then Jesus said to those Jews who believed Him, 'If you abide in My word, you are My disciples indeed. And you shall know the truth, and the truth shall make you free.'"

Abiding in God's word means to read it, feel it, be convicted by it, and finally, to do it. To make changes in our life does not make sense if we have not consulted the One who loves us enough to tell us the truth in all things. He will guide us in all we do and that includes resolutions for the coming year. He will assist us in keeping those resolutions. No one else on this planet will personally care if we keep our resolutions or not. He will. He loves us that much!

Reflections

Thursday   **Psalm 23:3 "He restores my soul; He leads me in the paths of righteousness for His name's sake."**

So what happens this year if your 'friends' see you break a New Year's Resolution? Nothing, did you say? You are right, but if you make a resolution to our Father, He loves you enough to care if you break it. His caring will restore your soul (forgive you), and He will put you back on the path of righteousness, all because you belong to Him. You are His child (His namesake).

Reflections

Friday   **Psalm 119:24**   **"Your testimonies also are my delight and my counselors."**

Know any good counselors or therapists who are free by the hour? Our Holy Father is! The best part is we can call Him any time day or night. He will pick up the phone. He will guide us and He knows <u>all</u> the answers. Take your list of resolutions to Him. Lift them to Him one by one. Let Him know by your words what you want to change and ask Him how He wants you to go about making the changes. He will be delighted and will set your anxieties to rest.

Reflections

Saturday   **Joshua 1:8**   **"This Book of Law shall not depart from your mouth, but you shall meditate in it day and night, that you may observe to do according to all that is written in it. For then you will make your way prosperous, and then you will have good success."**

There is only one book that can promise us prosperity and deliver on that promise. It is God's inspired word. The promises listed in this verse are more than any of us can ever hope for. We can gain both promises if we go to God daily, night and day. Read His words, meditate on His words, and then do His words. It will not let you down. We have His promises to make us prosperous and give us good success. Neither, of which, has He limited.

Reflections

Waiting

Sunday — **Psalm 27:14** "Wait on the Lord; be of good courage, and He shall strengthen your heart; Wait, I say, on the Lord!"

I have never counted, but I would be willing to claim that I remind myself: "love is patient" at least 1000 times a week. For me to wait on anything for any amount of time is arduous. But God always has good reason for asking us to do anything. Could be we are to wait because we are not ready; or maybe the 'it' is not ready for us. Could be to have 'it' now would cause harm, or maybe the 'it' just would not be as effective as He wishes according to His plans. So, I will continue to remind myself to wait with a glad heart and an even temper, because when 'it' arrives, 'it' will have all God's blessings attached.

Reflections

Monday — **Psalm 62:5 "My soul, wait silently for God alone, for my expectation is from Him."**

What are you waiting for today? Maybe a promotion, a letter, a raise, an understanding of someone or something that has happened in the past is what would set your mind at ease. Scripture tells us we actually wait with our soul. That tells me why waiting patiently is very important to us as individuals. By setting my wants aside and realizing my waiting is really from Him and not because of Him, I can now expect only the best. God does not pass out anything if it is not worth having.

Reflections

Tuesday Psalm 33:20 "Our soul waits for the Lord; He is our help and our shield."

If waiting is as hard for you as it is for me, think on the scripture above. While we are required to wait for many things in our daily lives, we are always shielded with God's love and help. A shield of any kind is for our protection and comfort. We have not been afforded a man-made shield, but instead, the covering of God Himself. Our protection or shield will cover every need. Thank God today for His help and shield whenever you must wait.

Reflections

Wednesday   **Psalm 130:5 "I wait for the Lord, my soul waits, and in His word I do hope."**

Did you realize our hope comes from waiting? I cannot ever remember putting hope and waiting in the same breath. The scripture tells us hope comes from waiting on the Lord. If we believe God is good and His love comes to us daily, then we must believe what He has asked us to wait on must be good and filled with His love. Praise Him today for being in all your waiting moments.

Reflections

Thursday — **Hebrews 10:23** "Let us hold fast the confession of our hope without wavering, for He who promised is faithful."

'Holding fast' indicates there is a time of waiting. This scripture tells us we are to wait without wavering. Wavering is to question the good or evil of a waiting situation. But God is faithful always, so it only stands to reason He will be faithful in our waiting. If we spend our waiting time making our own scenarios of how things will turn out, we are not waiting without wavering. We must confess to God that we are totally dependent on His decisions in our waiting, and thank Him for His love, patience with us, and His control in all our waiting.

Reflections

Friday   **Psalm 145:15 – 16**   **"The eyes of all look expectantly to You, and You give them their food in due season, You open Your hand and satisfy the desire of every living thing."**

We can expect God to answer our every need and that includes our times of waiting. God provided food, shelter, and water to the Israelites when they crossed the desert, so why do we not allow Him to answer our call when we are waiting. Their manna was given daily in the exact right amounts. If they took more than they ate that day, the manna was spoiled when they awakened. The same is true with our waiting. If we jump ahead of God's plan, our ending will be spoiled. It will not be in His perfect plan. Wait. You will be satisfied with your desires.

Reflections

Saturday — Habakkuk 2:3 "For the vision is yet for an appointed time; But at the end it will speak, and it will not lie. Though it tarries, wait for it; because it will surely come, it will not tarry."

This scripture is filled with so many promises, straight from God. Whatever we are waiting for and for however long we must wait, there is an appointed time. God Himself will reward our waiting. It is His vision we are waiting for always. Wait. It will not tarry.

Reflections

Safe In His Arms

I have a favorite picture of my daddy. It is a picture of me as a child in his arms. When I look at it, I see a warm smile on his face and a secure grin on mine. I enjoy looking back and remembering, not just my childhood but last year, last month, and even last week. One thing I can always remember is that whatever my situation, I am safe in my Father's arms.

Sunday   **1 Chronicles 16:10-12** "**Glory ye in his holy name: let the heart of them rejoice that seek the LORD. Seek the LORD and his strength; seek his face continually. Remember his marvelous works that he hath done, his wonders, and the judgments of his mouth;**"

A favorite song of mine is "YOU ALONE" written by Echoing Angels. The first words tell of one "Desperately wanting to just find a way, searching and seeking for someone to say, that it is alright and it is OK." Listening farther to the song, we realize that this person has found that Jesus ALONE is GOD. Verse 11 above tells us to "seek the LORD," seek His strength and His face, continually. We may not get the approval our flesh desires, but the soul can be filled with His love.

Reflections

Monday **Deuteronomy 4:29** "But if from thence thou shalt seek the LORD thy God, thou shalt find him, if thou seek him with all thy heart and with all thy soul."

The verse says, "From thence," which means 'from that place.' That place can be your desperate search for safety. By seeking with your whole heart and soul, you can actually find God. Once found, you can rest in His Arms. Your soul is full when you are dwelling with Jesus.

Reflections

Tuesday   Isaiah 57:2a "He shall enter into peace: they shall rest in their beds,"

In the second verse of YOU ALONE, "...I close my eyes and drift away to somewhere I remember — to a place I feel safe – I am in your arms." Have you ever closed your eyes and drifted away? Tired, sad, worried, wounded, and lonely, wanting to be held, wanting to feel secure? Drift into the love of Jesus Christ, and rest in His Arms.

Reflections

Wednesday II Corinthians 5:17 "Therefore if any man be in Christ, he is a new creature: old things are passed away; behold, all things are become new."

Sometimes we long for acceptance. God's Word tells us that Jesus forgives, and He accepts us as we are; something few others do. He gives us a clean slate to begin life anew.

Reflections

Thursday — **Proverbs 1:2 "To know wisdom and instruction; to perceive the words of understanding;"**

The song, "YOU ALONE" ends with, "You love me and want me to understand that YOU ALONE are GOD." To understand is to 'appreciate, value, and identify with.' When you feel NO ONE cares, know that God CARES.

Reflections

Friday **Jeremiah 30:22** "**And ye shall be my people, and I will be your God.**"

Wanting something does not give you satisfaction. Satisfaction is only realized when the 'want' becomes 'possession.' This possession is two sided: He possesses you, and you possess HIM. Only God completely satisfies. Let Him satisfy you today. Open your heart to Him.

Reflections

Saturday   **Psalm 95:6 "O come, let us worship and bow down: let us kneel before the LORD our maker."**

Ending the week with worship brings pleasure as well as excitement. Deepen your relationship with Christ by worshiping Him in praise, song, and prayer. Your strength may be weak and your heart broken and lonely, but rest in the arms of Jesus Christ. As you kneel before Him today, rest in the fact that you are SAFE in HIS ARMS.

Reflections

Scriptural Index

Scripture Book	Chapter Verse	Topic	Version	Title	Season	Day	Page
Old Testament							
Genesis	1:1	beginning	NKJ	The Beginning	Autumn	Sun	278
Genesis	1:1	created	NKJ	Elohim	Summer	Sun	103
Genesis	1:11	vegetation	NKJ	The Beginning	Autumn	Wed	281
Genesis	1:16-18	two great lights	NKJ	The Beginning	Autumn	Thur	282
Genesis	1:2	created	NKJ	The Beginning	Autumn	Sun	278
Genesis	1:21-22	creatures	NKJ	The Beginning	Autumn	Fri	283
Genesis	1:26	man (God made)	NKJ	The Beginning	Autumn	Sat	284
Genesis	1:26	man (Let Us make)	NKJ	Elohim	Summer	Tues	105
Genesis	1:27	created (God created man)	NIV	Designing Us	Autumn	Sun	264
Genesis	1:27	created	NKJ	Elohim	Summer	Wed	106
Genesis	1:27	created	NIV	Defining You	Winter	Sun	334
Genesis	1:28	dominion	NKJ	Elohim	Summer	Fri	107
Genesis	1:28	blessed	NKJ	Elohim	Summer	Thur	107
Genesis	1:3	God (said)	NKJ	The Beginning	Autumn	Mon	279
Genesis	1:3	light (God said)	NKJ	Elohim	Summer	Mon	104
Genesis	1:6-8	Second day	NKJ	The Beginning	Autumn	Tues	280
Genesis	11:27	Lord (had said..go)	KJ	Directions	Autumn	Mon	216
Genesis	15:12	horror	KJ	Sleep	Summer	Mon	181
Genesis	15:4	word (of the LORD)	NKJ	Who is in Control?	Spring	Sun	26
Genesis	16:2	children (from having)	NKJ	Who is in Control?	Spring	Sun	26
Genesis	17:1-2	blameless	NKJ	Who is in Control?	Spring	Mon	27
Genesis	2:21	flesh	KJ	Sleep	Summer	Sun	180
Genesis	2:3	blessed	NKJ	Elohim	Summer	Sat	108
Genesis	20:2	sister	NKJ	Who is in Control?	Spring	Tues	28
Genesis	20:5	conscience	NKJ	Who is in Control?	Spring	Wed	29
Genesis	28:16	Lord (in this place)	KJ	Sleep	Summer	Sat	186
Genesis	31:40	consumed	KJ	Sleep	Summer	Tues	182
Genesis	33:11	blessing	NKJ	Prosperity	Autumn	Sun	208
Exodus	1:14	bitter	NIV	Is it 'Worth it'?	Winter	Sun	327
Exodus	1:14	bondage	KJ	Is it 'Worth it'?	Winter	Sun	327
Exodus	12:31	serve	KJ	Is it 'Worth it'?	Winter	Tues	329
Exodus	13:21	guide	NIV	God's Provision in Your Wilderness	Winter	Sun	362
Exodus	14:13	afraid	NIV	God's Provision in Your Wilderness	Winter	Mon	363
Exodus	14:22	midst	KJ	Is it 'Worth it'?	Winter	Wed	330
Exodus	15:24	grumbled	NIV	God's Provision in Your Wilderness	Winter	Tues	364
Exodus	16:11	Lord (said)	NIV	God's Provision in Your Wilderness	Winter	Thur	366
Exodus	16:4	Lord (said)	NIV	God's Provision in Your Wilderness	Winter	Wed	365

Scripture Book	Chapter Verse	Topic	Version	Title	Season	Day	Page
Exodus	18:23	Command (thee so)	KJ	IF	Winter	Mon	300
Exodus	18:23	endure (able to)	KJ	IF	Winter	Mon	300
Exodus	18:23	wilt do	KJ	IF	Winter	Mon	300
Exodus	2:24	covenant	KJ	Is it 'Worth it'?	Winter	Mon	328
Exodus	2:24	groaning	KJ	Is it 'Worth it'?	Winter	Mon	328
Exodus	20:3	no other gods	NKJ	Adoration of Our Holy Father	Autumn	Fri	206
Exodus	34:8	bowed his head	NKJ	Adoration of Our Holy Father	Autumn	Wed	204
Exodus	34:8	worshipped	NKJ	Adoration of Our Holy Father	Autumn	Wed	204
Exodus	6:7	burdens	KJ	Know	Summer	Sun	173
Exodus	8:27	sacrifice	KJ	Ultimate Sacrifice	Summer	Sun	187
Exodus	8:27	wilderness	KJ	Ultimate Sacrifice	Summer	Sun	187
Leviticus	19:17	hate	NKJ	Love&Hate War&Peace	Winter	Mon	356
Numbers	11:6	soul (is dried)	KJ	Is it 'Worth it'?	Winter	Thur	331
Numbers	13:1	Lord (said)	NIV	God's Provision in Your Wilderness	Winter	Fri	367
Numbers	13:25	returned	KJ	Is it 'Worth it'?	Winter	Fri	332
Numbers	13:30	overcome	KJ	Is it 'Worth it'?	Winter	Sat	333
Deuteronomy	1:30	fight (for you)	NKJ	You are God's Specialty	Summer	Mon	146
Deuteronomy	1:30	fight (for you)	NKJ	Love&Hate War&Peace	Winter	Wed	358
Deuteronomy	3:22	fear	NKJ	Love&Hate War&Peace	Winter	Thur	359
Deuteronomy	30:19	choose life	KJ	For Sale	Spring	Mon	34
Deuteronomy	30:20	cleave (unto him)	KJ	For Sale	Spring	Mon	34
Deuteronomy	30:20	love the Lord	KJ	For Sale	Spring	Mon	34
Deuteronomy	30:20	obey (his voice)	KJ	For Sale	Spring	Mon	34
Deuteronomy	33:12	beloved (of the Lord)	NIV	Words	Autumn	Sat	228
Deuteronomy	33:12	rest	NIV	Words	Autumn	Sat	228
Deuteronomy	4:29	seek	KJ	Safe In His Arms	Winter	Mon	384
Deuteronomy	6:5	heart	NKJ	Adoration of Our Holy Father	Autumn	Sat	207
Deuteronomy	6:5	love the Lord	NKJ	Adoration of Our Holy Father	Autumn	Sat	207
Deuteronomy	6:5	soul	NKJ	Adoration of Our Holy Father	Autumn	Sat	207
Deuteronomy	6:5	strength	NKJ	Adoration of Our Holy Father	Autumn	Sat	207
Joshua	1:1	Lord (your God)	KJ	Directions	Autumn	Sat	221
Joshua	1:2	Get ready	KJ	Directions	Autumn	Wed	218
Joshua	1:8	law (book of)	KJ	Directions	Autumn	Fri	220
Joshua	1:8	meditate	KJ	Directions	Autumn	Fri	220
Joshua	1:8	Prosperous	KJ	Directions	Autumn	Fri	220
Joshua	1:8	successful	KJ	Directions	Autumn	Fri	220
Joshua	1:8	prosperous	NIV	God's Provision in Your Wilderness	Winter	Sat	368

Scripture Book	Chapter Verse	Topic	Version	Title	Season	Day	Page
Joshua	1:8	success (good)	NKJ	Keeping Resolutions	Winter	Sat	375
Joshua	1:9	courageous	KJ	Directions	Autumn	Thur	219
Joshua	1:9	Lord (with you)	KJ	Directions	Autumn	Thur	219
Joshua	1:9	strong	KJ	Directions	Autumn	Thur	219
Joshua	1:9	Terrified (not)	KJ	Directions	Autumn	Thur	219
Joshua	23:11	love the Lord	NKJ	Adoration of Our Holy Father	Autumn	Mon	202
Joshua	23:11	take heed	NKJ	Adoration of Our Holy Father	Autumn	Mon	202
Joshua	3:10	God (living)	KJ	Know	Summer	Wed	176
Joshua	3:3	follow	NIV	God's Provision in Your Wilderness	Winter	Sat	368
Joshua	4:22	children	KJ	Know	Summer	Fri	178
Judges	5:3	sing (I will)	NIV	Songs	Summer	Fri	122
1 Kings	11:38	Command (thee)	KJ	IF	Winter	Tues	301
1 Kings	11:38	hearken	KJ	IF	Winter	Tues	301
1 Kings	3:10	pleased (the Lord)	KJ	Speech	Spring	Sat	60
1 Kings	3:10	speech	KJ	Speech	Spring	Sat	60
2 Kings	20:1	sick (unto death)	KJ	Hezekiah - Added Days	Autumn	Intro	236
2 Kings	20:1	order (set thine house)	KJ	Hezekiah - Added Days	Autumn	Sun	236
2 Kings	20:2	prayed	KJ	Hezekiah - Added Days	Autumn	Intro	236
2 Kings	20:3	heart (perfect)	KJ	Hezekiah - Added Days	Autumn	Intro	236
2 Kings	20:3	wept	KJ	Hezekiah - Added Days	Autumn	Mon	237
2 Kings	20:3	walked	KJ	Hezekiah - Added Days	Autumn	Tues	238
2 Kings	20:4	word (of the LORD)	KJ	Hezekiah - Added Days	Autumn	Intro	236
2 Kings	20:5	heal	KJ	Hezekiah - Added Days	Autumn	Fri	241
2 Kings	20:5	heal	KJ	Hezekiah - Added Days	Autumn	Sat	242
2 Kings	20:5	tears (seen thy)	KJ	Hezekiah - Added Days	Autumn	Thur	240
2 Kings	20:5	prayer (have heard thy)	KJ	Hezekiah - Added Days	Autumn	Wed	239
2 Kings	20:6	deliver	KJ	Hezekiah - Added Days	Autumn	Intro	236
2 Kings	20:7	recovered	KJ	Hezekiah - Added Days	Autumn	Intro	236
1 Chronicles	16:10-12	glory	KJ	Safe In His Arms	Winter	Sun	383
1 Chronicles	16:10-12	judgment	KJ	Safe In His Arms	Winter	Sun	383
1 Chronicles	16:10-12	marvelous	KJ	Safe In His Arms	Winter	Sun	383
1 Chronicles	16:10-12	rejoice	KJ	Safe In His Arms	Winter	Sun	383
1 Chronicles	16:10-12	seek	KJ	Safe In His Arms	Winter	Sun	383
1 Chronicles	16:11	judgment	KJ	Ultimate Sacrifice	Summer	Wed	190
1 Chronicles	16:11	seek	KJ	Ultimate Sacrifice	Summer	Wed	190

Scripture Book	Chapter Verse	Topic	Version	Title	Season	Day	Page
1 Chronicles	16:11	strength	KJ	Ultimate Sacrifice	Summer	Wed	190
1 Chronicles	29:18	desire	NIV	Words	Autumn	Wed	225
1 Chronicles	29:18	loyal	NIV	Words	Autumn	Wed	225
1 Chronicles	4:10	evil (keep me)	KJ	Prayer of Jabez	Autumn	Fri	262
1 Chronicles	4:10	grieve	KJ	Prayer of Jabez	Autumn	Fri	262
1 Chronicles	4:10	called (on God)	KJ	Prayer of Jabez	Autumn	Mon	258
1 Chronicles	4:10	granted (God)	KJ	Prayer of Jabez	Autumn	Sat	263
1 Chronicles	4:10	be (with me)	KJ	Prayer of Jabez	Autumn	Thur	261
1 Chronicles	4:10	bless (me)	KJ	Prayer of Jabez	Autumn	Tues	259
1 Chronicles	4:10	enlarge (my coast)	KJ	Prayer of Jabez	Autumn	Wed	260
1 Chronicles	4:9	honorable	KJ	Prayer of Jabez	Autumn	Intro	257
1 Chronicles	4:9	sorrow	KJ	Prayer of Jabez	Autumn	Sun	257
2 Chronicles	12:1	law (forsook the)	NKJ	Prosperity	Autumn	Fri	213
2 Chronicles	12:1	strengthened	NKJ	Prosperity	Autumn	Fri	213
2 Chronicles	26:16	heart (lifted up)	NKJ	Prosperity	Autumn	Sat	214
2 Chronicles	5:14	glory	NKJ	You are God's Specialty	Summer	Sun	145
Job	Book of	Challenges (facing)	KJ	May'Flower'	Spring	Fri	87
Psalm	105:4	seek	NIV	Wisdom	Spring	Thur	72
Psalm	105:4	strength	NIV	Wisdom	Spring	Thur	72
Psalm	118:25	prosperity	NKJ	Passion Week	Spring	Wed	22
Psalm	119:105	light (unto my path)	NKJ	Keeping Resolutions	Winter	Sun	369
Psalm	119:11	word (I have hidden)	NIV	God's Provision in Your Wilderness	Winter	Mon	363
Psalm	119:11	heart (hidden in my)	NKJ	Keeping Resolutions	Winter	Mon	370
Psalm	119:142	everlasting	NIV	Father's Day	Spring	Fri	94
Psalm	119:142	righteousness	NIV	Father's Day	Spring	Fri	94
Psalm	119:24	delight	NIV	God's Provision in Your Wilderness	Winter	Fri	367
Psalm	119:24	delight	NKJ	Keeping Resolutions	Winter	Fri	374
Psalm	119:50	comfort	NIV	Defining You	Winter	Thur	338
Psalm	119:50	promise	NIV	Defining You	Winter	Thur	338
Psalm	119:50	suffering	NIV	Defining You	Winter	Thur	338
Psalm	120:6	hates	NKJ	Love&Hate War&Peace	Winter	Sat	361
Psalm	120:7	peace	NKJ	Love&Hate War&Peace	Winter	Sat	361
Psalm	124:1	Side (on our)	KJ	IF	Winter	Sun	299
Psalm	124:2	against (us)	KJ	IF	Winter	Sun	299
Psalm	127:1	vain, in	NKJ	Prosperity	Autumn	Mon	209
Psalm	13:6	sing (to the Lord)	NKJ	Week of Thanksgiving	Autumn	Mon	230
Psalm	13:6	sing	NKJ	Patience for Coming Events	Winter	Mon	342
Psalm	130:5	hope	NKJ	Waiting	Winter	Wed	379
Psalm	130:5	wait (for the Lord)	NKJ	Waiting	Winter	Wed	379
Psalm	130:7	hope	NIV	Jesus & the Seven RE's of Us	Spring	Mon	41

Scripture Book	Chapter Verse	Topic	Version	Title	Season	Day	Page
Psalm	136:1	mercy (endures forever)	NKJ	Week of Thanksgiving	Autumn	Sat	235
Psalm	136:1	thanks (give to the Lord)	NKJ	Week of Thanksgiving	Autumn	Sat	235
Psalm	136:1	mercy	NKJ	Patience for Coming Events	Winter	Sat	347
Psalm	136:1	thanks	NKJ	Patience for Coming Events	Winter	Sat	347
Psalm	139:13	created (my inmost being)	NIV	Designing Us	Autumn	Mon	265
Psalm	139:15	secret	NIV	Defining You	Winter	Mon	335
Psalm	145:16	desire	NKJ	Waiting	Winter	Fri	381
Psalm	145:16	satisfy	NKJ	Waiting	Winter	Fri	381
Psalm	146:8	sight	NIV	Senses	Winter	Sun	313
Psalm	17:6	hear (me, O God)	KJ	Speech	Spring	Mon	55
Psalm	17:6	speech	KJ	Speech	Spring	Mon	55
Psalm	18:1-3	deliverer	KJ	Letting Go & Letting God	Summer	Tues	154
Psalm	18:1-3	enemies	KJ	Letting Go & Letting God	Summer	Tues	154
Psalm	18:1-3	strength	KJ	Letting Go & Letting God	Summer	Tues	154
Psalm	18:1-3	deliverer	KJ	Letting Go & Letting God	Summer	Wed	155
Psalm	18:1-3	enemies	KJ	Letting Go & Letting God	Summer	Wed	155
Psalm	18:1-3	strength	KJ	Letting Go & Letting God	Summer	Wed	155
Psalm	22:4	delivered	NIV	Father's Day	Spring	Wed	92
Psalm	22:4	trust	NIV	Father's Day	Spring	Wed	92
Psalm	23:3	restores	NIV	God's Provision in Your Wilderness	Winter	Thur	366
Psalm	23:3	righteousness	NIV	God's Provision in Your Wilderness	Winter	Thur	366
Psalm	23:3	restore	NKJ	Keeping Resolutions	Winter	Thur	373
Psalm	23:5	cup	NKJ	His Refreshing Preparations	Summer	Fri	115
Psalm	23:5	Me (before)	NKJ	His Refreshing Preparations	Summer	Mon	111
Psalm	23:5	runs (over)	NKJ	His Refreshing Preparations	Summer	Sat	116
Psalm	23:5	prepare (Thou)	NKJ	His Refreshing Preparations	Summer	Sun	110
Psalm	23:5	oil	NKJ	His Refreshing Preparations	Summer	Thur	114
Psalm	23:5	enemies	NKJ	His Refreshing Preparations	Summer	Tues	112
Psalm	23:5	anoint	NKJ	His Refreshing Preparations	Summer	Wed	113
Psalm	26:7	thanksgiving	NKJ	Patience for Coming Events	Winter	Tues	343
Psalm	26:8	glory (dwells)	NKJ	Week of Thanksgiving	Autumn	Tues	231
Psalm	26:8	glory	NKJ	Patience for Coming Events	Winter	Tues	343
Psalm	27:14	strengthen	NKJ	Waiting	Winter	Sun	376

Scripture Book	Chapter Verse	Topic	Version	Title	Season	Day	Page
Psalm	27:14	wait (on the Lord)	NKJ	Waiting	Winter	Sun	376
Psalm	33:20	help	NKJ	Waiting	Winter	Tues	378
Psalm	33:20	shield	NKJ	Waiting	Winter	Tues	378
Psalm	33:20	waits (for the Lord)	NKJ	Waiting	Winter	Tues	378
Psalm	33:3	sing (to him a new song)	NIV	Songs	Summer	Thur	121
Psalm	34:1	bless	NKJ	You are God's Specialty	Summer	Sat	151
Psalm	34:8	Taste	NIV	Senses	Winter	Tues	315
Psalm	37:4	delight yourself	NKJ	Adoration of Our Holy Father	Autumn	Sun	201
Psalm	37:4	desires of your heart	NKJ	Adoration of Our Holy Father	Autumn	Sun	201
Psalm	37:4	anger	NKJ	Flowers in December	Winter	Thur	352
Psalm	37:4	harm	NKJ	Flowers in December	Winter	Thur	352
Psalm	37:4	love	NKJ	Flowers in December	Winter	Thur	352
Psalm	37:4	wrath	NKJ	Flowers in December	Winter	Thur	352
Psalm	37:5	commit (your way)	NIV	Words	Autumn	Mon	223
Psalm	37:6	righteousness	NIV	Words	Autumn	Mon	223
Psalm	37:7	patiently	NKJ	Patience	Spring	Thur	51
Psalm	37:7	prosper	NKJ	Patience	Spring	Thur	51
Psalm	37:7	rest	NKJ	Patience	Spring	Thur	51
Psalm	37:7	wicked	NKJ	Patience	Spring	Thur	51
Psalm	4:8	peace	KJ	Letting Go & Letting God	Summer	Sat	158
Psalm	4:8	safety	KJ	Letting Go & Letting God	Summer	Sat	158
Psalm	40:1	cry	NKJ	Patience	Spring	Fri	52
Psalm	40:1	waited	NKJ	Patience	Spring	Fri	52
Psalm	40:5	Lord (my God)	NKJ	Week of Thanksgiving	Autumn	Wed	232
Psalm	40:5	wonderful	NKJ	Patience for Coming Events	Winter	Wed	344
Psalm	46:7	refuge	NKJ	Flowers in December	Winter	Sun	348
Psalm	51:10	heart (create a clean)	KJ	For Sale	Spring	Tues	35
Psalm	51:10	spirit (renew a right)	KJ	For Sale	Spring	Tues	35
Psalm	57:1	mercy (have m on me)	NIV	Wisdom	Spring	Sun	68
Psalm	62:5	alone	NKJ	Waiting	Winter	Mon	377
Psalm	66:5	awesome	NIV	Jesus & the Seven RE's of Us	Spring	Fri	45
Psalm	68:30	delight	NKJ	Love&Hate War&Peace	Winter	Fri	360
Psalm	68:5	defender	NKJ	Our Father	Summer	Sun	138
Psalm	74:16	day (is yours)	NIV	Words	Autumn	Tues	224
Psalm	74:17	boundaries	NIV	Words	Autumn	Tues	224
Psalm	88:4	strength	KJ	Letting Go & Letting God	Summer	Tues	154
Psalm	9:1	praise	NKJ	Week of Thanksgiving	Autumn	Sun	229

Scripture Book	Chapter Verse	Topic	Version	Title	Season	Day	Page
Psalm	9:1	praise	NKJ	Patience for Coming Events	Winter	Sun	341
Psalm	9:2	rejoice	NKJ	Week of Thanksgiving	Autumn	Sun	229
Psalm	92:1	thanks (give, it is)	NKJ	Week of Thanksgiving	Autumn	Thur	233
Psalm	92:1	thanks	NKJ	You are God's Specialty	Summer	Sat	151
Psalm	92:1	thanks	NKJ	Patience for Coming Events	Winter	Thur	345
Psalm	92:4	triumph	NKJ	Week of Thanksgiving	Autumn	Thur	233
Psalm	95:6	worship	KJ	Safe In His Arms	Winter	Sat	389
Psalm	96:4	feared	NKJ	You are God's Specialty	Summer	Sat	151
Psalm	96:4	praised	NKJ	You are God's Specialty	Summer	Sat	151
Psalm	98:1	marvelous	NKJ	Week of Thanksgiving	Autumn	Fri	234
Psalm	98:1	victory	NKJ	Week of Thanksgiving	Autumn	Fri	234
Psalm	98:1	victory	NKJ	Patience for Coming Events	Winter	Fri	346
Proverbs	1:2	instruction	KJ	Safe In His Arms	Winter	Thur	387
Proverbs	1:2	understanding	KJ	Safe In His Arms	Winter	Thur	387
Proverbs	1:2	wisdom	KJ	Safe In His Arms	Winter	Thur	387
Proverbs	10:12	hatred	NKJ	Love&Hate War&Peace	Winter	Tues	357
Proverbs	16:32	anger	NKJ	You are God's Specialty	Summer	Wed	148
Proverbs	26:24	hates	NKJ	Love&Hate War&Peace	Winter	Sun	355
Proverbs	27:6	deceitful	KJ	Unquenchable Love	Summer	Tues	168
Proverbs	27:6	enemy	KJ	Unquenchable Love	Summer	Tues	168
Proverbs	27:6	faithful	KJ	Unquenchable Love	Summer	Tues	168
Proverbs	27:6	wounds	KJ	Unquenchable Love	Summer	Tues	168
Proverbs	3:24	afraid	KJ	Sleep	Summer	Fri	185
Proverbs	3:5	trust	NIV	Defining You	Winter	Wed	337
Proverbs	3:5	understanding	NIV	Defining You	Winter	Wed	337
Proverbs	3:5-6	trust	NIV	Phrases We Often Use	Winter	Sat	326
Proverbs	3:5-6	understanding	NIV	Phrases We Often Use	Winter	Sat	326
Proverbs	4:8	righteous	NIV	Defining You	Winter	Fri	339
Proverbs	6:9	arise	KJ	Sleep	Summer	Thur	184
Proverbs	6:9	sluggard	KJ	Sleep	Summer	Thur	184
Proverbs	7:21	speech	KJ	Speech	Spring	Sun	54
Proverbs	7:4	wisdom	NIV	Defining You	Winter	Sat	340
Ecclesiastes	7:14	adversity	NKJ	Prosperity	Autumn	Tues	210
Ecclesiastes	7:14	joyful	NKJ	Prosperity	Autumn	Tues	210
Ecclesiastes	7:9	angry	NKJ	Patience	Spring	Tues	49

Scripture Book	Chapter Verse	Topic	Version	Title	Season	Day	Page
Song of Solomon	8:7	condemned	KJ	Unquenchable Love	Summer	Sun	166
Song of Solomon	8:7	love	KJ	Unquenchable Love	Summer	Sun	166
Isaiah	1:18	sin	NIV	Jesus & the Seven RE's of Us	Spring	Tues	42
Isaiah	26:3	peace	NKJ	Flowers in December	Winter	Mon	349
Isaiah	26:3	trust	NKJ	Flowers in December	Winter	Mon	349
Isaiah	26:3	peace	NKJ	Love&Hate War&Peace	Winter	Thur	359
Isaiah	32:17	peace	NIV	Righteous	Spring	Fri	80
Isaiah	43:10	servant	KJ	Know	Summer	Sat	179
Isaiah	43:10	understand	KJ	Know	Summer	Sat	179
Isaiah	43:10	witnesses	KJ	Know	Summer	Sat	179
Isaiah	43:3	Lord (your God)	NKJ	Flowers in December	Winter	Fri	353
Isaiah	5:1	sing (for the one I love)	NIV	Songs	Summer	Wed	120
Isaiah	57:2	peace	KJ	Safe In His Arms	Winter	Tues	385
Isaiah	57:2	rest	KJ	Safe In His Arms	Winter	Tues	385
Isaiah	6:8	Lord (voice of)	NIV	Wisdom	Spring	Wed	71
Isaiah	6:8	Send	NIV	Wisdom	Spring	Wed	71
Isaiah	61:4	devastated	NIV	Jesus & the Seven RE's of Us	Spring	Wed	43
Isaiah	61:4	restore	NIV	Jesus & the Seven RE's of Us	Spring	Wed	43
Isaiah	63:16	redeemer	NKJ	Our Father	Summer	Tues	140
Isaiah	64:8	work (we are work of your hand)	NIV	Designing Us	Autumn	Thur	268
Isaiah	64:8	work (of your hand)	NIV	Jesus & the Seven RE's of Us	Spring	Thur	44
Isaiah	64:8	work (of your hand)	NKJ	Our Father	Summer	Mon	139
Jeremiah	1:5	Apart (set apart for a purpose)	NIV	Designing Us	Autumn	Tues	266
Jeremiah	18:4	marred	NIV	Designing Us	Autumn	Fri	269
Jeremiah	29:11	plans	KJ	Directions	Autumn	Sun	215
Jeremiah	29:11	evil (not)	NKJ	You are God's Specialty	Summer	Tues	147
Jeremiah	29:11	hope	NKJ	You are God's Specialty	Summer	Tues	147
Jeremiah	29:11	peace	NKJ	You are God's Specialty	Summer	Tues	147
Jeremiah	30:22	God (be your)	KJ	Safe In His Arms	Winter	Fri	388
Jeremiah	31:3	kindness	NKJ	Love&Hate War&Peace	Winter	Mon	356
Jeremiah	31:3	love	NKJ	Love&Hate War&Peace	Winter	Mon	356
Lamentations	3:26	hope	NKJ	Patience	Spring	Mon	48
Lamentations	3:26	salvation	NKJ	Patience	Spring	Mon	48
Lamentations	3:26	wait	NKJ	Patience	Spring	Mon	48
Ezekiel	34:24-26	blessing	KJ	Sleep	Summer	Wed	183
Ezekiel	34:24-26	covenant	KJ	Sleep	Summer	Wed	183
Ezekiel	34:24-26	peace	KJ	Sleep	Summer	Wed	183

Scripture Book	Chapter Verse	Topic	Version	Title	Season	Day	Page
Ezekiel	34:24-26	servant	KJ	Sleep	Summer	Wed	183
Daniel	3:17	rescue	NIV	Father's Day	Spring	Tues	91
Hosea	13:6	exalted (their heart was)	NKJ	Prosperity	Autumn	Thur	212
Hosea	4:7	glory (into shame)	NKJ	Prosperity	Autumn	Wed	211
Hosea	4:7	sinned (against ME)	NKJ	Prosperity	Autumn	Wed	211
Jonah	1:1	wickedness	KJ	Directions	Autumn	Tues	217
Jonah	1:1	word (of the LORD)	KJ	Directions	Autumn	Tues	217
Micah	1	word (of the LORD)	KJ	Micah	Winter	Sun	306
Micah	2	evil (time is)	KJ	Micah	Winter	Mon	307
Micah	2	iniquity (woe unto them)	KJ	Micah	Winter	Mon	307
Micah	3	answer (no answer of God)	KJ	Micah	Winter	Tues	308
Micah	3	Lips (cover their)	KJ	Micah	Winter	Tues	308
Micah	4	teach	KJ	Micah	Winter	Wed	309
Micah	4	walk (in his paths)	KJ	Micah	Winter	Wed	309
Micah	5	heard (have not)	KJ	Micah	Winter	Thur	310
Micah	6	done (what have I)	KJ	Micah	Winter	Fri	311
Micah	7	compassion (he will have)	KJ	Micah	Winter	Sat	312
Micah	7	iniquity (he will subdue)	KJ	Micah	Winter	Sat	312
Micah	7	sins (cast into seas)	KJ	Micah	Winter	Sat	312
Habakkuk	2:3	lie	NKJ	Waiting	Winter	Sat	382
Habakkuk	2:3	vision	NKJ	Waiting	Winter	Sat	382
Zephaniah	3:14	rejoice	NIV	Songs	Summer	Sun	117
Zephaniah	3:17	joy	KJ	May'Flower'	Spring	Sat	88
Zephaniah	3:17	love	KJ	May'Flower'	Spring	Sat	88
Zephaniah	3:17	rejoice	KJ	May'Flower'	Spring	Sat	88
Zephaniah	3:17	save	KJ	May'Flower'	Spring	Sat	88
Zechariah	9:9	rejoice	NKJ	Passion Week	Spring	Intro	19
Zechariah	9:9	salvation	NKJ	Passion Week	Spring	Intro	19
Malachi	2:10	create	NIV	Father's Day	Spring	Mon	90
New Testament							
Matthew	11:29	gentle	NIV	Wisdom	Spring	Fri	73
Matthew	11:29	humble	NIV	Wisdom	Spring	Fri	73
Matthew	11:29	learn	NIV	Wisdom	Spring	Fri	73
Matthew	11:29	rest	NIV	Wisdom	Spring	Fri	73
Matthew	12:50	will (Father in heaven)	NKJ	Our Father	Summer	Wed	141
Matthew	13:47	net	KJ	Letting Go & Letting God	Summer	Mon	153
Matthew	16:24	come (after me)	KJ	IF	Winter	Wed	302
Matthew	16:24	Cross (take up)	KJ	IF	Winter	Wed	302
Matthew	16:24	deny (himself)	KJ	IF	Winter	Wed	302
Matthew	16:24	Follow (me)	KJ	IF	Winter	Wed	302

Scripture Book	Chapter Verse	Topic	Version	Title	Season	Day	Page
Matthew	21:10-11	Jesus (This is)	NKJ	Passion Week	Spring	Thur	23
Matthew	21:4	King (is coming)	NKJ	Passion Week	Spring	Mon	20
Matthew	26:33	Stumble	NKJ	Adoration of Our Holy Father	Autumn	Thur	205
Matthew	26:73	betrayeth	KJ	Speech	Spring	Thur	58
Matthew	26:73	speech	KJ	Speech	Spring	Thur	58
Matthew	27:46	forsaken (My God…)	NKJ	From the Cross	Autumn	Wed	253
Matthew	27:5	afraid	NKJ	His Teaching Continues	Autumn	Mon	272
Matthew	27:57 - 60	Provision	NKJ	His Teaching Continues	Autumn	Sun	271
Matthew	5:18	fulfilled	NKJ	A Way of Life	Autumn	Sun	243
Matthew	5:18	heaven	NKJ	A Way of Life	Autumn	Sun	243
Matthew	5:22	angry	NKJ	A Way of Life	Autumn	Mon	244
Matthew	5:28	adultery	NKJ	A Way of Life	Autumn	Tues	245
Matthew	5:28	lust	NKJ	A Way of Life	Autumn	Tues	245
Matthew	5:32	adultery	NKJ	A Way of Life	Autumn	Wed	246
Matthew	5:32	divorce	NKJ	A Way of Life	Autumn	Wed	246
Matthew	5:37	evil (one)	NKJ	A Way of Life	Autumn	Thur	247
Matthew	5:4	blessed	NKJ	You are God's Specialty	Summer	Sun	145
Matthew	5:4	mourn	NKJ	You are God's Specialty	Summer	Sun	145
Matthew	5:42	Borrow	NKJ	A Way of Life	Autumn	Fri	248
Matthew	5:42	Give	NKJ	A Way of Life	Autumn	Fri	248
Matthew	5:44	love (your enemies)	NKJ	A Way of Life	Autumn	Sat	249
Matthew	7:20	fruits	KJ	Know	Summer	Thur	177
Matthew	7:8	knock	NIV	Jesus & the Seven RE's of Us	Spring	Sun	40
Matthew	7:8	seek	NIV	Jesus & the Seven RE's of Us	Spring	Sun	40
Matthew	9:17	wine	NIV	Designing Us	Autumn	Sat	270
Mark	11:1	disciples	NKJ	Passion Week	Spring	Sun	19
Mark	11:25	forgive	NKJ	Our Father	Summer	Thur	142
Mark	11:25	praying	NKJ	Our Father	Summer	Thur	142
Mark	11:8-10	King (is coming)	NKJ	Passion Week	Spring	Tues	21
Mark	4:38-40	calm	KJ	May'Flower'	Spring	Thur	86
Mark	4:38-40	faith	KJ	May'Flower'	Spring	Thur	86
Mark	4:38-40	fearful	KJ	May'Flower'	Spring	Thur	86
Mark	4:38-40	peace	KJ	May'Flower'	Spring	Thur	86
Mark	5:28	Touch	NIV	Senses	Winter	Thur	317
Luke	1:22	speak	KJ	Speech	Spring	Tues	56
Luke	10:19	power	NKJ	Flowers in December	Winter	Wed	351
Luke	10:9	enemy	NKJ	Flowers in December	Winter	Wed	351
Luke	11:9	ask	NIV	Defining You	Winter	Tues	336
Luke	11:9	knock	NIV	Defining You	Winter	Tues	336
Luke	11:9	seek	NIV	Defining You	Winter	Tues	336

Scripture Book	Chapter Verse	Topic	Version	Title	Season	Day	Page
Luke	12:15	greed	NIV	Wisdom	Spring	Sat	74
Luke	12:15	guard	NIV	Wisdom	Spring	Sat	74
Luke	15:8-10	rejoice	KJ	May'Flower'	Spring	Tues	84
Luke	15:8-10	repenteth	KJ	May'Flower'	Spring	Tues	84
Luke	15:8-10	seek	KJ	May'Flower'	Spring	Tues	84
Luke	18:27	impossible	NIV	Phrases We Often Use	Winter	Sun	320
Luke	18:27	possible	NIV	Phrases We Often Use	Winter	Sun	320
Luke	19:39	rebuke	NKJ	Passion Week	Spring	Fri	24
Luke	19:40	cry (stones would immediately)	NKJ	Passion Week	Spring	Fri	24
Luke	23:23	demanded	NKJ	Who is in Control?	Spring	Sat	32
Luke	23:34	forgive	NKJ	From the Cross	Autumn	Sun	250
Luke	23:43	paradise	NKJ	From the Cross	Autumn	Mon	251
Luke	23:43	truth	NKJ	From the Cross	Autumn	Mon	251
Luke	23:46	commit (my spirit)	NKJ	From the Cross	Autumn	Thur	254
Luke	24:7	delivered	NKJ	From the Cross	Autumn	Sat	256
Luke	24:7	delivered	NKJ	Who is in Control?	Spring	Sat	32
John	11:3	love	NKJ	Who is in Control?	Spring	Thur	30
John	11:4	death	NKJ	Who is in Control?	Spring	Fri	31
John	11:4	glory	NKJ	Who is in Control?	Spring	Fri	31
John	11:6	sick	NKJ	Who is in Control?	Spring	Thur	30
John	12:16	glorified	NKJ	Passion Week	Spring	Sat	25
John	14:1-4	come (again)	KJ	Our Mansion	Spring	Fri	66
John	14:1-4	believe	KJ	Our Mansion	Spring	Intro	61
John	14:1-4	receive	KJ	Our Mansion	Spring	Intro	61
John	14:1-4	troubled	KJ	Our Mansion	Spring	Intro	61
John	14:1-4	responsible	KJ	Our Mansion	Spring	Mon	62
John	14:1-4	way (ye know)	KJ	Our Mansion	Spring	Sat	67
John	14:1-4	Complete	KJ	Our Mansion	Spring	Sun	61
John	14:1-4	eternal (home)	KJ	Our Mansion	Spring	Thur	65
John	14:1-4	alone (not)	KJ	Our Mansion	Spring	Tues	63
John	14:1-4	honesty	KJ	Our Mansion	Spring	Wed	64
John	14:27	afraid	NKJ	Flowers in December	Winter	Tues	350
John	14:27	peace	NKJ	Flowers in December	Winter	Tues	350
John	15:12	love	KJ	Ultimate Sacrifice	Summer	Mon	188
John	15:13	friends	KJ	Ultimate Sacrifice	Summer	Intro	187
John	15:13	love	KJ	Ultimate Sacrifice	Summer	Intro	187
John	15:13	friends	KJ	Ultimate Sacrifice	Summer	Sat	193
John	15:13	love	KJ	Ultimate Sacrifice	Summer	Sat	193
John	15:13	friends	KJ	Unquenchable Love	Summer	Mon	167
John	15:13	love	KJ	Unquenchable Love	Summer	Mon	167
John	19:26	behold (your son)	NKJ	From the Cross	Autumn	Tues	252

Scripture Book	Chapter Verse	Topic	Version	Title	Season	Day	Page
John	19:30	finished (it is)	NKJ	From the Cross	Autumn	Fri	255
John	20:19	Peace (be with you)	NKJ	His Teaching Continues	Autumn	Tues	273
John	20:21	peace (to you)	NKJ	His Teaching Continues	Autumn	Wed	274
John	20:22	Holy Spirit	NKJ	His Teaching Continues	Autumn	Fri	276
John	20:29	believed	NKJ	His Teaching Continues	Autumn	Thur	275
John	20:29	blessed	NKJ	His Teaching Continues	Autumn	Thur	275
John	3:16	eternal (life)	NIV	Father's Day	Spring	Sun	89
John	3:16	loved	NIV	Father's Day	Spring	Sun	89
John	3:16	believeth (in him)	KJ	For Sale	Spring	Sat	39
John	3:16	life (everlasting)	KJ	For Sale	Spring	Sat	39
John	3:16	love (God so)	KJ	For Sale	Spring	Sat	39
John	3:16	everlasting	KJ	Ultimate Sacrifice	Summer	Sat	193
John	3:16	loved	NKJ	Love&Hate War&Peace	Winter	Tues	357
John	3:16	eternal life	NIV	Phrases We Often Use	Winter	Mon	321
John	3:16	loved (God so)	NIV	Phrases We Often Use	Winter	Mon	321
John	5:19	Son (can do)	NKJ	Our Father	Summer	Sat	144
John	6:44	come (to me)	NKJ	Our Father	Summer	Fri	143
John	8:32	truth	KJ	Know	Summer	Mon	174
John	8:32	truth	NIV	God's Provision in Your Wilderness	Winter	Wed	365
John	8:32	truth	NKJ	Keeping Resolutions	Winter	Wed	372
Acts	1:4	Promise	NKJ	What Waiting Can Bring	Summer	Sun	124
Acts	1:5	baptized	NKJ	His Teaching Continues	Autumn	Sat	277
Acts	1:5	Spirit (Holy)	NKJ	What Waiting Can Bring	Summer	Mon	125
Acts	1:6	restore	NKJ	What Waiting Can Bring	Summer	Tues	126
Acts	1:7	authority	NKJ	What Waiting Can Bring	Summer	Thur	128
Acts	1:7	know (times)	NKJ	What Waiting Can Bring	Summer	Wed	127
Acts	1:8	receive (power)	NKJ	What Waiting Can Bring	Summer	Fri	129
Acts	1:8	Spirit (Holy)	NKJ	What Waiting Can Bring	Summer	Fri	129
Acts	1:8	witnesses	NKJ	What Waiting Can Bring	Summer	Sat	130
Acts	17:26	determined (time)	NIV	Designing Us	Autumn	Wed	267
Romans	10:10	confession	NIV	Righteous	Spring	Sat	81
Romans	10:10	salvation	NIV	Righteous	Spring	Sat	81
Romans	10:17	faith	NIV	Father's Day	Spring	Thur	93
Romans	10:9	believe	KJ	IF	Winter	Sat	305
Romans	10:9	confess	KJ	IF	Winter	Sat	305

Scripture Book	Chapter Verse	Topic	Version	Title	Season	Day	Page
Romans	10:9	heart (believe in thine)	KJ	IF	Winter	Sat	305
Romans	12:8	leadership	NIV	Words	Autumn	Thur	226
Romans	15:4	comfort	NKJ	Patience	Spring	Wed	50
Romans	15:4	Patience	NKJ	Patience	Spring	Wed	50
Romans	16:20	grace	NKJ	Love&Hate War&Peace	Winter	Wed	358
Romans	16:20	peace	NKJ	Love&Hate War&Peace	Winter	Wed	358
Romans	3:23	glory (of God)	NIV	Senses	Winter	Fri	318
Romans	3:23	sinned	NIV	Senses	Winter	Fri	318
Romans	4:5	justifies	NIV	Righteous	Spring	Wed	78
Romans	5:3	glory	NKJ	Patience	Spring	Sat	53
Romans	5:3	tribulation	NKJ	Patience	Spring	Sat	53
Romans	5:8	love	NKJ	Love&Hate War&Peace	Winter	Sun	355
Romans	6:16	obey (him)	NIV	Words	Autumn	Sun	222
Romans	6:16	offer	NIV	Words	Autumn	Sun	222
Romans	6:16	righteousness	NIV	Words	Autumn	Sun	222
Romans	8:1	condemnation	NKJ	Freedom From the Laws of Sin	Autumn	Sun	285
Romans	8:1	flesh (according to)	NKJ	Freedom From the Laws of Sin	Autumn	Sun	285
Romans	8:1	Spirit	NKJ	Freedom From the Laws of Sin	Autumn	Sun	285
Romans	8:1	condemnation	NKJ	You are God's Specialty	Summer	Thur	149
Romans	8:1	flesh (walk)	NKJ	You are God's Specialty	Summer	Thur	149
Romans	8:10	Christ (in you)	NKJ	Freedom From the Laws of Sin	Autumn	Wed	288
Romans	8:14	Spirit (led by)	NKJ	Freedom From the Laws of Sin	Autumn	Thur	289
Romans	8:15	Abba, Father	NKJ	Freedom From the Laws of Sin	Autumn	Fri	290
Romans	8:15	Spirit (of adoption)	NKJ	Freedom From the Laws of Sin	Autumn	Fri	290
Romans	8:15	Spirit (of bondage)	NKJ	Freedom From the Laws of Sin	Autumn	Fri	290
Romans	8:26	intercession (Spirit makes)	NKJ	Freedom From the Laws of Sin	Autumn	Sat	291
Romans	8:26	weakness	NKJ	Freedom From the Laws of Sin	Autumn	Sat	291
Romans	8:3	flesh (weak)	NIV	Righteous	Spring	Thur	79
Romans	8:3	law	NIV	Righteous	Spring	Thur	79
Romans	8:6	carnally minded	NKJ	Freedom From the Laws of Sin	Autumn	Mon	286
Romans	8:6	Spiritual minded	NKJ	Freedom From the Laws of Sin	Autumn	Mon	286
Romans	8:9	flesh (in the)	NKJ	Freedom From the Laws of Sin	Autumn	Tues	287
Romans	8:9	Spirit (of God)	NKJ	Freedom From the Laws of Sin	Autumn	Tues	287
1 Corinthians	1:30	redemption	NIV	Righteous	Spring	Mon	76

Scripture Book	Chapter Verse	Topic	Version	Title	Season	Day	Page
1 Corinthians	1:30	sanctification	NIV	Righteous	Spring	Mon	76
1 Corinthians	1:30	wisdom	NIV	Righteous	Spring	Mon	76
1 Corinthians	14:15	sing (with my spirit)	NIV	Songs	Summer	Tues	119
1 Corinthians	14:33	confusion (God is not author of)	NKJ	He Gives Us Hope for Everyday	Spring	Thur	9
1 Corinthians	14:33	confusion (God is not author of)	NKJ	You are God's Specialty	Summer	Mon	146
1 Corinthians	14:33	peace	NKJ	You are God's Specialty	Summer	Mon	146
1 Corinthians	14:40	decently (things done)	NKJ	He Gives Us Hope for Everyday	Spring	Fri	10
1 Corinthians	14:40	order (things done)	NKJ	He Gives Us Hope for Everyday	Spring	Fri	10
2 Corinthians	1:3	Blessed (be the God)	NKJ	He Gives Us Hope for Everyday	Spring	Sun	5
2 Corinthians	1:3	Comfort (God of all)	NKJ	He Gives Us Hope for Everyday	Spring	Sun	5
2 Corinthians	1:3	Mercies	NKJ	He Gives Us Hope for Everyday	Spring	Sun	5
2 Corinthians	1:4	Comfort (those)	NKJ	He Gives Us Hope for Everyday	Spring	Mon	6
2 Corinthians	1:4	Comfort (us in all tribulation)	NKJ	He Gives Us Hope for Everyday	Spring	Mon	6
2 Corinthians	10:5	obedience	KJ	Letting Go & Letting God	Summer	Thur	156
2 Corinthians	12:9	grace	NIV	Phrases We Often Use	Winter	Fri	325
2 Corinthians	12:9	weakness	NIV	Phrases We Often Use	Winter	Fri	325
2 Corinthians	2:15	aroma	NIV	Senses	Winter	Wed	316
2 Corinthians	4:7	power	NKJ	He Gives Us Hope for Everyday	Spring	Sat	11
2 Corinthians	5:17	Christ (be in)	NKJ	He Gives Us Hope for Everyday	Spring	Wed	8
2 Corinthians	5:17	new (creation)	NKJ	He Gives Us Hope for Everyday	Spring	Wed	8
2 Corinthians	5:17	new	KJ	Safe In His Arms	Winter	Wed	386
2 Corinthians	5:21	righteousness	NIV	Righteous	Spring	Sun	75
2 Corinthians	5:7	faith (walk by)	NKJ	He Gives Us Hope for Everyday	Spring	Tues	7
2 Corinthians	7:4	glorying	KJ	Speech	Spring	Wed	57
2 Corinthians	7:4	speech	KJ	Speech	Spring	Wed	57
2 Corinthians	9:24	obtain	KJ	Letting Go & Letting God	Summer	Fri	157
Galatians	5:22	spirit (fruit of)	NKJ	Patience	Spring	Sun	47
Ephesians	2:20	corner stone	KJ	For Sale	Spring	Wed	36
Ephesians	3:19	knowledge	KJ	Unquenchable Love	Summer	Fri	171
Ephesians	3:19	love	KJ	Unquenchable Love	Summer	Fri	171
Ephesians	4:29	communication	KJ	Lips of Love	Spring	Mon	13
Ephesians	4:29	communication	KJ	Lips of Love	Spring	Sun	12
Ephesians	4:29	grace	KJ	Lips of Love	Spring	Sun	12
Ephesians	4:29	communication	KJ	Lips of Love	Spring	Tues	14
Ephesians	5:1-2	love	KJ	Unquenchable Love	Summer	Sat	172

Scripture Book	Chapter Verse	Topic	Version	Title	Season	Day	Page
Ephesians	5:1-2	offering	KJ	Unquenchable Love	Summer	Sat	172
Ephesians	5:1-2	sacrifice	KJ	Unquenchable Love	Summer	Sat	172
Ephesians	5:19	sing	NIV	Songs	Summer	Mon	118
Philippians	2:8	humbled	NKJ	Adoration of Our Holy Father	Autumn	Tues	203
Philippians	2:8	obedient	NKJ	Adoration of Our Holy Father	Autumn	Tues	203
Philippians	3:9	faith	NIV	Righteous	Spring	Tues	77
Philippians	4:8	pure	NKJ	Flowers in December	Winter	Sat	354
Philippians	4:8	true	NKJ	Flowers in December	Winter	Sat	354
Philippians	4:8	virtue	NKJ	Flowers in December	Winter	Sat	354
Colossians	1:9	knowledge	NIV	Phrases We Often Use	Winter	Wed	323
Colossians	1:9	understanding	NIV	Phrases We Often Use	Winter	Wed	323
Colossians	1:9	wisdom	NIV	Phrases We Often Use	Winter	Wed	323
Colossians	3:15	peace	NKJ	Love&Hate War&Peace	Winter	Fri	360
Colossians	4:6	speech	KJ	Lips of Love	Spring	Wed	15
Colossians	4:6	grace	KJ	Speech	Spring	Fri	59
Colossians	4:6	speech	KJ	Speech	Spring	Fri	59
1 Timothy	2:1	intercessions	KJ	Ultimate Sacrifice	Summer	Tues	189
1 Timothy	2:1	prayers	KJ	Ultimate Sacrifice	Summer	Tues	189
1 Timothy	2:1	thanks (giving of)	KJ	Ultimate Sacrifice	Summer	Tues	189
2 Timothy	1:17	love	NIV	Phrases We Often Use	Winter	Thur	324
2 Timothy	1:17	power	NIV	Phrases We Often Use	Winter	Thur	324
2 Timothy	1:7	fear	NKJ	You are God's Specialty	Summer	Wed	148
2 Timothy	1:7	love	NKJ	You are God's Specialty	Summer	Wed	148
2 Timothy	1:7	power	NKJ	You are God's Specialty	Summer	Wed	148
2 Timothy	2:15	study	KJ	May'Flower'	Spring	Sun	82
2 Timothy	4:2	prepared (be)	NIV	Words	Autumn	Fri	227
Titus	3:2	evil	KJ	Lips of Love	Spring	Thur	16
Titus	3:2	speak	KJ	Lips of Love	Spring	Thur	16
Titus	3:7	grace	NIV	Senses	Winter	Sat	319
Titus	3:7	justified	NIV	Senses	Winter	Sat	319
Hebrews	10:23	faithful	NKJ	Waiting	Winter	Thur	380
Hebrews	10:23	hope	NKJ	Waiting	Winter	Thur	380
Hebrews	10:23	promised	NKJ	Waiting	Winter	Thur	380
Hebrews	10:35-36	confidence	NKJ	You are God's Specialty	Summer	Thur	149
Hebrews	10:35-36	endurance	NKJ	You are God's Specialty	Summer	Thur	149
Hebrews	10:35-36	promise	NKJ	You are God's Specialty	Summer	Thur	149
Hebrews	10:35-36	reward	NKJ	You are God's	Summer	Thur	149

Specialty

Scripture Book	Chapter Verse	Topic	Version	Title	Season	Day	Page
Hebrews	11:1	faith	NIV	Wisdom	Spring	Tues	70
Hebrews	11:1	hope	NIV	Wisdom	Spring	Tues	70
Hebrews	11:11	faith (by)	NKJ	Faith	Summer	Wed	162
Hebrews	11:11	promise (faithful who had)	NKJ	Faith	Summer	Wed	162
Hebrews	11:11	strength (received)	NKJ	Faith	Summer	Wed	162
Hebrews	11:30	faith (by)	NKJ	Faith	Summer	Thur	163
Hebrews	11:30	walls (fell down)	NKJ	Faith	Summer	Thur	163
Hebrews	11:31	believe (not)	NKJ	Faith	Summer	Fri	164
Hebrews	11:31	faith (by)	NKJ	Faith	Summer	Fri	164
Hebrews	11:31	perish (did not)	NKJ	Faith	Summer	Fri	164
Hebrews	11:6	faith (without)	NKJ	Faith	Summer	Sun	159
Hebrews	11:6	rewarder	NKJ	Faith	Summer	Sun	159
Hebrews	11:6	seek (diligently. Him)	NKJ	Faith	Summer	Sun	159
Hebrews	11:8	faith (Abraham obeyed)	NKJ	Faith	Summer	Mon	160
Hebrews	11:8	Inheritance	NKJ	Faith	Summer	Mon	160
Hebrews	11:9	faith (by)	NKJ	Faith	Summer	Tues	161
Hebrews	11:9	promise (land of)	NKJ	Faith	Summer	Tues	161
Hebrews	12:1	patience	KJ	Letting Go & Letting God	Summer	Fri	157
Hebrews	12:1	patience	KJ	Ultimate Sacrifice	Summer	Thur	191
Hebrews	12:2	endured (the cross)	NKJ	Faith	Summer	Sat	165
Hebrews	12:2	faith (finisher)	NKJ	Faith	Summer	Sat	165
Hebrews	12:2	looking (unto Jesus)	NKJ	Faith	Summer	Sat	165
Hebrews	12:2	shame (despising)	NKJ	Faith	Summer	Sat	165
Hebrews	12:2	faith	KJ	Ultimate Sacrifice	Summer	Fri	192
Hebrews	12:2	joy	KJ	Ultimate Sacrifice	Summer	Fri	192
Hebrews	13:5	conversation	KJ	Lips of Love	Spring	Fri	17
Hebrews	13:5	conduct	NKJ	You are God's Specialty	Summer	Fri	150
Hebrews	13:5	covetousness	NKJ	You are God's Specialty	Summer	Fri	150
Hebrews	13:5	leave (never)	NKJ	You are God's Specialty	Summer	Fri	150
Hebrews	13:5	Forsake (never will I)	NIV	Phrases We Often Use	Winter	Tues	322
Hebrews	13:5	Leave (Never will I)	NIV	Phrases We Often Use	Winter	Tues	322
Hebrews	3:13	deceitful	KJ	Unquenchable Love	Summer	Wed	169
Hebrews	3:13	exhort	KJ	Unquenchable Love	Summer	Wed	169
James	1:23-25	blessed (in his deed)	KJ	May'Flower'	Spring	Mon	83
James	1:23-25	hearer	KJ	May'Flower'	Spring	Mon	83
James	1:23-25	liberty (perfect law of)	KJ	May'Flower'	Spring	Mon	83
James	4:14	life (what is)	KJ	Know	Summer	Tues	175
James	4:7	resist	NKJ	You are God's Specialty	Summer	Tues	147

Scripture Book	Chapter Verse	Topic	Version	Title	Season	Day	Page
James	4:7	submit	NKJ	You are God's Specialty	Summer	Tues	147
1 Peter	3:1	conversation	KJ	Lips of Love	Spring	Sat	18
1 Peter	5:5	humility	NIV	Wisdom	Spring	Mon	69
1 Peter	5:5	proud	NIV	Wisdom	Spring	Mon	69
1 Peter	5:7	care	KJ	Letting Go & Letting God	Summer	Sun	152
2 Peter	01:02	grace	NKJ	Keeping Resolutions	Winter	Tue	371
2 Peter	1:2	grace	NIV	God's Provision in Your Wilderness	Winter	Tues	364
2 Peter	1:2	peace	NIV	God's Provision in Your Wilderness	Winter	Tues	364
2 Peter	1:4	lust	NIV	God's Provision in Your Wilderness	Winter	Tues	364
2 Peter	2:18	allure	KJ	For Sale	Spring	Thur	37
2 Peter	2:18	flesh (lust of)	KJ	For Sale	Spring	Thur	37
1 John	1:9	Sins (confess)	KJ	For Sale	Spring	Sun	33
1 John	1:9	Sins (forgive)	KJ	For Sale	Spring	Sun	33
1 John	1:9	unrighteousness (cleanse from)	KJ	For Sale	Spring	Sun	33
1 John	3:17	compassion	KJ	Unquenchable Love	Summer	Thur	170
1 John	4:11	love (God so)	KJ	IF	Winter	Thur	303
1 John	4:11	love (one another)	KJ	IF	Winter	Thur	303
1 John	4:8	love (God is)	KJ	For Sale	Spring	Fri	38
Revelation	1:3	blessed (are those that hear)	NIV	Senses	Winter	Mon	314
Revelation	1:3	Heart (take to)	NIV	Senses	Winter	Mon	314
Revelation	13:9	hear (let him)	KJ	IF	Winter	Fri	304
Revelation	19:6	Hallelujah	NIV	Father's Day	Spring	Sat	95
Revelation	19:6	reigns	NIV	Father's Day	Spring	Sat	95
Revelation	22:12	reward	NIV	Jesus & the Seven RE's of Us	Spring	Sat	46
Revelation	3:7-13	hold (fast)	KJ	Church of Philadelphia	Summer	Fri	136
Revelation	3:7-13	strength	KJ	Church of Philadelphia	Summer	Mon	132
Revelation	3:7-13	overcometh	KJ	Church of Philadelphia	Summer	Sat	137
Revelation	3:7-13	Door (Open ... No man can shut)	KJ	Church of Philadelphia	Summer	Sun	131
Revelation	3:7-13	temptation	KJ	Church of Philadelphia	Summer	Thur	135
Revelation	3:7-13	Word (kept God's)	KJ	Church of Philadelphia	Summer	Tues	133
Revelation	3:7-13	Deny	KJ	Church of Philadelphia	Summer	Wed	134
Revelation	5:13	heard (then I)	NIV	Songs	Summer	Sat	123
Weekly Intro	intro	Adoration	NKJ	Adoration of Our Holy Father	Autumn	Intro	201
Weekly Intro	intro	Freedom	NKJ	Freedom From the Laws of Sin	Autumn	Intro	285
Weekly Intro	intro	Money	NKJ	Prosperity	Autumn	Intro	208

Scripture Book	Chapter Verse	Topic	Version	Title	Season	Day	Page
Weekly Intro	intro	For Sale (Are you)	KJ	For Sale	Spring	Intro	33
Weekly Intro	intro	Life today	NKJ	He Gives Us Hope for Everyday	Spring	Intro	5
Weekly Intro	intro	Re-Do	NIV	Jesus & the Seven RE's of Us	Spring	Intro	40
Weekly Intro	intro	Patience (pray for)	NKJ	Patience	Spring	Intro	47
Weekly Intro	intro	Faith	NKJ	Faith	Summer	Intro	159
Weekly Intro	intro	He Refreshes us	NKJ	His Refreshing Preparations	Summer	Intro	110
Weekly Intro	intro	If only…….What if	KJ	IF	Winter	Intro	299
Weekly Intro	intro	Choice (we have)	KJ	Micah	Winter	Intro	306

Topical Index

Scripture Book	Chapter Verse	Topic	Version	Title	Season	Day	Page
Romans	8:15	Abba, Father	NKJ	Freedom From the Laws of Sin	Autumn	Fri	290
Weekly Intro	intro	Adoration	NKJ	Adoration of Our Holy Father	Autumn	Intro	201
Matthew	5:28	adultery	NKJ	A Way of Life	Autumn	Tues	245
Matthew	5:32	adultery	NKJ	A Way of Life	Autumn	Wed	246
Ecclesiastes	7:14	adversity	NKJ	Prosperity	Autumn	Tues	210
Matthew	27:5	afraid	NKJ	His Teaching Continues	Autumn	Mon	272
Proverbs	3:24	afraid	KJ	Sleep	Summer	Fri	185
John	14:27	afraid	NKJ	Flowers in December	Winter	Tues	350
Exodus	14:13	afraid	NIV	God's Provision in Your Wilderness	Winter	Mon	363
Psalm	124:2	against (us)	KJ	IF	Winter	Sun	299
2 Peter	2:18	allure	KJ	For Sale	Spring	Thur	37
Psalm	62:5	alone	NKJ	Waiting	Winter	Mon	377
John	14:1-4	alone (not)	KJ	Our Mansion	Spring	Tues	63
Proverbs	16:32	anger	NKJ	You are God's Specialty	Summer	Wed	148
Psalm	37:4	anger	NKJ	Flowers in December	Winter	Thur	352
Matthew	5:22	angry	NKJ	A Way of Life	Autumn	Mon	244
Ecclesiastes	7:9	angry	NKJ	Patience	Spring	Tues	49
Psalm	23:5	anoint	NKJ	His Refreshing Preparations	Summer	Wed	113
Micah	3	answer (no answer of God)	KJ	Micah	Winter	Tues	308
Jeremiah	1:5	Apart (set apart for a purpose)	NIV	Designing Us	Autumn	Tues	266
Proverbs	6:9	arise	KJ	Sleep	Summer	Thur	184
2 Corinthians	2:15	aroma	NIV	Senses	Winter	Wed	316
Luke	11:9	ask	NIV	Defining You	Winter	Tues	336
Acts	1:7	authority	NKJ	What Waiting Can Bring	Summer	Thur	128
Psalm	66:5	awesome	NIV	Jesus & the Seven RE's of Us	Spring	Fri	45
Acts	1:5	baptized	NKJ	His Teaching Continues	Autumn	Sat	277
1 Chronicles	4:10	be (with me)	KJ	Prayer of Jabez	Autumn	Thur	261
Genesis	1:1	beginning	NKJ	The Beginning	Autumn	Sun	278

Scripture Book	Chapter Verse	Topic	Version	Title	Season	Day	Page
John	19:26	behold (your son)	NKJ	From the Cross	Autumn	Tues	252
John	14:1-4	believe	KJ	Our Mansion	Spring	Intro	61
Romans	10:9	believe	KJ	IF	Winter	Sat	305
Hebrews	11:31	believe (not)	NKJ	Faith	Summer	Fri	164
John	20:29	believed	NKJ	His Teaching Continues	Autumn	Thur	275
John	3:16	believeth (in him)	KJ	For Sale	Spring	Sat	39
Deuteronomy	33:12	beloved (of the Lord)	NIV	Words	Autumn	Sat	228
Matthew	26:73	betrayeth	KJ	Speech	Spring	Thur	58
Exodus	1:14	bitter	NIV	Is it 'Worth it'?	Winter	Sun	327
Genesis	17:1-2	blameless	NKJ	Who is in Control?	Spring	Mon	27
Psalm	34:1	bless	NKJ	You are God's Specialty	Summer	Sat	151
1 Chronicles	4:10	bless (me)	KJ	Prayer of Jabez	Autumn	Tues	259
John	20:29	blessed	NKJ	His Teaching Continues	Autumn	Thur	275
Genesis	1:28	blessed	NKJ	Elohim	Summer	Thur	107
Genesis	2:3	blessed	NKJ	Elohim	Summer	Sat	108
Matthew	5:4	blessed	NKJ	You are God's Specialty	Summer	Sun	145
Revelation	1:3	blessed (those that hear)	NIV	Senses	Winter	Mon	314
2 Corinthians	1:3	Blessed (be the God)	NKJ	He Gives Us Hope for Everyday	Spring	Sun	5
James	1:23-25	blessed (in his deed)	KJ	May'Flower'	Spring	Mon	83
Genesis	33:11	blessing	NKJ	Prosperity	Autumn	Sun	208
Ezekiel	34:24-26	blessing	KJ	Sleep	Summer	Wed	183
Exodus	1:14	bondage	KJ	Is it 'Worth it'?	Winter	Sun	327
Matthew	5:42	Borrow	NKJ	A Way of Life	Autumn	Fri	248
Psalm	74:17	boundaries	NIV	Words	Autumn	Tues	224
Exodus	34:8	bowed his head	NKJ	Adoration of Our Holy Father	Autumn	Wed	204
Exodus	6:7	burdens	KJ	Know	Summer	Sun	173
1 Chronicles	4:10	called (on God)	KJ	Prayer of Jabez	Autumn	Mon	258
Mark	4:38-40	calm	KJ	May'Flower'	Spring	Thur	86
1 Peter	5:7	care	KJ	Letting Go & Letting God	Summer	Sun	152
Romans	8:6	carnally minded	NKJ	Freedom From the Laws of Sin	Autumn	Mon	286
Job	Book of	Challenges (facing)	KJ	May'Flower'	Spring	Fri	87
Joshua	4:22	children	KJ	Know	Summer	Fri	178
Genesis	16:2	children (from having)	NKJ	Who is in Control?	Spring	Sun	26
Weekly Intro	intro	Choice (we have)	KJ	Micah	Winter	Intro	306
Deuteronomy	30:19	choose life	KJ	For Sale	Spring	Mon	34
2 Corinthians	5:17	Christ (be in)	NKJ	He Gives Us Hope for Everyday	Spring	Wed	8
Romans	8:10	Christ (in you)	NKJ	Freedom From the Laws of Sin	Autumn	Wed	288
Deuteronomy	30:20	cleave (unto him)	KJ	For Sale	Spring	Mon	34
Matthew	16:24	come (after me)	KJ	IF	Winter	Wed	302
John	14:1-4	come (again)	KJ	Our Mansion	Spring	Fri	66

Scripture Book	Chapter Verse	Topic	Version	Title	Season	Day	Page
John	6:44	come (to me)	NKJ	Our Father	Summer	Fri	143
Romans	15:4	comfort	NKJ	Patience	Spring	Wed	50
Psalm	119:50	comfort	NIV	Defining You	Winter	Thur	338
2 Corinthians	1:3	Comfort (God of all)	NKJ	He Gives Us Hope for Everyday	Spring	Sun	5
2 Corinthians	1:4	Comfort (those)	NKJ	He Gives Us Hope for Everyday	Spring	Mon	6
2 Corinthians	1:4	Comfort (us in all tribulation)	NKJ	He Gives Us Hope for Everyday	Spring	Mon	6
Exodus	18:23	Command (thee so)	KJ	IF	Winter	Mon	300
1 Kings	11:38	Command (thee)	KJ	IF	Winter	Tues	301
Luke	23:46	commit (my spirit)	NKJ	From the Cross	Autumn	Thur	254
Psalm	37:5	commit (your way)	NIV	Words	Autumn	Mon	223
Ephesians	4:29	communication	KJ	Lips of Love	Spring	Mon	13
Ephesians	4:29	communication	KJ	Lips of Love	Spring	Sun	12
Ephesians	4:29	communication	KJ	Lips of Love	Spring	Tues	14
1 John	3:17	compassion	KJ	Unquenchable Love	Summer	Thur	170
Micah	7	compassion (he will have)	KJ	Micah	Winter	Sat	312
John	14:1-4	Complete	KJ	Our Mansion	Spring	Sun	61
Romans	8:1	condemnation	NKJ	Freedom From the Laws of Sin	Autumn	Sun	285
Romans	8:1	condemnation	NKJ	You are God's Specialty	Summer	Thur	149
Song of Solomon	8:7	condemned	KJ	Unquenchable Love	Summer	Sun	166
Hebrews	13:5	conduct	NKJ	You are God's Specialty	Summer	Fri	150
Romans	10:9	confess	KJ	IF	Winter	Sat	305
Romans	10:10	confession	NIV	Righteous	Spring	Sat	81
Hebrews	10:35-36	confidence	NKJ	You are God's Specialty	Summer	Thur	149
1 Corinthians	14:33	confusion (God is not author of)	NKJ	He Gives Us Hope for Everyday	Spring	Thur	9
1 Corinthians	14:33	confusion (God is not author of)	NKJ	You are God's Specialty	Summer	Mon	146
Genesis	20:5	conscience	NKJ	Who is in Control?	Spring	Wed	29
Genesis	31:40	consumed	KJ	Sleep	Summer	Tues	182
Hebrews	13:5	conversation	KJ	Lips of Love	Spring	Fri	17
1 Peter	3:1	conversation	KJ	Lips of Love	Spring	Sat	18
Ephesians	2:20	corner stone	KJ	For Sale	Spring	Wed	36
Joshua	1:9	courageous	KJ	Directions	Autumn	Thur	219
Ezekiel	34:24-26	covenant	KJ	Sleep	Summer	Wed	183
Exodus	2:24	covenant	KJ	Is it 'Worth it'?	Winter	Mon	328
Hebrews	13:5	covetousness	NKJ	You are God's Specialty	Summer	Fri	150
Malachi	2:10	create	NIV	Father's Day	Spring	Mon	90
Genesis	1:2	created	NKJ	The Beginning	Autumn	Sun	278
Genesis	1:1	created	NKJ	Elohim	Summer	Sun	103
Genesis	1:27	created	NKJ	Elohim	Summer	Wed	106
Genesis	1:27	created	NIV	Defining You	Winter	Sun	334
Genesis	1:27	created (God created man)	NIV	Designing Us	Autumn	Sun	264
Psalm	139:13	created (my inmost being)	NIV	Designing Us	Autumn	Mon	265

Scripture Book	Chapter Verse	Topic	Version	Title	Season	Day	Page
Genesis	1:21-22	creatures	NKJ	The Beginning	Autumn	Fri	283
Matthew	16:24	Cross (take up)	KJ	IF	Winter	Wed	302
Psalm	40:1	cry	NKJ	Patience	Spring	Fri	52
Luke	19:40	cry (stones would immediately)	NKJ	Passion Week	Spring	Fri	24
Psalm	23:5	cup	NKJ	His Refreshing Preparations	Summer	Fri	115
Psalm	74:16	day (is yours)	NIV	Words	Autumn	Tues	224
John	11:4	death	NKJ	Who is in Control?	Spring	Fri	31
Proverbs	27:6	deceitful	KJ	Unquenchable Love	Summer	Tues	168
Hebrews	3:13	deceitful	KJ	Unquenchable Love	Summer	Wed	169
1 Corinthians	14:40	decently (things done)	NKJ	He Gives Us Hope for Everyday	Spring	Fri	10
Psalm	68:5	defender	NKJ	Our Father	Summer	Sun	138
Psalm	119:24	delight	NIV	God's Provision in Your Wilderness	Winter	Fri	367
Psalm	119:24	delight	NKJ	Keeping Resolutions	Winter	Fri	374
Psalm	68:30	delight	NKJ	Love&Hate War&Peace	Winter	Fri	360
Psalm	37:4	delight yourself	NKJ	Adoration of Our Holy Father	Autumn	Sun	201
2 Kings	20:6	deliver	KJ	Hezekiah - Added Days	Autumn	Intro	236
Luke	24:7	delivered	NKJ	From the Cross	Autumn	Sat	256
Psalm	22:4	delivered	NIV	Father's Day	Spring	Wed	92
Luke	24:7	delivered	NKJ	Who is in Control?	Spring	Sat	32
Psalm	18:1-3	deliverer	KJ	Letting Go & Letting God	Summer	Tues	154
Psalm	18:1-3	deliverer	KJ	Letting Go & Letting God	Summer	Wed	155
Luke	23:23	demanded	NKJ	Who is in Control?	Spring	Sat	32
Revelation	3:7-13	Deny	KJ	Church of Philadelphia	Summer	Wed	134
Matthew	16:24	deny (himself)	KJ	IF	Winter	Wed	302
1 Chronicles	29:18	desire	NIV	Words	Autumn	Wed	225
Psalm	145:16	desire	NKJ	Waiting	Winter	Fri	381
Psalm	37:4	desires of your heart	NKJ	Adoration of Our Holy Father	Autumn	Sun	201
Acts	17:26	determined (time)	NIV	Designing Us	Autumn	Wed	267
Isaiah	61:4	devastated	NIV	Jesus & the Seven RE's of Us	Spring	Wed	43
Mark	11:1	disciples	NKJ	Passion Week	Spring	Sun	19
Matthew	5:32	divorce	NKJ	A Way of Life	Autumn	Wed	246
Genesis	1:28	dominion	NKJ	Elohim	Summer	Fri	107
Micah	6	done (what have I)	KJ	Micah	Winter	Fri	311
Revelation	3:7-13	Door (Open ... No man can shut)	KJ	Church of Philadelphia	Summer	Sun	131
Hebrews	10:35-36	endurance	NKJ	You are God's Specialty	Summer	Thur	149
Exodus	18:23	endure (able to)	KJ	IF	Winter	Mon	300
Hebrews	12:2	endured (the cross)	NKJ	Faith	Summer	Sat	165
Psalm	23:5	enemies	NKJ	His Refreshing Preparations	Summer	Tues	112
Psalm	18:1-3	enemies	KJ	Letting Go & Letting God	Summer	Tues	154

Scripture Book	Chapter Verse	Topic	Version	Title	Season	Day	Page
Psalm	18:1-3	enemies	KJ	Letting Go & Letting God	Summer	Wed	155
Proverbs	27:6	enemy	KJ	Unquenchable Love	Summer	Tues	168
Luke	10:9	enemy	NKJ	Flowers in December	Winter	Wed	351
1 Chronicles	4:10	enlarge (my coast)	KJ	Prayer of Jabez	Autumn	Wed	260
John	14:1-4	eternal (home)	KJ	Our Mansion	Spring	Thur	65
John	3:16	eternal (life)	NIV	Father's Day	Spring	Sun	89
John	3:16	eternal life	NIV	Phrases We Often Use	Winter	Mon	321
Psalm	119:142	everlasting	NIV	Father's Day	Spring	Fri	94
John	3:16	everlasting	KJ	Ultimate Sacrifice	Summer	Sat	193
Titus	3:2	evil	KJ	Lips of Love	Spring	Thur	16
1 Chronicles	4:10	evil (keep me)	KJ	Prayer of Jabez	Autumn	Fri	262
Jeremiah	29:11	evil (not)	NKJ	You are God's Specialty	Summer	Tues	147
Matthew	5:37	evil (one)	NKJ	A Way of Life	Autumn	Thur	247
Micah	2	evil (time is)	KJ	Micah	Winter	Mon	307
Hosea	13:6	exalted (their heart was)	NKJ	Prosperity	Autumn	Thur	212
Hebrews	3:13	exhort	KJ	Unquenchable Love	Summer	Wed	169
Romans	10:17	faith	NIV	Father's Day	Spring	Thur	93
Mark	4:38-40	faith	KJ	May'Flower'	Spring	Thur	86
Philippians	3:9	faith	NIV	Righteous	Spring	Tues	77
Hebrews	11:1	faith	NIV	Wisdom	Spring	Tues	70
Weekly Intro	intro	Faith	NKJ	Faith	Summer	Intro	159
Hebrews	12:2	faith	KJ	Ultimate Sacrifice	Summer	Fri	192
Hebrews	11:8	faith (Abraham obeyed)	NKJ	Faith	Summer	Mon	160
Hebrews	11:11	faith (by)	NKJ	Faith	Summer	Wed	162
Hebrews	11:30	faith (by)	NKJ	Faith	Summer	Thur	163
Hebrews	11:31	faith (by)	NKJ	Faith	Summer	Fri	164
Hebrews	11:9	faith (by)	NKJ	Faith	Summer	Tues	161
Hebrews	12:2	faith (finisher)	NKJ	Faith	Summer	Sat	165
2 Corinthians	5:7	faith (walk by)	NKJ	He Gives Us Hope for Everyday	Spring	Tues	7
Hebrews	11:6	faith (without)	NKJ	Faith	Summer	Sun	159
Proverbs	27:6	faithful	KJ	Unquenchable Love	Summer	Tues	168
Hebrews	10:23	faithful	NKJ	Waiting	Winter	Thur	380
2 Timothy	1:7	fear	NKJ	You are God's Specialty	Summer	Wed	148
Deuteronomy	3:22	fear	NKJ	Love&Hate War&Peace	Winter	Thur	359
Psalm	96:4	feared	NKJ	You are God's Specialty	Summer	Sat	151
Mark	4:38-40	fearful	KJ	May'Flower'	Spring	Thur	86
Deuteronomy	1:30	fight (for you)	NKJ	You are God's Specialty	Summer	Mon	146
Deuteronomy	1:30	fight (for you)	NKJ	Love&Hate War&Peace	Winter	Wed	358
John	19:30	finished (it is)	NKJ	From the Cross	Autumn	Fri	255
Genesis	2:21	flesh	KJ	Sleep	Summer	Sun	180
Romans	8:1	flesh (according to)	NKJ	Freedom From the Laws of Sin	Autumn	Sun	285
Romans	8:9	flesh (in the)	NKJ	Freedom From the Laws of Sin	Autumn	Tues	287
2 Peter	2:18	flesh (lust of)	KJ	For Sale	Spring	Thur	37

Scripture Book	Chapter Verse	Topic	Version	Title	Season	Day	Page
Romans	8:1	flesh (walk)	NKJ	You are God's Specialty	Summer	Thur	149
Romans	8:3	flesh (weak)	NIV	Righteous	Spring	Thur	79
Joshua	3:3	follow	NIV	God's Provision in Your Wilderness	Winter	Sat	368
Matthew	16:24	Follow (me)	KJ	IF	Winter	Wed	302
Weekly Intro	intro	For Sale (Are you)	KJ	For Sale	Spring	Intro	33
Luke	23:34	forgive	NKJ	From the Cross	Autumn	Sun	250
Mark	11:25	forgive	NKJ	Our Father	Summer	Thur	142
Hebrews	13:5	Forsake (never will I)	NIV	Phrases We Often Use	Winter	Tues	322
Matthew	27:46	forsaken (My God...)	NKJ	From the Cross	Autumn	Wed	253
Weekly Intro	intro	Freedom	NKJ	Freedom From the Laws of Sin	Autumn	Intro	285
John	15:13	friends	KJ	Ultimate Sacrifice	Summer	Intro	187
John	15:13	friends	KJ	Ultimate Sacrifice	Summer	Sat	193
John	15:13	friends	KJ	Unquenchable Love	Summer	Mon	167
Matthew	7:20	fruits	KJ	Know	Summer	Thur	177
Matthew	5:18	fulfilled	NKJ	A Way of Life	Autumn	Sun	243
Matthew	11:29	gentle	NIV	Wisdom	Spring	Fri	73
Joshua	1:2	Get ready	KJ	Directions	Autumn	Wed	218
Matthew	5:42	Give	NKJ	A Way of Life	Autumn	Fri	248
John	12:16	glorified	NKJ	Passion Week	Spring	Sat	25
Romans	5:3	glory	NKJ	Patience	Spring	Sat	53
John	11:4	glory	NKJ	Who is in Control?	Spring	Fri	31
2 Chronicles	5:14	glory	NKJ	You are God's Specialty	Summer	Sun	145
Psalm	26:8	glory	NKJ	Patience for Coming Events	Winter	Tues	343
1 Chronicles	16:10-12	glory	KJ	Safe In His Arms	Winter	Sun	383
Psalm	26:8	glory (dwells)	NKJ	Week of Thanksgiving	Autumn	Tues	231
Hosea	4:7	glory (into shame)	NKJ	Prosperity	Autumn	Wed	211
Romans	3:23	glory (of God)	NIV	Senses	Winter	Fri	318
2 Corinthians	7:4	glorying	KJ	Speech	Spring	Wed	57
Jeremiah	30:22	God (be your)	NIV	Safe In His Arms	Winter	Fri	388
Joshua	3:10	God (living)	KJ	Know	Summer	Wed	176
Genesis	1:3	God (said)	NKJ	The Beginning	Autumn	Mon	279
Ephesians	4:29	grace	KJ	Lips of Love	Spring	Sun	12
Colossians	4:6	grace	KJ	Speech	Spring	Fri	59
2 Peter	1:2	grace	NIV	God's Provision in Your Wilderness	Winter	Tues	364
2 Peter	01:02	grace	NKJ	Keeping Resolutions	Winter	Tue	371
Romans	16:20	grace	NKJ	Love&Hate War&Peace	Winter	Wed	358
2 Corinthians	12:9	grace	NIV	Phrases We Often Use	Winter	Fri	325
Titus	3:7	grace	NIV	Senses	Winter	Sat	319
1 Chronicles	4:10	granted (God)	KJ	Prayer of Jabez	Autumn	Sat	263
Luke	12:15	greed	NIV	Wisdom	Spring	Sat	74
1 Chronicles	4:10	grieve	KJ	Prayer of Jabez	Autumn	Fri	262
Exodus	2:24	groaning	KJ	Is it 'Worth it'?	Winter	Mon	328

Scripture Book	Chapter Verse	Topic	Version	Title	Season	Day	Page
Exodus	15:24	grumbled	NIV	God's Provision in Your Wilderness	Winter	Tues	364
Luke	12:15	guard	NIV	Wisdom	Spring	Sat	74
Exodus	13:21	guide	NIV	God's Provision in Your Wilderness	Winter	Sun	362
Revelation	19:6	Hallelujah	NIV	Father's Day	Spring	Sat	95
Psalm	37:4	harm	NKJ	Flowers in December	Winter	Thur	352
Leviticus	19:17	hate	NKJ	Love&Hate War&Peace	Winter	Mon	356
Psalm	120:6	hates	NKJ	Love&Hate War&Peace	Winter	Sat	361
Proverbs	26:24	hates	NKJ	Love&Hate War&Peace	Winter	Sun	355
Proverbs	10:12	hatred	NKJ	Love&Hate War&Peace	Winter	Tues	357
Weekly Intro	intro	He Refreshes us	NKJ	His Refreshing Preparations	Summer	Intro	110
2 Kings	20:5	heal	KJ	Hezekiah - Added Days	Autumn	Fri	241
2 Kings	20:5	heal	KJ	Hezekiah - Added Days	Autumn	Sat	242
Revelation	13:9	hear (let him)	KJ	IF	Winter	Fri	304
Psalm	17:6	hear (me, O God)	KJ	Speech	Spring	Mon	55
Micah	5	heard (have not)	KJ	Micah	Winter	Thur	310
Revelation	5:13	heard (then I)	NIV	Songs	Summer	Sat	123
James	1:23-25	hearer	KJ	May'Flower'	Spring	Mon	83
1 Kings	11:38	hearken	KJ	IF	Winter	Tues	301
Deuteronomy	6:5	heart	NKJ	Adoration of Our Holy Father	Autumn	Sat	207
Romans	10:9	heart (believe in thine)	KJ	IF	Winter	Sat	305
Psalm	51:10	heart (create a clean)	KJ	For Sale	Spring	Tues	35
Psalm	119:11	heart (hidden in my)	NKJ	Keeping Resolutions	Winter	Mon	370
2 Chronicles	26:16	heart (lifted up)	NKJ	Prosperity	Autumn	Sat	214
2 Kings	20:3	heart (perfect)	KJ	Hezekiah - Added Days	Autumn	Intro	236
Revelation	1:3	Heart (take to)	NIV	Senses	Winter	Mon	314
Matthew	5:18	heaven	NKJ	A Way of Life	Autumn	Sun	243
Psalm	33:20	help	NKJ	Waiting	Winter	Tues	378
Revelation	3:7-13	hold (fast)	KJ	Church of Philadelphia	Summer	Fri	136
John	20:22	Holy Spirit	NKJ	His Teaching Continues	Autumn	Fri	276
John	14:1-4	honesty	KJ	Our Mansion	Spring	Wed	64
1 Chronicles	4:9	honorable	KJ	Prayer of Jabez	Autumn	Intro	257
Psalm	130:7	hope	NIV	Jesus & the Seven RE's of Us	Spring	Mon	41
Lamentations	3:26	hope	NKJ	Patience	Spring	Mon	48
Hebrews	11:1	hope	NIV	Wisdom	Spring	Tues	70
Jeremiah	29:11	hope	NKJ	You are God's Specialty	Summer	Tues	147
Psalm	130:5	hope	NKJ	Waiting	Winter	Wed	379
Hebrews	10:23	hope	NKJ	Waiting	Winter	Thur	380
Genesis	15:12	horror	KJ	Sleep	Summer	Mon	181
Matthew	11:29	humble	NIV	Wisdom	Spring	Fri	73
Philippians	2:8	humbled	NKJ	Adoration of Our Holy Father	Autumn	Tues	203
1 Peter	5:5	humility	NIV	Wisdom	Spring	Mon	69
Weekly Intro	intro	If only.......What if	KJ	IF	Winter	Intro	299

Scripture Book	Chapter Verse	Topic	Version	Title	Season	Day	Page
Luke	18:27	impossible	NIV	Phrases We Often Use	Winter	Sun	320
Hebrews	11:8	Inheritance	NKJ	Faith	Summer	Mon	160
Micah	7	iniquity (he will subdue)	KJ	Micah	Winter	Sat	312
Micah	2	iniquity (woe unto them)	KJ	Micah	Winter	Mon	307
Proverbs	1:2	instruction	KJ	Safe In His Arms	Winter	Thur	387
Romans	8:26	intercession (Spirit makes)	NKJ	Freedom From the Laws of Sin	Autumn	Sat	291
1 Timothy	2:1	intercessions	KJ	Ultimate Sacrifice	Summer	Tues	189
Matthew	21:10-11	Jesus (This is)	NKJ	Passion Week	Spring	Thur	23
Zephaniah	3:17	joy	KJ	May'Flower'	Spring	Sat	88
Hebrews	12:2	joy	KJ	Ultimate Sacrifice	Summer	Fri	192
Ecclesiastes	7:14	joyful	NKJ	Prosperity	Autumn	Tues	210
1 Chronicles	16:11	judgment	KJ	Ultimate Sacrifice	Summer	Wed	190
1 Chronicles	16:10-12	judgment	KJ	Safe In His Arms	Winter	Sun	383
Titus	3:7	justified	NIV	Senses	Winter	Sat	319
Romans	4:5	justifies	NIV	Righteous	Spring	Wed	78
Jeremiah	31:3	kindness	NKJ	Love&Hate War&Peace	Winter	Mon	356
Matthew	21:4	King (is coming)	NKJ	Passion Week	Spring	Mon	20
Mark	11:8-10	King (is coming)	NKJ	Passion Week	Spring	Tues	21
Matthew	7:8	knock	NIV	Jesus & the Seven RE's of Us	Spring	Sun	40
Luke	11:9	knock	NIV	Defining You	Winter	Tues	336
Acts	1:7	know (times)	NKJ	What Waiting Can Bring	Summer	Wed	127
Ephesians	3:19	knowledge	KJ	Unquenchable Love	Summer	Fri	171
Colossians	1:9	knowledge	NIV	Phrases We Often Use	Winter	Wed	323
Romans	8:3	law	NIV	Righteous	Spring	Thur	79
Joshua	1:8	law (book of)	KJ	Directions	Autumn	Fri	220
2 Chronicles	12:1	law (forsook the)	NKJ	Prosperity	Autumn	Fri	213
Romans	12:8	leadership	NIV	Words	Autumn	Thur	226
Matthew	11:29	learn	NIV	Wisdom	Spring	Fri	73
Hebrews	13:5	Leave(Never)	NIV	Phrases We Often Use	Winter	Tues	322
Hebrews	13:5	leave (never)	NKJ	You are God's Specialty	Summer	Fri	150
James	1:23-25	liberty (perfect law of)	KJ	May'Flower'	Spring	Mon	83
Habakkuk	2:3	lie	NKJ	Waiting	Winter	Sat	382
John	3:16	life (everlasting)	KJ	For Sale	Spring	Sat	39
James	4:14	life (what is)	KJ	Know	Summer	Tues	175
Weekly Intro	intro	Life today	NKJ	He Gives Us Hope for Everyday	Spring	Intro	5
Genesis	1:3	light (God said)	NKJ	Elohim	Summer	Mon	104
Psalm	119:105	light (unto my path)	NKJ	Keeping Resolutions	Winter	Sun	369
Micah	3	Lips (cover their)	KJ	Micah	Winter	Tues	308
Hebrews	12:2	looking (unto Jesus)	NKJ	Faith	Summer	Sat	165
Genesis	11:27	Lord (had said..go)	KJ	Directions	Autumn	Mon	216
Genesis	28:16	Lord (in this place)	KJ	Sleep	Summer	Sat	186

Scripture Book	Chapter Verse	Topic	Version	Title	Season	Day	Page
Psalm	40:5	Lord (my God)	NKJ	Week of Thanksgiving	Autumn	Wed	232
Exodus	16:11	Lord (said)	NIV	God's Provision in Your Wilderness	Winter	Thur	366
Exodus	16:4	Lord (said)	NIV	God's Provision in Your Wilderness	Winter	Wed	365
Numbers	13:1	Lord (said)	NIV	God's Provision in Your Wilderness	Winter	Fri	367
Isaiah	6:8	Lord (voice of)	NIV	Wisdom	Spring	Wed	71
Joshua	1:9	Lord (with you)	KJ	Directions	Autumn	Thur	219
Joshua	1:1	Lord (your God)	KJ	Directions	Autumn	Sat	221
Isaiah	43:3	Lord (your God)	NKJ	Flowers in December	Winter	Fri	353
Zephaniah	3:17	love	KJ	May'Flower'	Spring	Sat	88
John	11:3	love	NKJ	Who is in Control?	Spring	Thur	30
John	15:12	love	KJ	Ultimate Sacrifice	Summer	Mon	188
John	15:13	love	KJ	Ultimate Sacrifice	Summer	Intro	187
John	15:13	love	KJ	Ultimate Sacrifice	Summer	Sat	193
Song of Solomon	8:7	love	KJ	Unquenchable Love	Summer	Sun	166
John	15:13	love	KJ	Unquenchable Love	Summer	Mon	167
Ephesians	3:19	love	KJ	Unquenchable Love	Summer	Fri	171
Ephesians	5:1-2	love	KJ	Unquenchable Love	Summer	Sat	172
2 Timothy	1:7	love	NKJ	You are God's Specialty	Summer	Wed	148
Psalm	37:4	love	NKJ	Flowers in December	Winter	Thur	352
Jeremiah	31:3	love	NKJ	Love&Hate War&Peace	Winter	Mon	356
Romans	5:8	love	NKJ	Love&Hate War&Peace	Winter	Sun	355
2 Timothy	1:17	love	NIV	Phrases We Often Use	Winter	Thur	324
1 John	4:8	love (God is)	KJ	For Sale	Spring	Fri	38
John	3:16	love (God so)	KJ	For Sale	Spring	Sat	39
1 John	4:11	love (God so)	KJ	IF	Winter	Thur	303
1 John	4:11	love (one another)	KJ	IF	Winter	Thur	303
Matthew	5:44	love(enemies)	NKJ	A Way of Life	Autumn	Sat	249
Deuteronomy	6:5	love the Lord	NKJ	Adoration of Our Holy Father	Autumn	Sat	207
Joshua	23:11	love the Lord	NKJ	Adoration of Our Holy Father	Autumn	Mon	202
Deuteronomy	30:20	love the Lord	KJ	For Sale	Spring	Mon	34
John	3:16	loved	NIV	Father's Day	Spring	Sun	89
John	3:16	loved	NKJ	Love&Hate War&Peace	Winter	Tues	357
John	3:16	loved (God so)	NIV	Phrases We Often Use	Winter	Mon	321
1 Chronicles	29:18	loyal	NIV	Words	Autumn	Wed	225
Matthew	5:28	lust	NKJ	A Way of Life	Autumn	Tues	245
2 Peter	1:4	lust	NIV	God's Provision in Your Wilderness	Winter	Tues	364
Genesis	1:26	man (God made)	NKJ	The Beginning	Autumn	Sat	284
Genesis	1:26	man (Let Us make)	NKJ	Elohim	Summer	Tues	105
Jeremiah	18:4	marred	NIV	Designing Us	Autumn	Fri	269
Psalm	98:1	marvelous	NKJ	Week of Thanksgiving	Autumn	Fri	234
1 Chronicles	16:10-12	marvelous	KJ	Safe In His Arms	Winter	Sun	383
Psalm	23:5	Me (before)	NKJ	His Refreshing Preparations	Summer	Mon	111

Scripture Book	Chapter Verse	Topic	Version	Title	Season	Day	Page
Joshua	1:8	meditate	KJ	Directions	Autumn	Fri	220
2 Corinthians	1:3	Mercies	NKJ	He Gives Us Hope for Everyday	Spring	Sun	5
Psalm	136:1	mercy	NKJ	Patience for Coming Events	Winter	Sat	347
Psalm	136:1	mercy (endures forever)	NKJ	Week of Thanksgiving	Autumn	Sat	235
Psalm	57:1	mercy (have m on me)	NIV	Wisdom	Spring	Sun	68
Exodus	14:22	midst	KJ	Is it 'Worth it'?	Winter	Wed	330
Weekly Intro	intro	Money	NKJ	Prosperity	Autumn	Intro	208
Matthew	5:4	mourn	NKJ	You are God's Specialty	Summer	Sun	145
Matthew	13:47	net	KJ	Letting Go & Letting God	Summer	Mon	153
2 Corinthians	5:17	new	KJ	Safe In His Arms	Winter	Wed	386
2 Corinthians	5:17	new (creation)	NKJ	He Gives Us Hope for Everyday	Spring	Wed	8
Exodus	20:3	no other gods	NKJ	Adoration of Our Holy Father	Autumn	Fri	206
2 Corinthians	10:5	obedience	KJ	Letting Go & Letting God	Summer	Thur	156
Philippians	2:8	obedient	NKJ	Adoration of Our Holy Father	Autumn	Tues	203
Romans	6:16	obey (him)	NIV	Words	Autumn	Sun	222
Deuteronomy	30:20	obey (his voice)	KJ	For Sale	Spring	Mon	34
2 Corinthians	9:24	obtain	KJ	Letting Go & Letting God	Summer	Fri	157
Romans	6:16	offer	NIV	Words	Autumn	Sun	222
Ephesians	5:1-2	offering	KJ	Unquenchable Love	Summer	Sat	172
Psalm	23:5	oil	NKJ	His Refreshing Preparations	Summer	Thur	114
2 Kings	20:1	order (set thine house)	KJ	Hezekiah - Added Days	Autumn	Sun	236
1 Corinthians	14:40	order (things done)	NKJ	He Gives Us Hope for Everyday	Spring	Fri	10
Numbers	13:30	overcome	KJ	Is it 'Worth it'?	Winter	Sat	333
Revelation	3:7-13	overcometh	KJ	Church of Philadelphia	Summer	Sat	137
Luke	23:43	paradise	NKJ	From the Cross	Autumn	Mon	251
Romans	15:4	Patience	NKJ	Patience	Spring	Wed	50
Hebrews	12:1	patience	KJ	Letting Go & Letting God	Summer	Fri	157
Hebrews	12:1	patience	KJ	Ultimate Sacrifice	Summer	Thur	191
Weekly Intro	intro	Patience (pray for)	NKJ	Patience	Spring	Intro	47
Psalm	37:7	patiently	NKJ	Patience	Spring	Thur	51
Mark	4:38-40	peace	KJ	May'Flower'	Spring	Thur	86
Isaiah	32:17	peace	NIV	Righteous	Spring	Fri	80
Psalm	4:8	peace	KJ	Letting Go & Letting God	Summer	Sat	158
Ezekiel	34:24-26	peace	KJ	Sleep	Summer	Wed	183
Jeremiah	29:11	peace	NKJ	You are God's Specialty	Summer	Tues	147
1 Corinthians	14:33	peace	NKJ	You are God's Specialty	Summer	Mon	146
Isaiah	26:3	peace	NKJ	Flowers in December	Winter	Mon	349
John	14:27	peace	NKJ	Flowers in December	Winter	Tues	350

Scripture Book	Chapter Verse	Topic	Version	Title	Season	Day	Page
2 Peter	1:2	peace	NIV	God's Provision in Your Wilderness	Winter	Tues	364
Psalm	120:7	peace	NKJ	Love&Hate War&Peace	Winter	Sat	361
Isaiah	26:3	peace	NKJ	Love&Hate War&Peace	Winter	Thur	359
Romans	16:20	peace	NKJ	Love&Hate War&Peace	Winter	Wed	358
Colossians	3:15	peace	NKJ	Love&Hate War&Peace	Winter	Fri	360
Isaiah	57:2	peace	KJ	Safe In His Arms	Winter	Tues	385
John	20:19	Peace (be with you)	NKJ	His Teaching Continues	Autumn	Tues	273
John	20:21	peace (to you)	NKJ	His Teaching Continues	Autumn	Wed	274
Hebrews	11:31	perish (did not)	NKJ	Faith	Summer	Fri	164
Jeremiah	29:11	plans	KJ	Directions	Autumn	Sun	215
1 Kings	3:10	pleased (the Lord)	KJ	Speech	Spring	Sat	60
Luke	18:27	possible	NIV	Phrases We Often Use	Winter	Sun	320
2 Corinthians	4:7	power	NKJ	He Gives Us Hope for Everyday	Spring	Sat	11
2 Timothy	1:7	power	NKJ	You are God's Specialty	Summer	Wed	148
Luke	10:19	power	NKJ	Flowers in December	Winter	Wed	351
2 Timothy	1:17	power	NIV	Phrases We Often Use	Winter	Thur	324
Psalm	9:1	praise	NKJ	Week of Thanksgiving	Autumn	Sun	229
Psalm	9:1	praise	NKJ	Patience for Coming Events	Winter	Sun	341
Psalm	96:4	praised	NKJ	You are God's Specialty	Summer	Sat	151
2 Kings	20:2	prayed	KJ	Hezekiah - Added Days	Autumn	Intro	236
2 Kings	20:5	prayer (have heard thy)	KJ	Hezekiah - Added Days	Autumn	Wed	239
1 Timothy	2:1	prayers	KJ	Ultimate Sacrifice	Summer	Tues	189
Mark	11:25	praying	NKJ	Our Father	Summer	Thur	142
Psalm	23:5	prepare (Thou)	NKJ	His Refreshing Preparations	Summer	Sun	110
2 Timothy	4:2	prepared (be)	NIV	Words	Autumn	Fri	227
Acts	1:4	Promise	NKJ	What Waiting Can Bring	Summer	Sun	124
Hebrews	10:35-36	promise	NKJ	You are God's Specialty	Summer	Thur	149
Psalm	119:50	promise	NIV	Defining You	Winter	Thur	338
Hebrews	11:11	promise (faithful who had)	NKJ	Faith	Summer	Wed	162
Hebrews	11:9	promise (land of)	NKJ	Faith	Summer	Tues	161
Hebrews	10:23	promised	NKJ	Waiting	Winter	Thur	380
Psalm	37:7	prosper	NKJ	Patience	Spring	Thur	51
Psalm	118:25	prosperity	NKJ	Passion Week	Spring	Wed	22
Joshua	1:8	Prosperous	KJ	Directions	Autumn	Fri	220
Joshua	1:8	prosperous	NIV	God's Provision in Your Wilderness	Winter	Sat	368
1 Peter	5:5	proud	NIV	Wisdom	Spring	Mon	69
Matthew	27:57 - 60	Provision	NKJ	His Teaching Continues	Autumn	Sun	271
Philippians	4:8	pure	NKJ	Flowers in December	Winter	Sat	354
Luke	19:39	rebuke	NKJ	Passion Week	Spring	Fri	24
John	14:1-4	receive	KJ	Our Mansion	Spring	Intro	61
Acts	1:8	receive (power)	NKJ	What Waiting Can Bring	Summer	Fri	129
2 Kings	20:7	recovered	KJ	Hezekiah - Added Days	Autumn	Intro	236

Scripture Book	Chapter Verse	Topic	Version	Title	Season	Day	Page
Isaiah	63:16	redeemer	NKJ	Our Father	Summer	Tues	140
1 Corinthians	1:30	redemption	NIV	Righteous	Spring	Mon	76
Weekly Intro	intro	Re-Do	NIV	Jesus & the Seven RE's of Us	Spring	Intro	40
Psalm	46:7	refuge	NKJ	Flowers in December	Winter	Sun	348
Revelation	19:6	reigns	NIV	Father's Day	Spring	Sat	95
Psalm	9:2	rejoice	NKJ	Week of Thanksgiving	Autumn	Sun	229
Zephaniah	3:17	rejoice	KJ	May'Flower'	Spring	Sat	88
Luke	15:8-10	rejoice	KJ	May'Flower'	Spring	Tues	84
Zechariah	9:9	rejoice	NKJ	Passion Week	Spring	Intro	19
Zephaniah	3:14	rejoice	NIV	Songs	Summer	Sun	117
1 Chronicles	16:10-12	rejoice	KJ	Safe In His Arms	Winter	Sun	383
Luke	15:8-10	repenteth	KJ	May'Flower'	Spring	Tues	84
Daniel	3:17	rescue	NIV	Father's Day	Spring	Tues	91
James	4:7	resist	NKJ	You are God's Specialty	Summer	Tues	147
John	14:1-4	responsible	KJ	Our Mansion	Spring	Mon	62
Deuteronomy	33:12	rest	NIV	Words	Autumn	Sat	228
Psalm	37:7	rest	NKJ	Patience	Spring	Thur	51
Matthew	11:29	rest	NIV	Wisdom	Spring	Fri	73
Isaiah	57:2	rest	KJ	Safe In His Arms	Winter	Tues	385
Isaiah	61:4	restore	NIV	Jesus & the Seven RE's of Us	Spring	Wed	43
Acts	1:6	restore	NKJ	What Waiting Can Bring	Summer	Tues	126
Psalm	23:3	restore	NKJ	Keeping Resolutions	Winter	Thu	373
Psalm	23:3	restores	NIV	God's Provision in Your Wilderness	Winter	Thur	366
Numbers	13:25	returned	KJ	Is it 'Worth it'?	Winter	Fri	332
Revelation	22:12	reward	NIV	Jesus & the Seven RE's of Us	Spring	Sat	46
Hebrews	10:35-36	reward	NKJ	You are God's Specialty	Summer	Thur	149
Hebrews	11:6	rewarder	NKJ	Faith	Summer	Sun	159
Proverbs	4:8	righteous	NIV	Defining You	Winter	Fri	339
Psalm	37:6	righteousness	NIV	Words	Autumn	Mon	223
Romans	6:16	righteousness	NIV	Words	Autumn	Sun	222
Psalm	119:142	righteousness	NIV	Father's Day	Spring	Fri	94
2 Corinthians	5:21	righteousness	NIV	Righteous	Spring	Sun	75
Psalm	23:3	righteousness	NIV	God's Provision in Your Wilderness	Winter	Thur	366
Psalm	23:5	runs (over)	NKJ	His Refreshing Preparations	Summer	Sat	116
Exodus	8:27	sacrifice	KJ	Ultimate Sacrifice	Summer	Sun	187
Ephesians	5:1-2	sacrifice	KJ	Unquenchable Love	Summer	Sat	172
Psalm	4:8	safety	KJ	Letting Go & Letting God	Summer	Sat	158
Zechariah	9:9	salvation	NKJ	Passion Week	Spring	Intro	19
Lamentations	3:26	salvation	NKJ	Patience	Spring	Mon	48
Romans	10:10	salvation	NIV	Righteous	Spring	Sat	81
1 Corinthians	1:30	sanctification	NIV	Righteous	Spring	Mon	76
Psalm	145:16	satisfy	NKJ	Waiting	Winter	Fri	381

Scripture Book	Chapter Verse	Topic	Version	Title	Season	Day	Page
Zephaniah	3:17	save	KJ	May'Flower'	Spring	Sat	88
Genesis	1:6-8	Second day	NKJ	The Beginning	Autumn	Tues	280
Psalm	139:15	secret	NIV	Defining You	Winter	Mon	335
Matthew	7:8	seek	NIV	Jesus & the Seven RE's of Us	Spring	Sun	40
Luke	15:8-10	seek	KJ	May'Flower'	Spring	Tues	84
Psalm	105:4	seek	NIV	Wisdom	Spring	Thur	72
1 Chronicles	16:11	seek	KJ	Ultimate Sacrifice	Summer	Wed	190
Luke	11:9	seek	NIV	Defining You	Winter	Tues	336
Deuteronomy	4:29	seek	KJ	Safe In His Arms	Winter	Mon	384
1 Chronicles	16:10-12	seek	KJ	Safe In His Arms	Winter	Sun	383
Hebrews	11:6	seek (diligently. Him)	NKJ	Faith	Summer	Sun	159
Isaiah	6:8	Send	NIV	Wisdom	Spring	Wed	71
Isaiah	43:10	servant	KJ	Know	Summer	Sat	179
Ezekiel	34:24-26	servant	KJ	Sleep	Summer	Wed	183
Exodus	12:31	serve	KJ	Is it 'Worth it'?	Winter	Tues	329
Hebrews	12:2	shame (despising)	NKJ	Faith	Summer	Sat	165
Psalm	33:20	shield	NKJ	Waiting	Winter	Tues	378
John	11:6	sick	NKJ	Who is in Control?	Spring	Thur	30
2 Kings	20:1	sick (unto death)	KJ	Hezekiah - Added Days	Autumn	Intro	236
Psalm	124:1	Side (on our)	KJ	IF	Winter	Sun	299
Psalm	146:8	sight	NIV	Senses	Winter	Sun	313
Isaiah	1:18	sin	NIV	Jesus & the Seven RE's of Us	Spring	Tues	42
Ephesians	5:19	sing	NIV	Songs	Summer	Mon	118
Psalm	13:6	sing	NKJ	Patience for Coming Events	Winter	Mon	342
Isaiah	5:1	sing (for the one I love)	NIV	Songs	Summer	Wed	120
Judges	5:3	sing (I will)	NIV	Songs	Summer	Fri	122
Psalm	33:3	sing (to him a new song)	NIV	Songs	Summer	Thur	121
Psalm	13:6	sing (to the Lord)	NKJ	Week of Thanksgiving	Autumn	Mon	230
1 Corinthians	14:15	sing (with my spirit)	NIV	Songs	Summer	Tues	119
Romans	3:23	sinned	NIV	Senses	Winter	Fri	318
Hosea	4:7	sinned (against ME)	NKJ	Prosperity	Autumn	Wed	211
Micah	7	sins (cast into seas)	KJ	Micah	Winter	Sat	312
1 John	1:9	Sins (confess)	KJ	For Sale	Spring	Sun	33
1 John	1:9	Sins (forgive)	KJ	For Sale	Spring	Sun	33
Genesis	20:2	sister	NKJ	Who is in Control?	Spring	Tues	28
Proverbs	6:9	sluggard	KJ	Sleep	Summer	Thur	184
John	5:19	Son (can do)	NKJ	Our Father	Summer	Sat	144
1 Chronicles	4:9	sorrow	KJ	Prayer of Jabez	Autumn	Sun	257
Deuteronomy	6:5	soul	NKJ	Adoration of Our Holy Father	Autumn	Sat	207
Numbers	11:6	soul (is dried)	KJ	Is it 'Worth it'?	Winter	Thur	331
Titus	3:2	speak	KJ	Lips of Love	Spring	Thur	16

Scripture Book	Chapter Verse	Topic	Version	Title	Season	Day	Page
Luke	1:22	speak	KJ	Speech	Spring	Tues	56
Colossians	4:6	speech	KJ	Lips of Love	Spring	Wed	15
1 Kings	3:10	speech	KJ	Speech	Spring	Sat	60
Psalm	17:6	speech	KJ	Speech	Spring	Mon	55
Proverbs	7:21	speech	KJ	Speech	Spring	Sun	54
Matthew	26:73	speech	KJ	Speech	Spring	Thur	58
2 Corinthians	7:4	speech	KJ	Speech	Spring	Wed	57
Colossians	4:6	speech	KJ	Speech	Spring	Fri	59
Romans	8:1	Spirit	NKJ	Freedom From the Laws of Sin	Autumn	Sun	285
Galatians	5:22	spirit (fruit of)	NKJ	Patience	Spring	Sun	47
Acts	1:5	Spirit (Holy)	NKJ	What Waiting Can Bring	Summer	Mon	125
Acts	1:8	Spirit (Holy)	NKJ	What Waiting Can Bring	Summer	Fri	129
Romans	8:14	Spirit (led by)	NKJ	Freedom From the Laws of Sin	Autumn	Thur	289
Romans	8:15	Spirit (of adoption)	NKJ	Freedom From the Laws of Sin	Autumn	Fri	290
Romans	8:15	Spirit (of bondage)	NKJ	Freedom From the Laws of Sin	Autumn	Fri	290
Romans	8:9	Spirit (of God)	NKJ	Freedom From the Laws of Sin	Autumn	Tues	287
Psalm	51:10	spirit (renew a right)	KJ	For Sale	Spring	Tues	35
Romans	8:6	Spiritual minded	NKJ	Freedom From the Laws of Sin	Autumn	Mon	286
Deuteronomy	6:5	strength	NKJ	Adoration of Our Holy Father	Autumn	Sat	207
Psalm	105:4	strength	NIV	Wisdom	Spring	Thur	72
Revelation	3:7-13	strength	KJ	Church of Philadelphia	Summer	Mon	132
Psalm	18:1-3	strength	KJ	Letting Go & Letting God	Summer	Tues	154
Psalm	18:1-3	strength	KJ	Letting Go & Letting God	Summer	Wed	155
Psalm	88:4	strength	KJ	Letting Go & Letting God	Summer	Tues	154
1 Chronicles	16:11	strength	KJ	Ultimate Sacrifice	Summer	Wed	190
Hebrews	11:11	strength (received)	NKJ	Faith	Summer	Wed	162
Psalm	27:14	strengthen	NKJ	Waiting	Winter	Sun	376
2 Chronicles	12:1	strengthened	NKJ	Prosperity	Autumn	Fri	213
Joshua	1:9	strong	KJ	Directions	Autumn	Thur	219
2 Timothy	2:15	study	KJ	May'Flower'	Spring	Sun	82
Matthew	26:33	Stumble	NKJ	Adoration of Our Holy Father	Autumn	Thur	205
James	4:7	submit	NKJ	You are God's Specialty	Summer	Tues	147
Joshua	1:8	success (good)	NKJ	Keeping Resolutions	Winter	Sat	375
Joshua	1:8	successful	KJ	Directions	Autumn	Fri	220
Psalm	119:50	suffering	NIV	Defining You	Winter	Thur	338
Joshua	23:11	take heed	NKJ	Adoration of Our Holy Father	Autumn	Mon	202
Psalm	34:8	Taste	NIV	Senses	Winter	Tues	315
Micah	4	teach	KJ	Micah	Winter	Wed	309
2 Kings	20:5	tears (seen thy)	KJ	Hezekiah - Added Days	Autumn	Thur	240

Scripture Book	Chapter Verse	Topic	Version	Title	Season	Day	Page
Revelation	3:7-13	temptation	KJ	Church of Philadelphia	Summer	Thur	135
Joshua	1:9	Terrified (not)	KJ	Directions	Autumn	Thur	219
Psalm	92:1	thanks	NKJ	You are God's Specialty	Summer	Sat	151
Psalm	136:1	thanks	NKJ	Patience for Coming Events	Winter	Sat	347
Psalm	92:1	thanks	NKJ	Patience for Coming Events	Winter	Thur	345
Psalm	136:1	thanks (give to the Lord)	NKJ	Week of Thanksgiving	Autumn	Sat	235
Psalm	92:1	thanks (give, it is)	NKJ	Week of Thanksgiving	Autumn	Thur	233
1 Timothy	2:1	thanks (giving of)	KJ	Ultimate Sacrifice	Summer	Tues	189
Psalm	26:7	thanksgiving	NKJ	Patience for Coming Events	Winter	Tues	343
Mark	5:28	Touch	NIV	Senses	Winter	Thur	317
Romans	5:3	tribulation	NKJ	Patience	Spring	Sat	53
Psalm	92:4	triumph	NKJ	Week of Thanksgiving	Autumn	Thur	233
John	14:1-4	troubled	KJ	Our Mansion	Spring	Intro	61
Philippians	4:8	true	NKJ	Flowers in December	Winter	Sat	354
Psalm	22:4	trust	NIV	Father's Day	Spring	Wed	92
Proverbs	3:5	trust	NIV	Defining You	Winter	Wed	337
Isaiah	26:3	trust	NKJ	Flowers in December	Winter	Mon	349
Proverbs	3:5-6	trust	NIV	Phrases We Often Use	Winter	Sat	326
Luke	23:43	truth	NKJ	From the Cross	Autumn	Mon	251
John	8:32	truth	KJ	Know	Summer	Mon	174
John	8:32	truth	NIV	God's Provision in Your Wilderness	Winter	Wed	365
John	8:32	truth	NKJ	Keeping Resolutions	Winter	Wed	372
Genesis	1:16-18	two great lights	NKJ	The Beginning	Autumn	Thur	282
Isaiah	43:10	understand	KJ	Know	Summer	Sat	179
Proverbs	3:5	understanding	NIV	Defining You	Winter	Wed	337
Proverbs	3:5-6	understanding	NIV	Phrases We Often Use	Winter	Sat	326
Colossians	1:9	understanding	NIV	Phrases We Often Use	Winter	Wed	323
Proverbs	1:2	understanding	KJ	Safe In His Arms	Winter	Thur	387
1 John	1:9	unrighteousness (cleanse from)	KJ	For Sale	Spring	Sun	33
Psalm	127:1	vain, in	NKJ	Prosperity	Autumn	Mon	209
Genesis	1:11	vegetation	NKJ	The Beginning	Autumn	Wed	281
Psalm	98:1	victory	NKJ	Week of Thanksgiving	Autumn	Fri	234
Psalm	98:1	victory	NKJ	Patience for Coming Events	Winter	Fri	346
Philippians	4:8	virtue	NKJ	Flowers in December	Winter	Sat	354
Habakkuk	2:3	vision	NKJ	Waiting	Winter	Sat	382
Lamentations	3:26	wait	NKJ	Patience	Spring	Mon	48
Psalm	130:5	wait (for the Lord)	NKJ	Waiting	Winter	Wed	379
Psalm	27:14	wait (on the Lord)	NKJ	Waiting	Winter	Sun	376
Psalm	40:1	waited	NKJ	Patience	Spring	Fri	52
Psalm	33:20	waits (for the Lord)	NKJ	Waiting	Winter	Tues	378
Micah	4	walk (in his paths)	KJ	Micah	Winter	Wed	309
2 Kings	20:3	walked	KJ	Hezekiah - Added Days	Autumn	Tues	238

Scripture Book	Chapter Verse	Topic	Version	Title	Season	Day	Page
Hebrews	11:30	walls (fell down)	NKJ	Faith	Summer	Thur	163
John	14:1-4	way (ye know)	KJ	Our Mansion	Spring	Sat	67
Romans	8:26	weakness	NKJ	Freedom From the Laws of Sin	Autumn	Sat	291
2 Corinthians	12:9	weakness	NIV	Phrases We Often Use	Winter	Fri	325
2 Kings	20:3	wept	KJ	Hezekiah - Added Days	Autumn	Mon	237
Psalm	37:7	wicked	NKJ	Patience	Spring	Thur	51
Jonah	1:1	wickedness	KJ	Directions	Autumn	Tues	217
Exodus	8:27	wilderness	KJ	Ultimate Sacrifice	Summer	Sun	187
Matthew	12:50	will (Father in heaven)	NKJ	Our Father	Summer	Wed	141
Exodus	18:23	wilt do	KJ	IF	Winter	Mon	300
Matthew	9:17	wine	NIV	Designing Us	Autumn	Sat	270
1 Corinthians	1:30	wisdom	NIV	Righteous	Spring	Mon	76
Proverbs	7:4	wisdom	NIV	Defining You	Winter	Sat	340
Colossians	1:9	wisdom	NIV	Phrases We Often Use	Winter	Wed	323
Proverbs	1:2	wisdom	KJ	Safe In His Arms	Winter	Thur	387
Isaiah	43:10	witnesses	KJ	Know	Summer	Sat	179
Acts	1:8	witnesses	NKJ	What Waiting Can Bring	Summer	Sat	130
Psalm	40:5	wonderful	NKJ	Patience for Coming Events	Winter	Wed	344
Psalm	119:11	word (I have hidden)	NIV	God's Provision in Your Wilderness	Winter	Mon	363
Revelation	3:7-13	Word (kept God's)	KJ	Church of Philadelphia	Summer	Tues	133
Jonah	1:1	word (of the LORD)	KJ	Directions	Autumn	Tues	217
2 Kings	20:4	word (of the LORD)	KJ	Hezekiah - Added Days	Autumn	Intro	236
Genesis	15:4	word (of the LORD)	NKJ	Who is in Control?	Spring	Sun	26
Micah	1	word (of the LORD)	KJ	Micah	Winter	Sun	306
Isaiah	64:8	work (of your hand)	NIV	Jesus & the Seven RE's of Us	Spring	Thur	44
Isaiah	64:8	work (of your hand)	NKJ	Our Father	Summer	Mon	139
Isaiah	64:8	work (we are work of your hand)	NIV	Designing Us	Autumn	Thur	268
Psalm	95:6	worship	KJ	Safe In His Arms	Winter	Sat	389
Exodus	34:8	worshipped	NKJ	Adoration of Our Holy Father	Autumn	Wed	204
Proverbs	27:6	wounds	KJ	Unquenchable Love	Summer	Tues	168
Psalm	37:4	wrath	NKJ	Flowers in December	Winter	Thur	352

Authors Bios and Previous Writings

Kathleen Jones: I was eight years old when I accepted Christ as my Savior. As a wife and mother, I am often accused of "mothering" all with whom I spend time. Current activities in my local church include teaching adult bible studies, being a deacon, and being missions' team leader. When God impressed upon me to do a devotions book, I did not come to His understandings immediately. Because He loves me (and you) so sincerely, He has taught me to communicate His Words for daily life.

Maureen Eubank: I became a believer at the age of fourteen at a church summer camp. As a wife, mother, step-mother, and grandmother, I have a passion for women to know the Father intimately. For over ten years, I have been involved in all types of Women's Ministries. Bible study groups for women have met in my home. Knowing my own daily devotions have brought me to a greater understanding of the great "I AM," I could not help but say yes to Peggy and Kath when the book adventure began.

Peggy Seay: I accepted salvation through Jesus Christ in my late twenties. I am a wife, mother, and grandmother. Leading bible studies has been a part of my life for over twenty years. The age groups included toddlers through pre-college. My husband and I directed and worked with 'at-risk' youth for over four years. I continually build my intimate relationship with Jesus Christ by my own daily devotional studies, as well as being involved with various projects assisting women.

Collective Writing History: We began our writing experiences in the corporate world by writing instruction manuals for training and processing job responsibilities. Our website includes a variety of writings by each and ranges from in-depth studies to real life lessons. Kathleen has also written programs for parents to teach the creation of Godly habits to small children. In addition, she has created a manual and seminar for those who find themselves in that worldly debt cycle so prevalent today. Poetry is written for her own enjoyment, as well as 'special orders' for those who want to present a personal note to a loved one. Maureen writes teachings for her in-home bible studies and women's ministry duties to include mentoring programs and divorce recovery. Peggy, too, has written many of her own bible studies and classroom lessons which are used for groups and individuals. She is currently writing a women's self-help book on the issues involved with the many phases a woman goes through in her lifetime.